ALSO BY VALERIE TAYLOR

What's Not Said

What's Not True

What's Not Lost

a WHALE *of a* MURDER

A WHALE of a MURDER

A Venus Bixby Mystery

VALERIE TAYLOR

This is a work of fiction. Names, characters, places, and incidents either are the product of the author's imagination or are used fictitiously. Any resemblance to actual persons, living or dead, is entirely coincidental.

Copyright © 2023, Valerie Taylor

All rights reserved. No part of this publication may be reproduced, distributed, or transmitted in any form or by any means, including photocopying, recording, digital scanning, or other electronic or mechanical methods, without the prior written permission of the publisher, except in the case of brief quotations embodied in critical reviews and certain other noncommercial uses permitted by copyright law. For permission requests, please contact Aspetuck Publishing.

All company and/or product names, logos, trademarks, and/or registered trademarks are the property of their respective owners.

Edited by Melissa Norton Carro
Cover and book design by Danna Mathias Steele

Published 2023

ISBN: 979-8-9865995-2-6 (paperback)
ISBN: 979-8-9865995-3-3 (ebook)

Library of Congress Control Number: 2023919833

For information, contact:
Aspetuck Publishing
159 High HL
Shelton, CT 06484

Printed in the United States of America

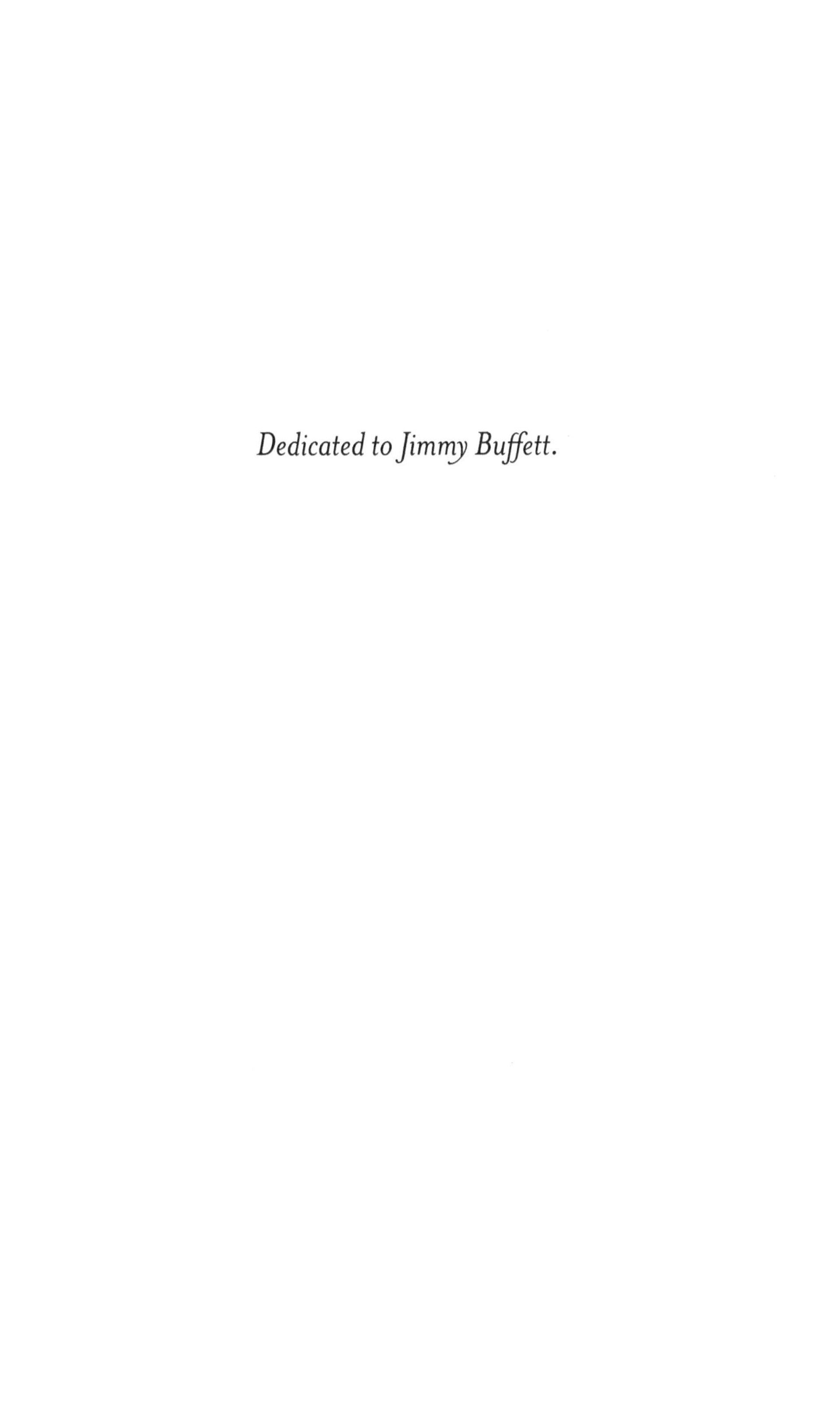

Dedicated to Jimmy Buffett.

CHAPTER ONE

The Chatham Crossing Chronicle
"Song and Dance Lady" Tap Danced Around Whaling Museum Murder Investigation

By: Daniel DaRosa, Investigative Reporter

Monday morning, July 5, 2010. Early Saturday, Venus Bixby, widow of lifelong and beloved Chatham Crossing resident Paul Bixby, tripped and fell strolling through the lush Gardens of the Sofia Silva Whaling Museum just hours before neighbors and friends were scheduled to gather there to celebrate her fiftieth birthday.

That wasn't the only calamity at the museum that day. The much anticipated birthday party of the summer had to be postponed indefinitely due to the sudden death of Margaret "Maggie" McGee, manager of the museum's gift shop. Though unconfirmed, sources close to the investigation said the police are treating this as a homicide.

As it turns out, according to an anonymous tipster, Ms. Bixby may have been the last to see Ms. McGee alive in the gardens that morning. All we can report at this juncture is that Ms. Bixby told a friend she hadn't the foggiest idea if the victim was "alive and kicking" when she tumbled over a pair of orange platform shoes and broke her thumb.

Like the birthday festivities, efforts by the always diligent Chatham Crossing police to take a full statement from Ms. Bixby were delayed until she sleeps off the pain medication.

Hazard to guess what song Ms. Bixby will sing when that happens?

For up-to-the-minute investigation details and the date and time of the rescheduled birthday bash, follow this story.

Print and digital editions.

CHAPTER TWO

On any given Saturday afternoon, bumper-to-bumper traffic choked the streets of the historic district of Chatham Crossing, especially during the summer. Proprietors, like me, welcomed the congestion. After all, it was our lifeblood.

But it was Saturday morning, the second day of the extended July 4th holiday weekend. Our streets were relatively deserted and quite traversable. So, why in the world were the police tailgating the ambulance I was riding in, attracting undue attention and making more of a fuss than my thumb deserved?

Surely, one blaring emergency vehicle should be enough to clear the streets, if necessary, when the destination was only five blocks away. Besides, with no traffic lights to negotiate in the direction we were heading, there was little to slow this rescue transport down.

Though smaller in acreage than Quincy and twice the size of Nantucket, Chatham Crossing had ample stop signs to manage traffic flow and only one contentious stop light in all of our cozy town.

That's because ten years or so ago the Town Committee created a controversy that still hangs around today. They voted six to five to install a traffic light at the start of Wharf Way, the main entrance to our enclave from the highway. A half dozen misinformed citizens thought the light, which now blinked *caution* at least ten hours a day, by the way, would regulate the inflow of tourists stopping in Chatham Crossing on their way to or from their vacations on the Cape.

Cape Cod, that is.

Shouldn't the Town Committee have known Oldies & Goodies was then, and has always been, the main attraction and destination of most of those "invaders," as the Committee called them, who made an annual pilgrimage to Chatham Crossing?

I called them my "amigos and amigas." That's friends in Portuguese. I knew this because soon after moving here after graduating from Providence College of Art with high honors and my diploma in art history, I worked ardently to pick up a few useful words and phrases from the residents whose families settled here decades ago. Actually, make that centuries ago.

Growing up in California, I'd never heard of Chatham Crossing. I only discovered this charming town after *twenty-one* museums rejected my application for even an entry level docent position. As I was about to slide another résumé into the mailbox across the street from my apartment in Providence, my best friend pulled my hand back. She had a better idea: her boyfriend had a friend who knew a guy that would sweep me off my feet.

Which, of course, he did.

Paul Bixby was like no other guy I'd dated in college. For one thing, he was five years older than me. Hardly a problem. But that he shared the same first name as my father made me pause and consider if this was a sign I should pay attention to or shrug it off as an annoying coincidence.

At over six feet tall, Paul towered at least a foot over me. Perhaps I could differentiate him from my father by calling him "Tall Paul," like the 1959 hit by Annette. That wouldn't do either, for I worried he'd consider me childish. Or maybe, if my family came East for my graduation, I could avoid name confusion altogether by introducing him with: "I'd like you to meet PB." However, as soon as my sister's squeaky voice reverberated through my head, I tabled that idea. I could just hear her: "PB&V sitting in a tree." Sherrie would get a kick out of mimicking how our initials sounded astoundingly like peanut butter and jelly. Geez. Speaking of being childish.

I was determined to come up with a clever, yet meaningful, nickname for Paul. As an art history major, that shouldn't be an overwhelming assignment for me, should it?

After all, there was so much more to him than his first name. Boyishly handsome, Paul's disheveled, dark walnut hair begged to be finger-combed (by me, of course) and his full luscious lips beckoned to be kissed (also by me). His square chin, prominent forehead, and deep blue inset eyes reminded me of Kevin Costner. Be still my heart.

But, oh, it was the way he moved that summoned up an image of Fred Astaire in *Top Hat*—one of my mother's favorite movies she watched each year when it aired on network television. In black and white, of course.

Every Friday and Saturday night for the four weeks after our first date, we laced up our dancing shoes. We'd trot arm-in-arm into his favorite club in Providence, where he taught me to be his Ginger Rogers.

On the fifth Friday night, as *Twenty-two* and I sat across from each other at Friendly's ice cream parlor, getting ready to share a banana split, he handed me a dainty white box. No wrapping paper, no ribbon. As I held the gold necklace with the Two to Tango pendant up to the light, Paul simply said, "Marry me." Since I'd learned in short order, this was a man who spoke more with his feet than with his words, I interpreted what he said as more of a command than a question.

To be honest, I was both relieved *and* disappointed that my dream of being a museum curator would be postponed until some future time. Tossing one's career aspirations aside to marry the love of her life was still the most accepted and expected path for a young woman to follow in the late 1970s. Given a choice.

With little fanfare, I grabbed the stem of the lone cherry, popped the juicy red fruit in my mouth, and mumbled, "I guess I won't be needing those résumés any longer."

Two years later on the twenty-second of June 1982, I married *Twenty-two*, becoming Venus Bennett Bixby. As a result, the monogrammed charms, gold-plated circle pins, and white Peter Pan collared blouses I'd collected in my late teens and early twenties were still usable and fashionable. If I said so myself.

A prudent and prophetic New Englander, Paul assumed correctly that I'd agree to set up our home in Chatham Crossing, the town in which he grew up and still lived. Bordering both Massachusetts and Rhode Island, in some ways Chatham Crossing reminded me of my hometown. Although, there was no way would I choose, or need, to move back to San Francisco. I could get fog, ocean air, sea spray, and the rank smell of dead fish right here in a more charming and quaint seaside town with quite the history. Having Paul's arms curled around me each morning was the icing on the cake … the cherry on top.

To be honest, I had no desire to return to a place where I'd have to constantly defend my choices in life. Unlike my sister who'd stayed in California and became a respectable teacher, I'd traipsed all the way across the country to attend art school and came up empty, with no solid employment prospects after graduation. Why would I subject myself to that abuse? Leaving my baggage, but not my heart, in San Francisco was a simple decision.

When we were first married, there was no need for me to do the whole nine-to-five work routine. Nor did I care to. The two skirted suits I'd bought in anticipation of job interviews—one navy, the other somewhat lighter blue than navy—still had tags hanging from them when I packed to move from Providence to Chatham Crossing.

I counted myself fortunate. Paul worked hard to provide for us. Though he'd earned an accounting degree, he, too, didn't use his education. Well, not technically. Like me, he was a trust fund baby. In his mid-twenties, just before we met, he'd opened Decades of Dance Studio. After we married, six days a week he'd spend his mornings researching and writing a book about the history of dance. He dedicated his afternoons and evenings teaching the art of ballroom dancing to children and adults of all ages.

The seventh day he spent with me, under the covers. Lucky Paul. His artistic and manly drives were being fulfilled. As for me, though, after a time, I began fidgeting around the house. Restless as the wind off the bay, I worked my way through the *Better Homes and Gardens New Cookbook* and rearranged the linen closet more times than I'd care to admit.

What about me? Whatever am I to do?

Not surprisingly, with dancing central to our lives, so was music. Soon, music claimed its place alongside my interest in art history. One morning as Paul worked in his study, I brought him his second cup of Chock Full O'Nuts coffee, combed my fingers through his locks and whispered in his ear, "Twenty-two, what is your favorite song today?"

"Venus," he said. After taking a sip of coffee, he added, "by Frankie Avalon." Of course he said that. Always the wife-pleaser.

From that day forward, I greeted Paul with the same question. He quickly came to expect it, always having an oldies tune on the tip of his tongue. About a month later, when I gave him a peek into my notebook where I'd started a list of his responses, he stood up from his desk, wrapped me in his arms, dipped me, and asked, "Why?"

"You never know," I winked, gave him a kiss and a loving shove, and headed outside first to sweep the porch that wrapped around the front of the house and then the inside of the cottage, which was vacant, but still a dust-collector.

One evening shortly thereafter, between bites of his favorite steak and mashed potatoes dinner, he casually mentioned Sam's Shoes across the street from his studio was going out of business. Most people were buying their footwear from department stores or at the mall in Providence in those days. "A sign?" he asked.

I laughed, saying the only sign going up would be "For Lease."

It didn't seem like a wise time to start a new business, although I had to admit the location was perfect. With its historic, yet restored, facades, Morgan Street—the only remaining cobblestoned street in town—was a shopper's paradise with unique boutiques, restaurants, a bookstore, jewelry store and the like. Running perpendicular to Wharf Way, the four-way stop sign at the intersection in those days also pointed drivers to shopping and parking, both of which were ample. Kudos to whoever was on the Town Committee then for considering the needs of both residential and tourist traffic.

While Paul polished off two scoops of Neapolitan ice cream, saving strawberry for last, I reminded him that each of us had just invested a quarter of our trust funds to buy and restore both the Craftsman style house and the adjacent cottage. We fondly christened this four-bedroom beauty "Hilltop," because it sat high up on the northern edge of Chatham Crossing's historic center. Soon after moving in, we had it painted an Italian Basil with sandy and ruby accents. With its eat-in gourmet kitchen, refinished oak floors, window seats in both the living and dining rooms, and tiled fireplace, I imagined living there for the rest of my life. Add to all that comfy-coziness were the views from our Adirondack rockers on the wraparound porch and the second-story sunroom. It seemed the coast of Chatham Crossing with its bustling piers and docks was there for our singular pleasure. Life couldn't be grander.

That evening, I daydreamed as I hand washed the dishes. *Could it be my time? Time to define who I am?*

Humming the song "Tall Paul" and swaying rhythmically from side to side, as I often did when doing chores, I felt Paul's strong hands on my hips and his warm nose nuzzle that sweet triggering spot on my neck he discovered early in our relationship. As always, his actions spoke louder than his words.

The dishes waited until morning.

CHAPTER THREE

Since I first opened my very own establishment more than twenty years ago, I've proudly observed that Oldies & Goodies operates like a magnet. Neither long lines of SUVs nor minivans with kayaks and bike racks hanging off of them like Christmas decorations—or one measly traffic light—would stop music fanatics from getting their fill of the oldies and goodies my store was famous for. At least I hoped they wouldn't.

Why would they? After all, few stores like mine existed any longer in Massachusetts. Perhaps not even in the entire US of A. Thanks to the digital world and to smartphones—and the wide variety of music apps to choose from—oldies music was just one click away.

Yet, be still my heart, vinyl records and cassette tapes were still coveted like the newest iPhone release.

I often wondered if there was some yet unexplored correlation between families who vacationed on the Cape and oldies music. Were they a nostalgic bunch trying to relive the good old days when sunshine and lollipops ruled their summers? Or were they simply trying to justify holding on to their Victrola, turntable, or record player? Whatever they called it nowadays. Or perhaps it was their favorite CD player (that's compact disc, for those of you young 'uns) that drove them to take a detour to Chatham Crossing every summer? I believed they rationalized there was no way they should have to recycle their outdated equipment when there were stacks and racks of music always waiting for them to snatch up for a song at my unique shop.

If I let myself imagine overflowing recycling centers, my throat would dry up like a desert, and a prickly chill would rush up my spine. What would I do with my life if that ever happened?

Begrudgingly, though, I had to admit it, Oldies & Goodies wasn't the only drawing card.

The town had history.

Granted, most of it was captured within the halls, walls, and glass displays of the Sofia Silva Whaling Museum, located just four blocks from my store. Named for the wife of Fernando Silva, who possessed a private collection of artifacts—maritime logs, drawings, artwork, statues, and whale tales—the SSWM, as it was common-ly referred to, anchored majestically adjacent to Wharf Way on the corner of Bradford and Center Streets. Early on, Center Street was indeed the middle of the town. Yet, alas, the good fortune and evolution of the whaling in-dustry and all the commerce needed to support it pushed the heartbeat of the town farther from the center.

Despite the constant expansion of Chatham Crossing, the museum remained rooted to its original location, tak-ing up an entire town block. Over the years as curators acquired more and more treasures, SSWM was forced to build up instead of out. There was simply no way to expand a town block outward—although I wouldn't have put it past the Town Committee to attempt to do so.

Back in the day, Sofia Silva had her thumb on the Town Committee. She convinced the all-male advisory group at the time to protect the history of an industry that had once prospered in Chatham Crossing. Though not fond of considering a woman's eccentric impulses, they ultimately agreed, and SSWM broke ground in 1806. Of course, it didn't hurt that Sofia's husband Fernando headed the Town Committee at the time.

In retrospect, if I were on the Town Committee ten years ago, as I should have been after all I'd done to put Chatham Crossing "on the map," I would've given two thumbs *down* to installing that traffic light. Yet, obviously, if the meeting were held today, I'd only be able to give just one thumb down, considering the current state of my digits.

Given the chance, I would present just the facts. And, then, the eleven-members would have to admit the truth. There'd been no accidents at the intersection of Wharf Way and Morgan Street where they insisted the light needed to be strung.

No accidents ever. Never ever.

In fact, there were so few automobile accidents in Chatham Crossing that ten years ago the local paper eliminated a weekly section on the last page that donned the catchy headline, Chatham Crossing Car Crashes. With none to report, they simply wrote, "Sem Acidentes. Mantenha o bom trabalho." Ordinarily, that would've been a respectful nod to the Portuguese community, except that around the turn of the twenty-first century,

Portuguese families only accounted for about 15 percent of the population in Chatham Crossing.

Thankfully, some tactful reporter at *The Chatham Crossing Chronicle*—referred to as *The Chronicle*—had the good presence of mind to add in small print below, "No accidents. Keep up the good work," for the rest of us English-is-our-only-language residents.

Ahead of the Town Committee voting yea or nay on the light, I asked Carole, "Can't your bloody husband stop this nonsense? Where's their evidence a light is needed?"

Carole Duffy—that's Carole with an 'e'—was the other half of Oldies & Goodies. Well, not really half. She was my best amiga, not a part owner. Actually, not an owner at all. When I first opened my store, my stock was limited. All I needed was someone like Carole, a friend who'd volunteer to give me a hand when she wasn't otherwise occupied. Over time, as years became decades, songs naturally shifted from the current charts and became oldies. As my inventory and the number of regular customers grew, so did the hours Carole spent at the store. Naturally, I offered to compensate her for her time there. When that happened, according to my accountant, she became a sub-contractor.

Our relationship changed again one day about five years ago as the peak summer season wound down. I think it must have been a Wednesday, because it was the slowest day of the week for Carole's catering business. That's when she made me an offer I simply couldn't refuse.

As I was about to clamp a checklist to my Lucite clipboard, Carole offered to take the inventory of the leftover candy on the shelves and tidy them up a bit. Customarily, whatever I couldn't sell by the first few weeks of October, I'd give away to witches, pirates, and parrots, and then take the cost off my taxes as a donation.

As Carole crouched down to dust the lowest shelf, she hemmed and hawed and suggested I replace the candy counter with a bakery counter.

"Your customers can get Hershey bars and Red Hots anywhere. But locally baked cookies—now that would be something they'd drool over and remember us for," Carole began her pitch. "And cookies, well, most cookies, won't melt in the summer heat!"

While I was grateful to Carole for taking on the dusting chore, I needed time to think. Where was this out-of-the-blue proposal coming from? We'd never talked about it before. She'd never let on she had this concept swirling in her brain. Biding my time to respond, I removed my work glasses—the ones I bought at Costco—and held them up to the fluorescent lights, as if the perfect response would magically appear through them.

"The name of the store could remain the same," Carole pressed her idea.

I nodded. Why would I change the name of my store to accommodate a chocolate chip cookie? Was Carole nuts? Nevertheless, having known her for as long as I did, I figured she'd been thinking about this for a while. I wanted her to know I valued her for more than her cleaning skills.

As a lifelong townie and the owner of Carefree Catering, Carole was by far the most popular and affluent caterer in Chatham Crossing. Come to think of it, she was the only caterer— and my very first friend (besides

Paul) when I moved there. All of that should count for something, shouldn't it?

"Oh! Carol," I started singing Mr. Sedaka's hit song. I paused, and then gave her a two thumbs up and a great big smile. And with that, I agreed to open a store within the store. *Bixby's Dozen* emerged fully baked.

Consenting to Carole's cookie proposal was my way of finally forgiving her for not interceding on behalf of myself and the other proprietors in town when it came to the traffic light project. She happened to be married to the long-time mayor, the Honorable Simon Duffy. You'd think she would've had some clout regarding the subject.

It seemed she wasn't as influential as Sofia Silva was with Fernando. The light was hung and to this day swings with the wind that comes off Buzzard's Bay.

Perhaps I was wrong to dispute Carole. She was right, it seemed, about the cookies and the light. In search of their favorite treats, both residents and tourists alike continued to swarm like bees to a hive. Traffic light be damned.

"Are we there yet?" I shouted up to Tommy, the ambulance driver. I'd known Tommy for going on fifteen years, I figured. "Two-left-feet-Tommy" was Paul's nickname for him. We kept that respectfully, though, between ourselves.

I was glad they wheeled me into Tommy's vehicle. I didn't recognize the driver of the other ambulance; the one that transported Maggie wherever she needed to be treated. Lord only knew what she was looking for in the bushes. Budd Nickerson whisked me out of the gardens and into this rescue car so quickly, I didn't have the chance to check on her. I hoped she was okay and that I didn't break her ankle when I tripped over her. Apparently, she didn't listen when I warned her the day before that wearing those platform shoes could be the death of her.

"Hang in there, Ms. Bixby. We'll be there before you can name all the members of Pearl Jam."

"If you're trying to distract me from this pain and keeping it bleeping freezing in here—"

Then, just like that, sirens screeched to a halt mid-wail. Rear doors cranked open, and the gurney on which I was partially sitting on, partially laying on, slid out onto the pavement. The July humidity smacked my face, briefly making me wish I was back inside the ambulance.

"Unstrap me, Tommy. I can walk in from here." After all, Chatham Crossing Clinic, a.k.a. The Cube for short, was a walk-in clinic.

"I can take it from here," a voice approaching from my right announced as I got to my feet.

"Oh, hi, Detective Donovan, don't they need you back at the museum?" Tommy asked.

CHAPTER FOUR

"Ruby slippers," I declared. "That's the first thing I thought of this morning when I realized I'd tripped over a pair of shoes as I walked through the museum's gardens. Ruby slippers."

"Wait. What? Next you'll tell me, Ms. Bixby, that you began to sing—what was that song? 'We're Off To See The Wizard?'" Detective Oscar Donovan chuckled as he clutched my right elbow, guiding me through The Cube's sliding glass doors.

"It's Venus, Oscar. No reason to be formal here. We've known each other way too long."

He nodded, hesitantly.

"Just because music is my life doesn't mean I automatically launch into song at the drop of a hat with little forethought. And for your information, if I had started singing, I would've sung 'Over The Rainbow.' Much more my style, wouldn't you agree?"

Truth be told, doing my best Judy Garland was the last thing on my mind as I flew over orange platform shoes, landing very unladylike on the garden's walkway. Thank goodness I decided to wear black knit capri pants instead of a skirt. Otherwise, it wouldn't have been a pretty sight and my knees would have been a bloody mess.

My Kate Spade black and creme vinyl cross-body bag helped break my fall to a point. The thumb on my left hand, which I'd looped through the chain link strap, absorbed the brunt of my stumble. That's why I was sitting in The Cube's waiting room with Detective Donovan surrounded by posters of whaling ships and a bulletin board crammed with pictures of menacing pirates children had colored while waiting their turns to have their cuts and bruises patched up.

I glanced at my right wrist, which miraculously survived. The minuscule images of the Beatles on the face of my limited edition watch stared back at me. The hands falsely showed it was two-thirty. They would remain stuck at that time for however long it took me to make the watch tick again. Who knew when the battery died? I could've chosen a working timepiece that morning from among my collection of two dozen watches, but since this was a special day, I just had to wear one of my Beatles' watches.

It brought me back, way back, to when Paul and I visited Liverpool twenty years before. Celebrating my thirtieth birthday in London, I insisted we do a day trip to Liverpool. "Why not?" Paul had shrugged.

While shopping there, I couldn't decide between two Beatles' watches.

"Get both," Paul proposed as he waved his palm across the two that caught my fancy and handed his platinum AMEX card to the store's proprietor. Such a sweet and generous man he was. To me. To everyone. And did I say, such a talented dancer?

Doing a slight two-step shuffle in my bedroom that morning, I sighed and grinned at the memories I'd always cherish. I tried to fasten the watch with the brown strap and teal blue face. Had my wrists ballooned in the last two decades? Weren't wrists just bones? I ended up wearing the one with the black leather strap instead. Probably my favorite, anyway.

Interrupting my thoughts, Oscar sang, "Because, because …" Apparently, he enjoyed showboating his vocal skills, or lack thereof. I patted his knee and gave him a wink and a nod.

"But do tell, dear Oscar, what is *your* favorite song today?" That made him pause, at least for the moment.

I inhaled deeply. Instead of a fresh breath to ease the pain percolating from my throbbing thumb, I got a whiff of my sister. A combination of irises and roses. But it couldn't be Sherrie. She'd called earlier from San Francisco so she could be the first to wish me a happy birthday. After all, she was my twin. She developed this annoying habit since Paul passed. I couldn't bear to make her quit or let her in on a little secret—that on this particular birthday, someone of the male persuasion had beat her to the punch.

I looked up. Praise be. There'd be no encore for Oscar. I was saved by Jeanne, the on-duty nurse practitioner. I should've known it wasn't Sherrie. She couldn't be in two places at once and had her own birthday celebration to attend to.

"Actually," Jeanne sang, "*we are off* to one of the examination rooms. Come with me, Ms. B."

"But wait. I need to talk with her. She might know—"

"It can wait." I lifted the hat Oscar set on the coffee table and placed it cockeyed on his head, tapping its brim. "Catch me later."

Jeanne gave me a slight lift onto the examining table and promptly sat on a black swivel stool in front of a computer. I was cold again. Not sure if it was the air conditioning or if the shock from my ill-timed tumble was creeping under my skin. Shivering, I asked for a tissue. My nose twitched. From the perfume? Or perhaps a warning?

"So, Jeanne, what is your favorite song today?"

"Excuse me? You already asked me that."

"So I did." I licked my lips and briefly shut my eyes, trying to recall the day's events so far. I let loose a massive sigh.

"Okay, then, Ms. B. What brings you back here this morning? Another piece of cotton lodged in your ear?" She grabbed the here-let's-have-a-look instrument and stepped toward me, the tiny light aimed and ready to probe.

"Very funny, Jeanne, but not quite." I lifted my right arm, palm up toward her. I hoped she interpreted my gesture to mean I wanted her to stop—not that I was giving her a high-five.

I totally got why she might think I was there for a repeat performance or perhaps a follow up. Just a few hours earlier as The Cube opened its doors, I'd scurried in with an embarrassing predicament. After listening to Sherrie's rendition of the birthday song, including the "run around the room" verse our parents always added, I had showered for the first time that day. More than likely, I'd shower again before the party that night. One can never be too clean.

While tending to my ears, I noticed one of the cotton swabs, typically situated at the end of the little white stick, was missing. Excuse me?

I looked on the vanity. I knelt on the beige Berber carpet and patted around with both palms. Nothing. I emptied the clear plastic jar that stored the unused swabs and panicked. Where the heck did it go?

In my ear? But which one? Gently, I touched the inner part of each ear, fretting though, that by doing so, I'd shove the little piece of fiber even further into the ear canal. Still, I found nothing. I searched for a hand mirror in my two vanity drawers, making a mental note to clean them out the first chance I got. There was no reason to keep Paul's old toothbrushes or razors any longer. Maybe it was time to suggest to Budd Nickerson that we spend even more nights at my place, rather than in the cottage. He could bring his own toothbrush, or I could give him one of the dozen in the box designated "For Teeth" in the linen closet.

Unfortunately, my mirror idea lacked any prospect of success. What was I thinking? If Budd hadn't left for work while I showered, he could've checked it out for me. *Coulda, woulda ...* whatever.

I realized I needed a professional with the right tools for the job to peer into my ears and remove the little nemesis. Not how I planned to spend my Saturday, this Saturday of all days. But life didn't always go as planned.

Speaking of plans. I thought I'd open Oldies & Goodies early. I'd given Carole permission to use the back room at the store as a launching pad that day and offered to lend a helping hand, if needed, before I went for my mani/pedi. She'd asked both the catering and cookie crews to be there starting at eight-thirty. As an incentive, she'd buy a couple of Starbucks Coffee Travelers so there was no need for them to stop for their morning boost. She wanted to be sure the food and decorations were all ready and accounted for. Her plan was to have the non-perishables shuttled over to the museum early in the day, so she could be sure everything was organized and displayed to absolute perfection.

Before heading to The Cube for what I didn't realize at the time would be my first visit of the day there, I had called Carole and asked her to do me a favor.

"You'll never guess what's happened."

"Don't worry, I'll open the store before I head over to the museum."

Relieved, yet confident I could always count on Carole, I hopped into Jitter Bug and drove to The Cube.

They'd just turned on the fluorescent lights and unlocked the door. As the first patient of the day, I was attended to immediately by Jeanne, the same nurse practitioner who was standing in front of me now, holding that same lighted scope.

"You won't need that."

"I didn't need it this morning either." Jeanne laughed at what she must have perceived as her idea of a joke.

"Okay. So, there was no cotton in my ears. Must have been a fluke, an error in manufacturing. I'll be more careful in the future."

I held up my left hand. My thumb was an odd shape: clearly gnarled and awkward looking. And throbbing to beat the band. "Think this warrants a trip to The Cube?"

"How in God's name—"

"I tripped over Maggie McGee at the museum."

"Maggie McGee. The manager of the gift shop?"

"Yes, but she wasn't in the gift shop when I tripped over her. That would be ridiculous."

Jeanne stood, her mouth opened, evidently waiting for me to explain.

"In the museum gardens," I continued. "After you gave my ears a clean bill of health earlier, I went for a mani-pedi. See."

Jeanne was all ears as I waved my fingers the best I could without incurring too much pain, displaying the nine beautiful mauve nails still intact.

"My fiftieth birthday party is tonight, you know, in the museum's gardens." I paused and then launched into the first verse of Ricky Nelson's "Garden Party."

Jeanne nodded and twirled her index finger in a circular go-on gesture.

"I went there to check how the preparations were coming along. The decorations and food. Much to my surprise, not much had been set up. And it was already mid-morning."

Jeanne handed me a pill and a cup of water. "Here, this should help your pain."

I slugged it down in one gulp.

"Okay, but why the police escort? I know you're a VIP in town, but—"

"Good question. I really haven't a clue why Detective Donovan is here."

"It's hardly needed for a fractured thumb. Of course, we won't know if it's a Rolando or Bennett fracture until we look at the X-ray."

I tilted my head, thinking about what she just speculated. "So, it's either a Tony Orlando or Tony Bennett fracture?"

Jeanne guffawed. "Do you associate everything with music, Ms. B?"

"Why not? Isn't it what the world needs now? Better than believing a fracture was named after me."

"Why would—"

"Bennett's my maiden name."

"Well, neither Tony nor you are associated with naming this anatomical situation. And it's *Rolando*, not Orlando. The Bennett fracture is a clean break. If the bone is shattered into several pieces, it's Orlando. I mean Rolando. See, now you've got me saying it."

About twenty minutes later, Jeanne and I stared at the lighted Xray view box.

"What's the diagnosis?"

"Well, let's just say your thumb is also your maiden name. And that's a good thing. We'll fix you right up—"

With one good hand, I rifled through my bag to retrieve my phone. I placed it on the exam table and awkwardly texted Carole.

Ull nvr gess whts hppnd NOW.

I heard. Poor Maggie.

CHAPTER FIVE

When Maggie McGee stepped out of her second-floor rental apartment early that Saturday morning, she noticed the humidity, but not the fellow in the parking lot below spit shining his candy apple red Mustang. After she'd shooed him out of her bed at 2 a.m., Maggie wasn't sure what kind of reception she'd get from him … considering. He'd wanted to stay until dawn, but she knew if she let him linger, she'd be late for work. And that would never do. Not that day of all days. If she had stayed at his place downstairs as usual, she could've easily snuck out when he dozed off.

"Good morning, sunshine," he called up to her, forcing her to look his way.

"Hey, there! You're up early." She couldn't have ignored him even if she wanted to. She heard him loud and clear, just as she did the night before, when they'd clinked their drinks—his a Captain Morgan and coke, hers a glass of ginger ale with extra ice—and he offered a toast.

"Here's to tomorrow. A day that'll change lives forever," he'd pronounced the evening before. The sweet smell of vanilla and spiced rum wafted out of his glass and through the air.

She had been about to explore exactly what he meant by that. Whose lives? Why forever? But the server arrived with their seafood platter, which they ordered as an appetizer, but which was sufficient to be the meal. Distracted by taking her share of jumbo shrimp and fish taco bites and his slurping back raw oysters (never her favorite), she had let his nebulous toast slide. Rightly or wrongly, she had assumed he was heralding the debut of the brand new cookie he had baked for the party at the museum. In the weeks leading up to that day, all he'd say when she asked what he'd come up with was, "It's a secret."

"Not drinking tonight?" he'd asked, jutting his chin toward her soda.

Such was not the case when she first met him the Friday before Valentine's Day. She'd had a buzz on that night. Her colleagues from SSWM started celebrating the end of the week shortly after work at the Whaler's Watch Pub, just a quick walk across the street from the museum. Back then, Maggie would start off the evening ordering the house red wine to save money. Almost without fail, by the second round, some dude would start buying her drinks hoping to score a place to bunk for the night. She always disappointed them. Until … this happened.

Gently pushing aside the latest chap who had his wallet out, a tall, good-looking guy in a cowboy sort of way with a dimpled chin and eyes that sparkled when he smiled, introduced himself. "Good evening, young lady. I'm Roger P. Drake. I hear you've got a thing for whales."

"Is that your best pickup line?" she asked, feeling only a little sorry for the previous guy who'd lost his chance.

Evidently it was his best, because it worked. Though Roger P. Drake looked vaguely familiar, she couldn't place him. So she allowed him to loop his arm through hers and usher her to a two-seater table in the darkest corner of the pub. He had a swagger about him that melted her typical reserve. Helped along, too, was the wine glass that appeared never to be empty. Without divulging specifics, Maggie shared her story about her recent move from Maine to Massachusetts and how she loved her new job at the museum. Refreshingly, Roger P. Drake seemed to hang on her every word.

"What about you?" she asked.

He was a newcomer to town, arriving just a few months before she did. Short on background details just as she was, he said, "I'm a chef by training, a cook by circumstance, a baker by stroke of good fortune." As she was about to ask the difference between a chef and a cook, Roger added, "Didn't you see the newspaper just before Christmas? I'm one of *Bixby's Dozen*." She reminded him she just moved there after New Year's and had been too busy settling in and starting her new job.

"Tell me all about the humpbacks," he murmured, leaning across the table and slipping his long fingers along her wrist under her sweater sleeve.

Since she'd only been managing the gift shop at the museum for little over a month, she admitted she had a lot yet to learn about whaling. What did he want to know?

"Everything! Initially, I moved here to research and write a book about the history of whalers. But in my spare time, I've volunteered to read to kids in the elementary school. Guess what I've discovered?"

"Can't imagine. What?" Reading to kids was not high on Maggie's bucket list, but the fact that this guy did made him one of the most interesting guys she'd ever met.

"Even though most of them were born right here where the history of this place is most likely in their DNA, these kids want to know more. Not just about the ships that went to sea, but about the men who lived and died for a whale oil trade that had faded away. And, of course, about their families. And were pirates for real?"

"What did you say your name was?"

He smiled without answering. So, she recalled it on her own and filed it away. That was not the time to go there. When he lifted her left hand and asked if she was married, she dodged his question. "It depends on how you define married."

He grabbed her L.L. Bean parka, slipped her arms through it, and led her out into the twenty-degree, clear sky night.

"Now what?" Maggie asked, bouncing from one foot to the other, trying to stay warm.

"Take me home," Roger said, drawing her close in and kissing her forehead.

She pulled on her wool cap, and together they stumbled down the hill to her apartment building.

"You live here?"

"Uh, yeah?"

"So do I. How have we not met?"

That was the start of their Friday night routine they dubbed *Soup and Shag*. No commitments. Just good food and a great romp in the hay, almost always at his place. Until …

CHAPTER SIX

As she turned to lock her apartment door on Saturday morning, Maggie heard, "Can I give you a lift?" She almost accepted Roger's offer, but the smell of rotten eggs just about made her gag. The sun came up two hours ago. She realized the culprits making her queasy were the July heat and the ninety-degree humidity soaking into the seaweed that washed up along the docks.

"No, thanks. I could use the walk."

"Be like that."

She gulped and her eyebrows lifted above her sunglasses. For a moment, she considered his snarky tone and wondered whether there was a hidden meaning in his remark. Briefly, she thought about turning around and heading back inside to rethink her next move. But she couldn't let him or the pungent sea breeze distract her. That would only delay the inevitable. She had to get a move on and, after all, she only had herself to blame for Roger's attitude. And dealing with the funky air was the price she paid for listening to Robin Ritchie, the lady from Sailing Ships Realty that rented Maggie the place.

"So close to the bay, you'll save a bundle on electricity when the dog days roll in this summer. No need for air conditioning," Robin had said.

Back in January, that made logical sense to Maggie. As she waited for the condo she was buying at Harbor View Cove to be ready in September, the prospect of saving money appealed to her. About ten blocks north of the shoreline, her new place would be far enough away from the stink. Maggie was confident the stench wouldn't blow all the way up toward her new home. Besides, it was the best investment, perhaps the only investment, she'd ever make in her life. If she couldn't afford anything within historic Chatham Crossing, she justified at the time, owning a piece of real estate bordering it was second best.

What was the saying? Location, location, location? Yet, Maggie had to admit, the view of Buzzards Bay from the living area of her current studio apartment was mesmerizing, even in the dead of winter. There was always something, or someone, moving around on the wharf and the docks. And since the Sofia Silva Whaling Museum was just up the hill, she could walk to her new job, allowing her to save the cash in her savings accounts. Plural.

Yet, after a week of almost unbearable temperatures, Maggie had second thoughts. She half expected her clothes to melt permanently onto her skin. *Was saving $2.79 on a gallon of gas worth it?*

"Less than two months until the closing," she mumbled, slinging the canvas tote bag with the word Vacationland plastered on the front over her shoulder. As the queen of penny-pinchers, Maggie knew full well she wouldn't drive to work after the move in September either. The Old Town

Trolley stopped on Buzzards Bay Boulevard, a half a block from what would be her new front door and would drop her off just thirty-three steps away from the entrance to the museum. Before buying the condo, Maggie had done a dry-run and counted the steps. Kudos to the realtor: she'd gotten that one perk right.

Though Maggie could walk the 2,000 steps from the rental apartment to work in less than ten minutes, after Roger left in the wee hours of the morning, Maggie set her Baby Ben alarm clock for an hour earlier than normal. She could've set the alarm on her cell phone, but the clock had sentimental value. Setting it was a habit she'd held onto. The clock was one of the few things she'd taken when she and Brian split. During their brief four and half year marriage, she regularly annoyed him by winding the clock before bed each night. He'd say: "If you don't stop that shit, I'm going to throw you and that damn clock out." She'd roll away from him and turn off the light.

As the world turned, she beat Brian to the punch. Just after the Christmas holiday, Maggie hauled herself, her inheritance, and the Tick-Tock out of Maine and away from Brian's cheating heart. The new year meant a new life for her.

Given her choice, Maggie would've arrived at work by dawn that morning. Without a key, though, she had to wait until the caretaker showed up to let her into the premises. She suggested they meet at seven. He countered by a half hour later. They compromised at quarter past.

With each step up the slope, Maggie set aside all thoughts of Roger and reminded herself this was her big day. An opportunity to show *everyone* she was more than just a measly old sales clerk. *Everyone*—meaning Sandra "Sadie" Hawkins, the museum's curator, and the entire Chatham Crossing A-list.

Over the last few days Maggie kept a tissue in her pocket so she could blot the occasional tear that meandered down her cheek. When Maggie went into Sadie's office the previous Saturday to leave the gift shop receipts report for the day, she caught a glimpse of an engraved invitation, which she was sure Sadie had purposely left visible on her desk. She imagined Sadie had sent everybody who was anybody in town the gold leaf invitation to the big event in the gardens scheduled for that evening. She recalled it as if she'd written it herself.

We request your esteemed presence on Saturday, July 3, 2010
For a joyous dual celebration
In honor of Venus Bixby, as she turns half a century!
and
To unveil SSWM's newest and most exciting acquisition!
Please be punctual. Festivities begin at 6 o'clock in the evening.
Garden party attire an absolute must!

Maggie remembered thinking no one needed to explain who Venus Bixby was. Everyone knew her, because Venus Bixby made sure everyone knew her. Even a newcomer like Maggie. Unlike so many middle-aged women often were, Venus wasn't shy about telling the world she was turning fifty. For the past month, all the local radio station played was sixties music. Between sets, WCCR aired not-so-veiled advertising spots about Oldies & Goodies, Venus's shop that seemed to draw nostalgic crowds no matter the season.

Concurrent with all the hoopla organized by Venus herself, Maggie heard the purveyor of the "goodies" part of the store, a.k.a. *Bixby's Dozen*, recognized a chance to capitalize on the festivities as well. Rumor had it, Carole Duffy emailed the thirteen cookie bakers who were at her beck and call with an assignment. As she tried to make a new life in Chatham Crossing, Maggie refrained from engaging in water cooler chitchat and spreading gossip. Still, she doubted, yet couldn't ignore, what she'd over-heard: Carole had given marching orders to her bakers to "create something singularly exceptional for Chatham Crossing's first lady."

So when Carole showed up at the museum gift shop on Friday with a Lucite clipboard in one hand and a Mont Blanc pen in the other, Maggie recognized the opportuni-ty to put the rumor to a test. "Oh, Carole," she said, "is it true you refer to Ms. Bixby as Chatham Crossing's first lady?"

With that, the clipboard soared across the gift shop like a frisbee, just missing Maggie, but knocking over the entire display of black and white whale and gray shark stuffed animals, and landing softly on top of a stack of fleece blankets. The white-lined pad that disengaged from the clipboard, along with Carole's pen, scraped the tile floor and slid under a display of postcards with pictures of current and past museum exhibits, famous whaling cap-tains, and notorious pirates.

"Wherever did you hear that?" Carole crossed her arms in a huff, reminding Maggie of a female version of Mr. Clean. Somehow, she suppressed a laugh.

"As the mayor's wife, that makes *me* the town's first lady," Carole groused. "And it's Mrs. Duffy to you."

Brushing off this slight, which Maggie sadly had become accustomed to, she scooted past Carole, and began rescuing the felled merchandise. "Just being new in town, *Mrs. Duffy*," she said with a snort, "and having met Ms. Bixby on more than one occasion, I could understand why people hold her in such—" She handed Carole the lined pad and noticed the heading on the checklist, *S&DL 50*th. Maggie wondered whose business Carole was truly promoting? The Song and Dance Lady's or her own?

"Thought I'd double check. Knowing who's who is—" Maggie turned her gaze toward Carole and away from the checklist.

"Well, now you know." Carole spun on her heels. "It might behoove you to busy yourself with whatever chores Sadie's assigned you for the shindig tomorrow night rather than spreading rumors that have nothing to do with you."

Maggie watched Carole march down the hall, more than likely toward Sadie's office, which was situated smack in the middle of the main floor. The inconspicuous closed circuit television system installed throughout most of the museum apparently was not enough for Sadie. From the one-way window, she kept a watchful eye not only on the precious, irreplaceable exhibits but also on the staff and visitors. Nothing got past Sadie.

Maggie inhaled deeply and let out a full exhale that could've been heard had anyone been within earshot.

"Nothing to do with you," she repeated under her breath what Carole had said. *That about sums things up, doesn't it?* She lowered her eyes to the floor and tried to shake it off.

But that was difficult. *Chores. The paid help.* That was what Maggie's life in Chatham Crossing amounted to if Carole's attitude toward her was any indication of how others viewed her. That exchange with the mayor's wife only doubly confirmed what Maggie already suspected.

She wasn't *anybody.* The week before the incident with Carole, it was Sadie who made sure she received that message, but not an invitation, loud and clear. After all, many townies still considered Maggie a stranger in Chatham Crossing. A newcomer. An interloper.

If this was really going to be her new life, she'd have to earn her stripes.

As she sat on the wooden bench with black varnished arms and legs waiting for the man with the key, Maggie tapped her left foot, deciding whether to slip out of her green Converse and into her platforms. If she did that before he arrived, she'd save time once inside the museum. She could get right to work on her *chores.* She was determined today would be *her* celebration, *her* unveiling.

Just you watch, first ladies of Chatham Crossing, whoever you are.

Maggie sensed Budd Nickerson before he rounded the corner of the building to where she was perched. He whistled, "Don't Worry Be Happy." Quite the giveaway. Budd adopted Bobby McFerrin's hit as his signature song during their tenure working together at Chadborn's in Maine. Whenever he was out of earshot of Franklin Chadborn, the master of the house, he'd whistle while he waited to butler. On more than one occasion, Maggie implored him to stop. She was neither happy doing her wifely duties at home nor as secretary to Mr. Chadborn. And, thus, she had much to worry about.

Budd halted mid-stride to the right of the bench, along with his tune.

"What are you so happy about this morning, Budd?"

"And a good morning to you, too, Ms. Margaret." He never took to calling her Maggie, a holdover from his butler days, she figured. It pleased her that he showed her some respect and kept their relationship somewhat professional. Maybe it was simply his way of reminding her of the mutual secret society they'd established post-Chadborn.

"You really should buy one of ours," Budd said. He gestured his clean-shaven chin toward Maggie's tote bag that sat untouched on the space next to her on the bench. As he unlocked the side entrance to the museum, he added, "Gracious, girl. You're not in Maine anymore."

"Girl?" she mumbled, grabbing her belongings. Perhaps she was wrong about the way he viewed her. She brushed past him, turned around and walked backward. "You really should mind your own beeswax. I'm not paid enough."

Maggie stopped and settled down on one of the two armchairs conveniently positioned in the hall leading to the lobby so tired museumgoers could take a load off their feet if need be. She popped off her sneaks with a flip of her big toe against each heel, and slipped into her platform shoes, recently bought half-price at Target (which she'd taken to wear daily at work). "If the high and mighty Mrs. Hawkins has a problem with me carrying my shoes in this bag, she could just as easily give me one."

"Or maybe you'd just take it."

"I'd never do that, and you know it. Speak for yourself. You never did tell me why you bolted from Chadborn's."

"I'll tell you my secret, if you tell me yours. Like how'd you have enough money to buy into that new con-do complex?"

"Wouldn't you like to know?" she teased. Working closely together in Maine, she'd confided in Budd about Brian's evil ways, even though he'd witnessed Brian in action himself on occasion. But that was about as personal as it got between them. She'd kept close to the vest any information about her financial situation, especially about the money her rich aunt had bequeathed her.

"What I do know is … you're late."

"Not that late." Budd winked.

"What? Did you get it on this morning? Do a little mambo with the Song and Dance Lady?" Maggie shot him a flirty grin. "Is that why you're whistling? Tell me, Mr. Nickerson, did you flash dance for her or perhaps sing happy birthday to her *au naturel*?"

"I'd lower your voice. Mrs. Hawkins is probably in her office already. Big day today."

Maggie heard whispers among the museum's staff in the breakroom about Budd and Venus hooking up, but she never engaged in the banter or spoke up to confirm what she knew to be true. Though Budd had implied that living in the cottage on the Hilltop grounds had its advantages, she'd keep his confidence as long as he wanted her to. She owed him one.

"Is Venus excited?" Maggie asked as they walked together toward the museum's gift shop. She stepped to one side, giving Budd room to bend down to unlock the store's gate. As the keeper of the keys, on any normal day he would've already opened the gate and had the lights on ahead of her arrival. She'd only have to find him wandering somewhere in the museum to get the cash register drawer out of the safe. How long did it take for Sadie to trust Budd with that task? Perhaps after that weekend, Sadie would trust Maggie enough to make opening each morning easy-peasy for her. Time would tell.

"Excited? Seems to be. She was just hopping into the shower—" Budd caught himself. "Oops."

Maggie winked. "Gotcha!"

"Do you have any clue what the big reveal is?" he asked, an obvious attempt to change the subject.

"Ooh … the secret unveiling." Maggie went along with it, making a horrific face and scary noise like Jack Nicholson did in *The Shining*. She busied herself ensuring the stuffed animals were secure after yesterday's tumble, then added, "How would I know? I just work here."

"Me too."

"You want to know what I think?" Maggie faced Budd with her hands on her hips.

"Always."

"I think it's a hoax. There's no *BIG* reveal. Sadie hated the idea that Venus was going to be the center of attention. So she's dragged something out of the archives, something that people haven't seen in a while to make a splash with. Alleging something that was old is actually new and ultra-valuable."

"That's ridiculous."

"We'll see. I've heard Sadie and Venus are both vying for a seat on the Town Committee. Who do you think is more important to the town? The curator of the Sofia Silva Whaling Museum or the Song and Dance Lady?"

"You have to ask?"

CHAPTER SEVEN

Early Friday night, Carole Duffy climbed into bed with the singular goal of getting a restful night's sleep ahead of the big day. Saturday would be her moment to shine, to showcase not only the sumptuous spreads of Carefree Catering but also the wizardry of her team of cookie bakers. She'd planned every detail—starting with the menu, then the tablecloths and decorations, and culminating with the exact presentation of the banquet right down to the arrangement of the cookie trays. When she and Venus discussed all of Carole's plans, Venus suggested placing an Oldies & Goodies sign next to the cookie display. There was so much to do, Carole somehow forgot to add that task to her checklist.

As she drifted to sleep, her interaction with Maggie McGee that afternoon played havoc with her mind. She hadn't shared their conversation with anyone. Not her husband. Certainly not Venus.

That anyone in town would ever think Carole would refer to Venus as the first lady of Chatham Crossing was utterly ridiculous. Fortunately, she set the record straight with Maggie before such a bizarre notion made its way through the community. Unfortunately, she missed her chance to ask Maggie who she'd heard it from. Whoever started, or was spreading, that rumor ought to be smacked alongside the head. Not literally, of course.

Maggie was right about one thing. Carole had instructed her team, well, her team leaders, to create unique cookies for the event. Her goal, however, was more about shining a light on herself than it was in creating a tribute to Venus. To ensure the bakers came through like a charm, she divided them up—three teams had three bakers; one had four. To liven things up, Carole assigned each team a leader. She wanted to give each team a name but left it to the teams themselves to handle should they be interested in having a contest, a friendly competition.

Carole loved her thirteen cookie bakers and approached the selection process super-seriously. Since she transformed the candy counter in Venus's store to *Bixby's Dozen* five years ago, many local bakers locked horns during the selection process. Between Thanksgiving and Christmas each year, Carole held a bake-off to fill any vacancy caused by anyone resigning or moving away since the end of September. At the end of last year there were two spots to fill.

In an unusual move, a couple of weeks before the big event at the museum, Carole invited four bakers to her home to form the teams and give them their assignment. She'd selected the team leaders not just for their creative baking prowess, but to demonstrate to one and all how she valued the diversity of her team. She scanned her list for just the right ingredients—take one Portuguese, add a millennial, mix in a baby boomer, and stir in some spice. She circled, in order: Billy Bomba, Cecilia Powers, Helen Davis, and Roger P. Drake.

As the mayor, Carole's husband would have preferred the bakers meet at Venus's store instead of their home. Even though Carole ran Carefree Catering out of the state-of-the-art kitchen she had built in the basement of their home, Simon didn't share Carole's rationale that inviting more people into their home would improve his chances to be re-elected to another term. According to Simon, his success transcended hers.

Suffice it to say, Carefree Catering didn't need a promotional boost to stay a winner either. Events both large and small in Chatham Crossing, as well as in the surrounding towns, sought Carole's culinary expertise and party planning skills. Throughout that corner of Massachusetts, Carole's twenty-five-year reputation was untarnished.

Her idea to replace the candy counter with cookies was brilliant (even if she said so herself, which she did at every opportunity). When tourists stopped by Oldies & Goodies, even if they bought nothing Venus was hawking, they always walked out with a bagful of cookies. This gave Carole, or whoever was working the counter that day, the opportunity to slip a business card into their bag or box, introducing Carefree Catering.

Yet Carole wanted more. She dreamed if she built enough interest on the Cape, she could expand her catering business, perhaps even doubling its size. Chatham Crossing would remain the central hub—the Cape, a satellite. If all went well, she might be able to open her own storefront, just like Venus had. She had her eye on Roger P. Drake, one of the newest cookie bakers, as a real go-getter who might help her take Carefree Catering to a new level. When that happened, *Bixby's Dozen* would become a burden, too much for her to handle. She could easily pass it on to someone else in town who was willing to put up with the owner of Oldies & Goodies.

Venus's birthday bash, coupled with the big reveal Sadie had planned, could make that dream come true. Sadie had invited the town managers of most of the towns on the Cape—towns close to them, like Bourne and Falmouth, as well as those farther out, like Dennis and Provincetown. By the end of Saturday night, everyone would be buzzing about Carefree Catering, and *Bixby's Dozen* would be an afterthought. Absolutely nothing could go wrong … if Carole had anything to do with it.

Carole's deep sleep was rudely interrupted. She rolled to her left to grab and answer her phone. "Venus? What time is it?"

"Are you still in bed, Carole? Don't tell me you're still in bed. Do you realize what day it is?"

Carole bit her tongue. Obviously, it was Venus's day. And she was at the clinic because she lost an argument with a cotton swab. Just like Venus to draw even more attention to herself. She'd be in her glory at the party.

Carole swung her legs out of bed, assuring Venus she had everything under control. She'd get to the store asap and everything would be just dandy. She recognized Venus's heavy breathing. She was known to hyperventilate. Especially when things didn't go her way.

"Calm yourself, girl. I've got this."

CHAPTER EIGHT

If creating a competition between the four team leaders was a goal of Carole's, she failed miserably. At least according to Helen Davis. As the eldest among the four, Helen enjoyed promoting an attitude of camaraderie, not just among those Carole cherry-picked for this mission of hers, but among the entire *Bixby's Dozen* staff. And she wasn't shy about voicing her opinions believing permission to do so came with age.

Last year, as the seasons changed and September morphed into October, Helen took to her bed for a week with a cold. "Doctor's orders," she'd told Carole, who showed up one day to check on her status. Over the cup of hot chicken broth, which she'd brought for Helen, Carole confided about her dream to expand Carefree Catering onto the Cape.

"What'll happen to Bixby's—" Helen's eyes watered at the thought of it closing down.

"Don't you worry your pretty little head about that. I'll just spin it off, like those banking giants do in Providence and Boston." Helen frowned at this. She couldn't fathom what the banks were up to, except that every few years she'd get a new ATM card in the mail and have to stop whatever she was doing and activate it.

"Oh, no! You won't give it to Venus to run, will you? She has her hands full." Helen covered her mouth and coughed.

"Not on your life. Anyway, we both know Venus is looking for other fish to fry." Carole grabbed the box of tissues that sat on the nightstand next to a blood pressure cuff and placed it alongside Helen.

"And they all involve getting her hooks into the museum, am I right?"

"That you are. So I have a little surprise for you, Helen. You must get yourself out of that king size bed as soon as you can. I need you."

"I'll try." Helen sneezed, thankful Carole didn't question her need for such a large bed since her husband was long gone, or mention the men's slippers that rested alongside hers at the foot of it.

"What's the surprise?" She sneezed again. "Sneezes always come in pairs. Why is that?" She tucked the used Kleenex under the covers where a large mound had formed under the bedspread.

"Hold onto your jammies, Helen. You are in line to inherit *Bixby's Dozen*." Carole squealed with delight. "So, don't go and die on me just yet."

Helen had no intention of dying. She'd earned her stripes, not just as the longest-standing member of *Bixby's Dozen,* but also as somewhat of a master chef. She was damned proud of both her cooking skills and her cookie contributions, even though it seemed no one other than Carole recognized her for it. Her day would come.

Wherever she ventured around town—to the market, the hairdresser, The Cube—Helen carried a vintage binder, the blue cloth kind; the only kind available when she was growing up. The binder was her trademark. She'd heard whispers that some folks in town believed instead of rosary beads, they would bury her with the binder. Despite their jibber-jabbering, Helen clutched it to her chest as if it contained maps to a trove of hidden treasure, or maybe her bank account passwords. No one knew for sure because she never opened it in public. Truth was, Helen stored all her original recipes—cookies, brownies, and whatever—in there, not in a computer file somewhere at home. She'd seen the stories on TV about hacking and computer theft. If she took over Carole's cookie business, she'd find a publisher worthy of her recipes. And, indeed, a prime outlet to sell her cookbook would be *Bixby's Dozen*. Perhaps with the transfer from Carole to her, she'd be able to change its name. Less Bixby, more Davis. *Davis's Dozen*. Yeah, that's the ticket.

Last December, on the Tuesday morning before Christmas, Helen waltzed into Oldies & Goodies at half-past eleven. She carried her binder safely in a tote bag that was so worn one of the canvas handles was threadbare. She arrived forty-five minutes early so she could grab the only padded armchair at the table in the back room that served as a meeting room when it wasn't crowded with Tupperware cookie bins. It was a momentous occasion. Carole would announce the winners of the bake-off precisely at 12:15—the time specifically set so those who would be on their lunch break would have time to get to the store. Helen could feel her blood pressure mounting. No blood pressure cuff required to confirm that. Whoever joined them would uniquely shape the team for the coming year and perhaps for years to come when she was destined to be in charge. She just had a feeling.

"My aunt had one of those," Roger P. Drake said when Helen met him for the first time that day. Just a week ago, she'd tasted over twenty cookie samples, and his was one of her top two choices.

As they all gathered at the assigned time, they took the empty seats surrounding Helen. Moving clockwise—to her left, there was Roger, Billy, Cecilia, and Carole. Since Roger and Cecilia were the only two at the table not already part of *Bixby's Dozen*, it didn't take a rocket scientist to figure out who won the bake-off. Nevertheless, the anticipation of the announcement grew as they continued making small talk over Elvis' Christmas Album playing in the background. When Venus walked in carrying a platter of cookies, Helen caught her eye and mouthed a request of her. "Turn it down a tad?" Though she loved the King of Rock 'n Roll, she was afraid she'd miss out on the table talk surrounding her.

Helen figured Roger's comment about his aunt was a silly attempt to impress her. She was a judge, after all. "Now what was it you were saying?"

"She tried to get me to use one of those binders for school, but I preferred pocket folders instead. I had one color for each subject," he said, picking up where he'd left off before Venus dropped by. He reached out to touch and scratch the binder's rough fabric.

When she pulled it back, Roger pointed to the quote on the binder's backside. "Gettin' good players is easy. Gettin' them to play together is the hard part," he read aloud. "Now, who said that?" He massaged his clean-shaved chin.

Somewhat defensively, Helen placed the binder out of harm's way on her lap, not on the table where it would be dangerously near Roger's long, calloused fingers. She'd never seen such hard-worn hands before on a dough puncher. As one of the most critical tools of the trade, master bakers protected their hands at all costs. For the first time, she looked closely at one of the town's newest residents. She hoped Billy was too busy uselessly flirting with Cecilia to notice her interest in the new guy.

The week before when she sampled Roger's entry in the bake-off, she'd checked around with a few of her friends at the Senior Center to see if anyone knew him. Everyone shrugged. "People come and go around here, Helen; you know that. There's always work to be had on the docks," was the best anyone could come up with. Beyond that, she learned he moved into town in September and was renting an apartment near the wharf. Alone. Oh, and that he drove a shiny new Mustang. Color: candy apple red. Clearly not someone who wished to move around under the radar, unnoticed.

But when he strolled into the back room twenty minutes early, taking the seat next to Helen, it was Roger's height she first noticed. He had to duck to not hit the low doorframe and when he pulled up the rickety metal chair beneath him, his knees spread like a wishbone, almost rubbing against hers. His black cowboy boots rested squarely flat on the floor, while Helen's gray orthopedic boots dangled unmoored. Her toes could touch the floor only if she gave it the good old college try. She hoped her tweed slacks were long enough to cover her black compression knee highs.

"You must be Mrs. Davis?" he'd asked, offering her his right hand. "I'm Roger P. Drake." Baffled at first as to how he knew who she was, Helen ultimately realized he would've already met Carole, and Cecilia was young enough to be Helen's daughter, or maybe granddaughter. Under either scenario, Cecilia was too young to be a *Bixby's Dozen* judge.

With introductions out of the way, it was Roger's long dark brown hair (pulled back in a ponytail), his well-trimmed (yet animated) eyebrows Helen could see peeking out beneath the baseball cap he wore, the twinkle in his eye, and the sparkle of the diamond he sported in just one ear, that reminded her of that pirate. *What's his name?* One never knew when a delay recalling names would be a red flag worth reporting to one's physician. Helen breathed a silent sigh of relief when it came to her in two flashes. *Jack Sparrow. That's it.*

"Why Casey Stengel said it, of course, now I recall," Roger said, removing his black and gold two-toned cap and plunking it down on the table in front of him.

Momentarily confused and about to say "No, Jack …", Helen blinked and tried to focus on the other three at the table. She soaked in the aroma of the decaffeinated green tea with mango Carole had ready for her when she arrived and willed the tea's aroma to overpower the spicy and woody smell coming from the man sitting to her left. *Ralph Lauren Polo.* She'd recognize her late-husband's favorite cologne anywhere.

"Who's Casey Stengel?" Cecilia Powers asked, showing her millennial-ness.

"Only the best Yankees manager ever," Helen said, relieved she'd gotten her groove back.

A sudden gasp reverberated through the room and interrupted Helen's chance to showcase her sports acumen. At least temporarily.

"Thought you were a Red Sox fan these days, Lena," Billy said. Billy Bomba and Helen had been friends since she moved to Chatham Crossing twenty years ago after her husband died and was the only person who could call her Lena. The town scuttlebutt was that the Welcome Wagon package Billy, who was fifteen years her junior, delivered to her contained more than coupons to the local hardware store. So far there was no expiration date to whatever had grown between them.

"I am, Billy, you know that." She looked up from her binder and winked at him. He blew her a quick kiss.

Helen reached across Roger and swiveled his hat toward her for a better look. The gold embroidered 'P' gave her pause. Did that refer to his middle name? She traced the gold fabric with her index finger. He didn't pull the hat away. Instead, he smiled and said, "Pittsburgh Pirates. But I'm sure *you* know that."

"Ah," she bowed her head toward him. *Perhaps Pittsburgh is a second clue to this mysterious man's background.* She'd already picked up on the fact that he had an aunt he probably lived with growing up. She grinned at the thought of making notes in pencil in her address book, not the binder, of course, under W for Who's Who in town. She'd wait until the real Roger P. Drake revealed himself to memorialize his name in ink.

With her wits back, Helen lifted her binder, turning it toward Cecilia. "Is it safe to assume you know who Helen Keller is?"

Unlike Roger, Cecilia was not a newbie to Chatham Crossing. In fact, she was born and raised there, and then returned four years ago after graduating from Boston University with a degree in art history. In her teen years, she became chummy with the Bixby's—taking Paul's dance lessons and working part time for Venus. To hear Venus tell it, after graduation, Cecilia listened to her advice and set up an appointment with Sandra Hawkins at the SSWM. What Cecilia didn't know was that she was a shoo-in for a docent-in-training position based almost entirely on the glowing recommendation from Venus. Nice to know people in high places. Just after the first season where she received high marks from tourists and academics alike for her knowledge, good humor, and enthusiasm for all things whales, Cecilia became a full-fledged docent. A paid position with benefits.

Cecilia lowered her dark blue rimmed glasses and squinted at the binder's black lettering. "Alone we can do so little, together we can do so much," she read. She looked around the table for affirmation. "She said that? Awesome."

Carole confirmed the Helen Keller quote and moved on to announce that Roger and Cecilia made the cut and would join the other eleven members of *Bixby's Dozen*.

"But with Roger and me, by my count, that makes thirteen, right?" Cecilia's greenness showed.

"What do you think a baker's dozen is?" Roger teased.

"Oh, yeah. I forgot. I'm so excited. Thank you." Cecilia stamped her feet and placed her arms across her chest. "I'm looking forward to working with all of you."

If you asked Helen, she'd say Cecilia had her sights set on more than just *Bixby's Dozen*. Rumor had it, she'd recently told Venus—who told Carole, who told Helen—her dream was to manage the museum gift shop. Evidently, Cecilia believed given her art history background, she could double the sales in the shop given half a chance. The coffee table books and videos provided a much higher profit margin than stuffed animals and T-shirts. Naturally, rumor also had it Venus promised to put in a good word for her. But, of course, she would.

"We're just baking cookies, Cecilia, not striving for world peace," Carole said.

"Oh, but it's just as important to me, at least. You know what they say?" Cecilia asked.

"Do tell," Helen retorted, tilting her head in Cecilia's direction.

"Find a group of people who challenge and inspire you, spend a lot of time with them, and it will change your life," Cecilia answered gleefully.

Helen imagined this young girl fell asleep each night with visions of the museum gift shop dancing incessantly through her head.

"Who said that?" Helen asked, half expecting Cecilia had made it up.

"Why Amy Poehler, of course. The star of *Parks and Recreation*! Don't you know?"

Helen didn't have a clue. And looking around the table, she didn't think anyone else did either. Her eyes settled on Billy, begging him to save her and the conversation.

"Each monkey has its own branch," was all he could come up with.

So, in mid-June, as Helen sat in the mayor's residence, she thought about how it didn't surprise her that Carole chose the four of them to coordinate the dessert (that is, cookies) for the gala at the museum Independence Day weekend. Well, not really a gala, more like a neighborhood party. It was her way of rewarding them for a job well done. Thus far that summer, the cookies created by Helen, Billy, Roger, and the youngster were flying out of the display cases.

Helen knew Carole was counting on them to do her proud. But that wasn't the half of it. She further believed a successful event at the SSWM would finally launch Carole's plans to expand her catering business and hand off *Bixby's Dozen* to her, precisely the way she'd presented the scheme to Helen between sneezes last October. You couldn't fault her for having her own visions of sugar plums—or rainbow cookies—dancing in her head. Could you?

As she waited for the others to join her downstairs in Carole's custom kitchen, Helen opened her binder and flipped to the sheet protector containing the article announcing the team last December. She read it as if for the first time. Following a string of grunts and groans, she vowed next time Daniel DaRosa of *The Chronicle* wrote about the town's cookie business, he'd come to her for a quote.

CHAPTER NINE

The Chatham Crossing Chronicle
Bixby's Dozen Fills the Void

By: Daniel DaRosa, Investigative Reporter

December 22, 2009. **BREAKING NEWS!** A collective sigh of relief swept through Chatham Crossing yesterday. So much so, the Christmas lights strung across the historic district swayed, and the bells hanging on doorways jingle jangled with the news *Bixby's Dozen* will remain true to its name. At least for the coming year.

Not that there was ever really any doubt. With twenty-two entrants, this year's highly anticipated bake-off surely provided the necessary ingredients to yield fresh bakers to fill the void left by two residents who, for whatever reason, took their culinary talents elsewhere.

This reporter caught up with a few of those responsible for this story following the big announcement.

In thanking the judges for lending their expertise to this year's contest, Carole Duffy, big cheese of *Bixby's Dozen,* said, "The process of searching for perfection among such confectionary delights could have crumbled without Billy Bomba and Helen Davis. I am grateful they put their heads and tastebuds together to select two residents to join the team. This is testimony not only to the winners but also to Billy and Helen's eagerness to recognize a Chatham Crossing native and to welcome a newcomer."

So whose cookies will we be savoring after the New Year?

It appears in her spare time, Cecilia Powers, long-time resident and docent at the Sofia Silva Whaling Museum (a.k.a. SSWM), has broadened her training and competencies to include not just art history but also the art of baking. One can only assume she took to heart the story of how Vincent Van Gogh's sister-in-law and brother encouraged him to become a bookkeeper or a *baker* after he'd been sacked as an art dealer. Unlike Van Gogh's unstable and early career in the art world, Ms. Powers's tenure at SSWM seems to be secure. We're confident she'll surprise us with her cookies and do nothing as drastic as loping off her ear.

The other half of this duo is Roger P. Drake. His name may not be familiar, but odds are you've seen his candy apple red Mustang about town. When I asked Mrs. Duffy to give us the scoop on him, all she said was, "Not sure where he comes from. Perhaps he'll tell us his story through the cookies he bakes."

So, there you have it, cookie lovers of Chatham Crossing. As we look forward to saying good-bye to one year and welcoming a new one, this news is not quite out with the old and in with the new. You'd have to agree, though, having the last mystery of the year solved leaves the community feeling satisfied and excited about good things to come.

Of course, news about *Bixby's Dozen* would not be fully baked without hearing from the proprietor of Oldies & Goodies herself. When asked if she'd personally entered the bake-off this year, Venus Bixby said, "You're kidding, right? If a recipe says, 'Preheat oven,' I close the damn cookbook."

Print edition.

CHAPTER TEN

As usual, none of the museum staff were darting around among the ships and whale displays when Sadie Hawkins arrived early on the Friday morning of the July 4th holiday weekend. First thing she did, even before heading into her office, was check to be sure the gift shop gate was closed and the lights off. If Margaret McGee, the recently hired manager, was already there, the caretaker would've let her in and he'd be somewhere in the building starting his daily chores as well.

But with the coast clear, Sadie climbed the three flights of stairs to the uppermost level of the museum. When she got to the top, she checked her Fitbit. Besides the 4,500 steps she clocked before, during, and after her two-mile pre-work walk, she'd added another 700 on her way into the building and up the stairs. "Good for me," she mumbled. "Halfway there."

However, stair climbing was not the usual way Sadie increased her typical daily step goal or started her day. On most mornings, her routine included a two or three-mile walk about town and to work, a twenty-minute meditation in the museum gardens, and then the first of her hourly rounds among the cultural and historical objects and documents she cherished. By the time she'd lock up at the end of a day, she'd have already met or exceeded her objective. Every step Sadie took after that was gravy. Too bad she couldn't flip them over into the next day's count.

Slightly winded, Sadie regretted foregoing her quietude in the gardens that morning. With her long list of to-dos to get ready for Saturday night, there would be no chance of her fitting in some quiet time. Standing in front of the door labeled Central Storage, she fumbled with the keys on the Harry Potter key ring. In her haste, she dropped it on the gray and white tile. The dozen keys clanged. She hurriedly bent over to retrieve them, and on rising, she exhaled what oxygen remained in her lungs. After a sharp glance over her shoulder to be certain she was still alone, she found the key to the main door, made her way inside, and shut the door behind her.

Only one other person had a key to Central Storage. Budd Nickerson, the caretaker. From time to time, he needed access to contents stowed there, especially if one exhibit was closing down and being replaced by another. To Sadie's surprise and consternation, the gift shop manager had asked for a key just days after she hired her in January.

"I need access to the inventory, Mrs. Hawkins," Margaret McGee said, pitching her request one Monday morning as Sadie stop by the gift shop as she made her rounds.

"Sorry to disappoint you, Margaret, only Mr. Nickerson—"

"It would make everything so much easier for me and Budd. Oh, and you can call me Maggie."

"You just got here, Margaret. Don't get ahead of your-self. All in due time," Sadie had replied. She turned to leave Maggie alone to do her job, but not before stopping to refold a stack of children's T-shirts. She considered asking her how well she'd known Budd when they worked together in Maine. Wouldn't Venus Bixby love to know? And how Sadie would relish being the one to wipe Venus's effervescence off her face. That would be priceless. But Sadie let the exchange with Margaret pass. She had an entire world-renowned museum under her wing. Venus had two small-scale local businesses that relied on limited resident and tourist support to keep the lights on. Sadie's confidence grew by the day. Rest assured, she'd be the next person chosen to be on the powerful Town Committee. *All in due time.*

As she stepped into Central Storage, Sadie welcomed the cool air that smacked her face. The temperature in there was climate controlled at the required 65 degrees and the humidifiers were set at 45 percent. Since no one was looking, she lifted her right armpit and took a whiff. Could she count on the unscented deodorant she'd rolled on after showering that morning to protect her from the combination of sticky July air and the stair climb?

There was no need for Sadie to hurry now that she was safely inside, closeted and undetectable by any of the staff. Her plan to arrive forty-five minutes ahead of her usual time worked like a charm.

Neither Budd nor Maggie—when she went into Central Storage accompanied by him—knew of Sadie's personal storage cabinet. She'd had it built into the wall when she was hired five years ago. In it, she kept the most highly prized museum possessions. Most had been on display in years past, but she kept several to rollout when she decided it was in the museum's, and her, best interest to do so.

In early May, Venus and her close friend Carole Duffy submitted a formal written request to the museum's board of directors to celebrate Venus's fiftieth birthday on Saturday, July 3, at the museum. The request contained one specific condition. The party had to be held in the museum's award-winning gardens.

Initially, Sadie balked at the idea. No can do. For two reasons.

They'd never had a birthday party in their beautiful gardens. That's why year after year the Gardens of Sofia Silva Whaling Museum were celebrated as one of the top three museum gardens in the country, often taking top spot.

Sadie envisioned over-indulgent partygoers stomping through the lilacs, disposing of unwanted wine in the juniper bushes, spitting semi-chewed hors d'oeuvres surreptitiously in the hydrangeas—all the while the transgressors justifying to themselves that they were just adding useful fertilizer.

"Noth-nothing to be a-afraid of, Mrs. Haw-hawkins," Jeremy Roserun, the master gardener, tried to reassure her when she interrupted him one day and shared the party request and her nightmare with him. Surely, he'd side with her on this one. But no. He looked away from her and continued weeding.

She sighed so loudly Jeremy must have heard, but he didn't let on. "Maybe you're right, Jeremy, we're all upstanding individuals here in Chatham Crossing. I'm sure everyone will be on their best behavior. Great opportunity for the museum and all of us to be in the spotlight."

Yet, it was that spotlight that caused Sadie the most angst of all. Why would she willingly put Venus center stage? Didn't her obsession with oldies music give her enough notoriety? Everyone loved oldies, no matter what their age. Even Sadie unwittingly drank the Kool-Aid after Venus's husband died. In an unplanned display of kindness and empathy toward Venus as she grieved, Sadie asked if she had any mindfulness music selections to recommend? Within twenty-four hours Venus emailed her a meditation playlist containing only Beatles songs. Reluctantly, Sadie had to admit—Venus knew her stuff.

And so did Sadie.

She recognized an opportunity when she saw one staring in her face. As chairperson of the museum board, Sadie had the clout to ensure the museum got its fair share of the limelight. It was due time to reveal one of the museum's most valuable possessions. One of its best-kept secrets. An acquisition that museums around the world would have given their sharks' teeth to obtain. But they hadn't. Sadie had.

Without disclosing her ultimate scheme, Sadie put the party request to a vote by the museum's board. "Given that Ms. Bixby is an honorary member of the board, and Carole Duffy's husband is our mayor, I recommend approval of their application. After all, it's just one night. What could go wrong?" And that was that.

Sadie summoned the party planners to her office and let the other shoe drop. The museum (meaning Sadie) had one condition for the use of the gardens. On the night of the event, one of the museum's newest acquisitions must be unveiled, and Sadie would be the one doing the honors.

"Cool beans," Venus said, with a disinterested shrug.

"Do tell us what it is," Carole chirped like a canary.

"It's a surprise!"

The time had come to set the final wheels in motion. Sadie unlatched the crate and sifted through the packing popcorns. She retrieved a pair of white gloves from her hip pocket, slipping them on before lifting her ticket to ride out of its protective casing.

CHAPTER ELEVEN

Joy filled the air in Chatham Crossing whenever the July 4th holiday weekend began on a Friday. I felt it in my bones. I witnessed it in the Oldies & Goodies cash register receipts.

Without a doubt, this particular weekend was the busiest and most profitable for all the local businesses, not just mine. The other two popular weekends were naturally, Memorial Day, which was simply called *The Start*; and Labor Day, logically and sadly labeled *The End*. In its usual infinite wisdom, the Town Committee plastered billboards along the highways into town in early May and August to attract tourists, while installing a traffic light to slow them down once they got there.

Up until then, no one in the community had similarly, or successfully, branded the July 4th weekend itself, despite it being such a uniquely American holiday.

Taking matters into their able hands, *The Chronicle* ran a naming contest back in March, hoping to distract residents from one of the coldest, wettest months of the year, and to provide a bit of frivolity and competition as well. Two of the top contenders were *Midway* and *Halfway*.

A short, but not so sweet, letter to the editor, shot down *Midway*.

"What the H-E double hockey sticks are you thinking?" The anonymous scribe ranted, "Even though few World War II veterans walk along our shore these days, *Midway* could stir negative emotions for residents or visitors alike. Keep trying."

Another townie objected strenuously to *Halfway*, writing, "Have you ever ridden in a car with a ten-year-old? Do the words, 'Are we there yet?' mean anything to you?"

In my humble opinion, which I shared in an email to my friend Daniel DaRosa at the paper, "*Halfway* doesn't cut it. No one wants to admit the summer is halfway over. Never. Ever."

I was of the mind at the time that my opinion influenced, and ultimately convinced, both interested parties in the naming contest to shelve the idea until next year. Who knew what excitement was in store for charming Chatham Crossing that could prompt our creative citizenry to finally solve this nagging problem?

So, as was my custom ahead of any holiday, I reviewed my list of temporary staffing requirements to be sure Oldies & Goodies would be well organized over the Fourth. I'd need to focus on my birthday celebration. To make sure all bases would be covered, I shared my staffing plans with Carole, assuming she'd staff *Bixby's Dozen* however it made sense to her.

Lucky for me, the recruitment process was as easy as stealing candy from a baby, which of course, I would never do. As my business grew, Paul's dance studio across the street always provided me with a steady stream of temporary hires, no matter what the season. All I needed to do was tack up a Help Wanted poster on the bulletin board inside the studio and wait. In the case of this July 4th weekend, it took less than twenty-four hours for my email box to overflow with applications from high school kids and college students home for the summer.

Three years ago, about a month after Paul suddenly collapsed and died of heart failure while demonstrating how to break-dance to a class of nine-year-olds at Decades of Dance Studio, I handled my grief by having the outdoor sign above his pride and joy removed and hung in his honor inside Oldies & Goodies. Then, to commemorate his lifelong service to the town and memorialize my nickname for him, I changed the name of the studio to "It Takes Twenty-Two …"

In a stroke of creative genius, the designer at the local sign shop painted the image of a couple in a cross-step tango dip just after the ellipsis in the name. There was no reason to finish the thought. Everyone seemed to catch the tango reference. Close friends, like Carole, recognized the double meaning immediately, especially given the necklace I never removed. If he were still here, I think Paul would've applauded the name change and sung my praises by simply saying, "Very cool."

With a quick calculation, I concluded I'd need a team of eleven to staff Oldies & Goodies over the July 4th weekend.

The Help Wanted sign I posted inside "It Takes Twenty-Two …" listed my hiring criteria for those highly coveted part-time opportunities as:

1. In the email subject line, answer this: "What's your favorite song today?" 2. Must Love Cats.

As it turned out, one dance student must have told another, as I received well over one hundred emails the day after the advertisement went up. Not only did this process help me with staffing, but it also provided me with a bit of education in pop culture. Insight or a pulse, if you will, into the listening habits of today's kids. Their favorite song needn't be what I considered an oldie but goodie. In fact, I liked it better if it were a contemporary melody that I'd have to check out on iTunes. It was essential for me to stay "with it" when it came to music.

"Besides," I'd told Carole when she challenged me on my thought process, "junior employees today are the repeat customers of tomorrow."

While overall I did not judge the applicants by their favorite songs, their love of cats was a downright absolute qualification. Naturally, everyone professed to adoring cats. I doubted that to be entirely true. Some responses seemed a bit devious, some appeared slightly confused.

Many attached pictures to their emails, claiming the kitties to be their own. My suspicions arose when more than a few of the responses posted photos that were clearly of the same cat, more than likely downloaded from the Internet. I applauded those that did that for their ingenuity and their desire to be hired. Nevertheless, I scratched their name off my long list of possible hires.

There were a handful who thought I meant must love *Cats*, the Broadway play. I should've known what I'd find before opening their email when "Memory" was their favorite song. Obviously, those in this category seldom visited Oldies & Goodies; otherwise they would've easily grasped what I meant by the second qualification. I started an "out of touch" list.

So, why the *Must Love Cats* criterion? Because of Sonny and Cher, of course. Not the famous 1960s duo, but my two yellow tabbies, whom I adopted six months earlier. Initially, I named them after that musical pair to carry on a family tradition. My hippy-dippy parents named my twin sister Sherrie and me after songs that were popular in the early sixties. I didn't appreciate their inspiration during my formative years. Would you, if you were in my go-go boots? Sherrie and I were teased non-stop throughout our elementary school days. Yet, now as the proprietor of a highly successful music store, the value of naming my feline pair something that reinforced the image of my enterprise was not lost on me.

I adopted Sonny and Cher from a reputable, and extraordinarily thorough, agency all the way up in Newburyport, a small town in northeastern Massachusetts. They put me through the wringer when evaluating whether I'd be a good parent to two cats. They conducted a comprehensive background check on me, as well as an extensive interview, trying to uncover my true motives for adopting. Since I believed honesty was the best policy, I indicated on my application that I wanted them to guard my store.

"But they're not dogs," the agency manager cried out during a phone conversation.

I invited her to drive south to Chatham Crossing to check out the premises and see for herself. I was sure she'd agree historic buildings, like the one I leased, were magnets for real life Mickies and Minnies. This was especially the case since a sizable portion of the merchandise in my storefront was dessert; a prime target for mice living in dens nearby.

Moving on from that line of inquiry, I learned that rather than a quick call to our local police to find out if I had a *rap* sheet, the agency manager conducted a Google search. The closest thing she discovered was an interview I did for a Providence newspaper where the reporter asked whether I stocked *rap* music in my store?

"Certainly," I'd offered in the interview, "as rap becomes old—" The adoption agency interviewer chuckled as she quoted me, apparently satisfied I wasn't an ax murderer. And with that, the case of Venus Bixby, potential cat owner, was closed. The entire process convinced me adopting pets shouldn't be so difficult.

The next day, I drove to Newburyport, picked up Sonny and Cher, and then settled them down in the store. *The Chronicle* even included them in the monthly list of new residents in Chatham Crossing, listing Oldies & Goodies as their address. Nothing could be finer than free advertising!

Soon, I realized I needed a cat sitter; someone responsible. Perhaps a reliable high schooler who'd swing by each afternoon to tend to the cats' daily needs and entertain them. Someone I could trust. Not just with the kitty cats, but someone who wouldn't help themselves to the merchandise while having free rein at the store.

One afternoon after a board meeting at the Sofia Silva Whaling Museum, I shared my cat sitter idea with Sadie Hawkins. I inquired about her opinion of the new woman she'd hired in January to manage the museum gift shop. Perhaps she'd be interested in some part time work to add to her income.

"What's Maggie McGee's story?"

"You probably know as much about her as I do. Aren't she and Budd BFFs?"

"I wouldn't go so far as to say that," I said with a bit of a gulp. "He tells me he helps her out whenever he can. Unpacking inventory and stocking shelves. Not much beyond that. Unless you …"

I started to ask Sadie if she knew something I didn't know about Budd. She'd met him before I ever did. After she offered him the museum caretaker position, he needed a place to live. Since she'd heard I was thinking about renting the cottage after Paul had passed away, she suggested I consider renting to Budd. Who better to rent to than a man who was good with his hands? She failed to mention he was also easy on the eyes. Maybe an inch or two taller than Paul, shaggy brown hair, with green eyes like the promise of springtime. I discovered all that myself soon enough.

When Sadie rolled her eyes and waved me off, I figured she was just trying to stir up trouble, insinuate there was fire when, in fact, no smoke billowed at all.

Then, much to my surprise, Sadie recommended her daughter Hannah, who was in her junior year at the local public high school. Unbeknownst to Sadie, this was like manna from heaven for me; a gift.

Though they slept most of the day, when the front door chimed at 2:10 p.m., Sonny and Cher instinctively knew their BFF was in the building. They loved her so much. She was so dependable, exceeding my expectations of a high schooler. She reminded me of me. Needless to say, I gave Hannah more responsibility within the store and a two-dollar an hour raise after only one month on the job.

But I must confess to having an ulterior motive in hiring her. I needed to thaw my relationship with Sadie. Get in her good graces. Try to build a relationship with her that, for some strange reason, never grew beyond our museum connection.

For some time, especially after Paul died, I had my eye on the museum gift store—acquiring it would expand my retail footprint in town. I hoped Sadie would graciously open doors for me to do that directly through the SSWM board. But the few times I raised it with her, she changed the subject.

If I couldn't persuade Sadie directly, perhaps if I were a member of the Town Committee, I could submit the necessary paperwork requesting they explore the possibility. If they agreed my idea had merit, they could pressure Sadie so ultimately it would happen. No matter which path I took toward owning the gift shop, Sadie's support was critical to achieving that goal.

The gift shop was top of my mind because Budd raised it last evening during our weekly Thursday date night dinner at my house. It was my week to prepare the meal, but it kind of slipped my mind; I was just so busy party planning. I gave him a thumbs up, which he couldn't see through the phone, when he called and offered to swap weeks with me. As we were on our last bites of his sweet-and-smoky cedar planked salmon with wild rice and broccoli on the side, he brought up Maggie. Before he went any further, I held up my wineglass. As he poured my favorite Pinot Grigio, he shared good news he'd learned from Maggie. Following the Memorial Day weekend, summer sales at the gift shop were off to a fairly good start.

"She has some thoughts on how to boost sales," Budd said. "Ways to spruce up the displays and reposition promotional items for more visibility. Cross-sell slow-moving items. She'd like to present her ideas to Sadie."

"Why doesn't she?" I salivated at the prospect of taking ownership of a shop that was already thriving.

"Easier said than done. Sadie tends to blow her off."

"I gather you don't." I pinched my lips together as soon as the words escaped my mouth. Sadie's implication from a couple of months ago roared back into my mind. I'd never confronted Budd.

"What's that supposed to mean?"

I explained to him as best as I could recall how Sadie had intimated he and Maggie may have had an untoward relationship when they worked together in Maine.

"Hogwash. I don't play in the sandbox where I work. Especially with married women."

"What about now? Isn't she divorced?"

He asserted he didn't know about that, pushed his chair back, and cleared the table while I sat there gobsmacked. The silverware banged against the plates as he dropped everything into the sink. He slipped on his Birkenstocks and grumbled as he slammed the screen door.

Standing at the kitchen sink, I watched him cross the backyard to the cottage, swinging his arms in an obvious huff. I could have stopped him, but I didn't. And he didn't have second thoughts, never turning back to see me through the window. Customarily, on canoodle nights (like Thursday was supposed to be—instead of dinner and a movie, dinner and canoodling), Budd would leave the cottage's outside light on for no particular reason. Maybe it reminded him of a habit of looping a towel over the doorknob during his college years. On that night, in less than three seconds after he'd entered the cottage, the yard went dark. I gathered he didn't plan to return to play in my sandbox either.

Over the rest of the evening, I obsessed more about the extent of his and Maggie's friendship than I did about missing a night of making whoopee. *The gentlemen doth protest too much, me thinks.*

An uneasy feeling lingered when I got up Friday morning. I couldn't shake it, even after breakfast. I looked across the yard to get a sense of Budd's whereabouts, but the morning sun bouncing off his windows made it impossible to determine whether any lights were on. No calls or messages appeared on my phone from him, either.

The only way to sort this out was to confront the other half of the accused pair. Find out once and for all if Budd and Maggie were merely BFF or FWB, as Sadie had suggested.

My schedule for the day was already full. To squeeze in a visit to the museum gift shop required I keep my check-in with the weekend crew at Oldies & Goodies short and sweet. To my relief, no one had backed out of their commitments or asked to reschedule their assigned hours.

When I arrived at the store, Hannah was already one step, or maybe two, ahead of me. Sonny and Cher had eaten and were curled up on their individual beds at the front of the store, waiting for the sun to pour through the windows. She'd gathered the crew, reviewing the schedule not just for that day, but also for the next. When they saw me, they launched into "Happy Birthday." I raised the palm of my right hand. "You're a day early!"

"Just in case we don't see you tomorrow," Hannah said.

"Do you know something I don't, young lady?" Everyone giggled.

Quite contrary to the music section of the store, the *Bixby's Dozen* side appeared unusually quiet. I could see through the glass display cases that customers would have a wide choice of delicious cookies and other baked goods to choose from. Not surprised. Carole always had everything buttoned up and ready to go.

"I think I'll head over to the museum. Check in with your mom," I told Hannah, not revealing I was really going there to see Maggie, not Sadie. A white lie never hurts, right? "I assume she's there?"

"She left the house early. So, your assumption is most likely spot on."

I gave Hannah two thumbs up after I opened the cookie display case and filled a bag with an assortment. I assumed Maggie wasn't allergic to nuts.

"Don't worry. We've got this," Hannah added, paying no mind to what I was doing. After all, I did own the place.

As I headed out the back door to my car, I passed Helen Davis in the parking lot. She was red in the face and carrying a tote bag with knitting needles sticking out of the top.

"Morning, Helen. You in charge here today?"

"Can't talk now, Venus. But yes, just until Carole shows up."

"Where she at? The dentist?"

Helen skidded to a stop. "Where do you think she is? At the museum! Where else would she be with your bash just a day away? You know Carole! Everything must go off without a hitch." She lifted both shoulders to the sky and a box of Kleenex toppled end over end out of her tote bag to the ground. Some people don't leave home without their AMEX card. In Helen's case, it was Kleenex.

"You okay, Helen?" I bent down and retrieved the box for her.

She snatched it from me in a blink of an eye. As she turned to enter the store, I swore I heard a bit of gas escape. I let it pass unmentioned, confident it wasn't me.

"I'll be fine when I find my binder. It better be here, that's all I've got to say." The bells hanging on the screen door chimed, ending our conversation. "Have any of you cookie-stealers seen …"

I heard Helen loud and clear and made a mental note to advise Helen my staff steals nothing. At least I trusted even if they saw me help myself to the goodies, they wouldn't assume that privilege extended to them just because they worked there.

CHAPTER TWELVE

By the time I arrived at the museum Friday morning, it buzzed in the quiet sort of way museums do. Within seconds of entering the lobby, I smacked into a line of people of all shapes and sizes waiting to buy tickets. I worked my way around them, scanning faces. I didn't recognize anyone—probably all out of towners. To my left, I could hear a tour group shuffling between galleries adhering to Cecilia Powers's directive: "Right this way." Feeling sprightly, I grinned, amazed at how these twenty-somethings could juggle multiple interests. For Cecilia, it was whales and cookies. Who would've ever imagined such a heterogeneity in someone so young?

Delaying my primary mission, I slipped past the room Cecilia's tour group had piled into and stopped at the diorama of Chatham Crossing back in its whaling days. Before going further, I needed a plan. Who should I tackle first? Maggie or Sadie? I checked my phone, wishing to see a message waiting from Budd, explaining why he bolted the night before. He better not expect me to make the first move. I didn't walk out on him. Of course, there was more than a fifty-fifty chance I could bump into him right there among the rare antiquities. For all I knew, he could be spying on me, peeking through the glass display cases. I looked about. If Sadie was in her office, she could see me as I wandered around at sixes and sevens. Maybe she and Budd were together, wondering why the devil I was there.

Whatever. As I scrolled through my emails, out of the corner of my eye, I saw Carole speed past me. Where was she going in such a hurry? To meet with Sadie? I didn't call out to stop her. She probably didn't notice me since she expected me to be at the store. Out of mind. Out of sight.

No messages from Budd, text or otherwise. I decided a little chat with Maggie should be first on my agenda. I opened my purse, checking I hadn't accidentally left the cookies in the car.

On the way back through the lobby, it occurred to me I should have thought this through. What would I say to her? Where should I start?

As I approached the gift shop, I saw a woman bent over retrieving something from a low cabinet. Actually, I could only see a pair of shapely legs balancing on a pair of orange platform shoes. Oh, to be young again and have the shape for a mini-skirt. When Maggie stood, the hem of the sea green smock she wore with SSWM embroidered on the pocket touched just above her knees, camouflaging what was underneath. Protecting her jewels, as it were.

At a loss for how to begin, I let out what was swirling in my mind. "Good Friday morning, Maggie! You know, those shoes could kill ya." I pointed to her platforms.

She laughed. "What? These old things?" She picked up a T-shirt she'd fetched from below and folded it. "Can

I help you with something, Ms. Bixby? I didn't expect to see you here today."

"Do call me Venus. Actually, I brought you something. Figured you could use some sugar energy."

"If the lobby is any indication," she said, jutting her chin in that direction, "you could be a lifesaver. Thanks."

Maggie accepted the bag and slid it gingerly behind the counter next to a blue Yeti water bottle that looked vaguely familiar. If I wasn't mistaken, it was similar in both brand and color to the bottle Budd gave me on May first. "It's May, it's May," he'd sung. "The thirsty month of May." I laughed at his attempt to sing one of my favorite songs from *Camelot.*

"The word is lusty, not thirsty," I'd giggled at the time.

"Thirsty, lusty, whatever," he laughed and swung me around for a kiss. "We all could use a refresher come spring."

At the time, I thought *we* meant him and me, not Maggie and him. Suddenly, I wasn't so sure. Did he pull her in close and dance with her too?

I tried to suppress my suspicious thoughts by twirling the postcard stand. What reason could I give for buying postcards, thereby prolonging my visit? Ah, of course, Lexi.

I slipped one card out of the rack and held it up toward Maggie. "My niece," I said. "Lexi, in San Francisco. A teenager. Perhaps if I send a series of postcards every two weeks, I could entice her to get on a plane and come out for a visit." I narrowed my eyes, just thinking. There was no reason Maggie should give a hoot about Lexi, so I kept the rest of my thoughts on the subject to myself. I could handle a teenager. I did every day at the store. If push came to shove, I'd put her to work. Hannah could work the register, and Lexi could take care of the cats. Surely, she loved cats! Didn't everyone?

"Have you come to see Budd?" Maggie interrupted my plan and guided me down a path I wasn't quite ready to take.

With that question, I focused on pictures of scrimshaw, pirates, and whalers.

Ultimately, I bit the bullet ever so slightly. "Did he stop by to see you this morning?"

"Yes, he did. Budd comes by to see me every morning. Like clockwork. Just like he did when we worked together in Maine."

"Right. Maine."

"I owe him big time."

"Why do you—?" I started to ask as seven rowdy boys, wearing various Red Sox and Yankees caps, and three chaperones stormed the shop. Scooting past them, I placed the five postcards and three singles on the counter. "Keep the change. I'll catch you later," I said. "Would love to hear more about your time with Budd, uh, in Maine." I backed out between the displays, almost tripping over my own feet, when it was my mouth that was all tangled up. Part of me wanted the chance to ask Maggie what her favorite song was, but I was afraid she'd start singing a song from *Camelot*.

CHAPTER THIRTEEN

Though they knew I was at The Cube after I fell at the museum that Saturday morning, neither Budd nor Carole showed up there to take me home. Jitter Bug was at the museum. I'd parked in one of the spaces marked specifically for board members, even though that privilege did not extend to honorary members, like me.

When I'd called Carole she told me yellow crime scene barrier tape was wrapped around almost the entire building, except for the front door. "All it needs now is a big bow," she said.

"A crime? Who thinks it's a crime?"

"Well, the police must."

"Maybe she tripped over her own shoes, like I tripped over her shoes."

"I don't have a clue what happened. All I can tell you is the museum's closed until further notice."

"No party then, I guess."

"Venus, you are insufferable! Margaret McGee is dead! Do you really think celebrating your birthday is an appropriate response?"

"What about all the food?"

"I'm hanging up."

With confirmation from Carole that Maggie had, in fact, died, I understood why Budd didn't follow my ambulance to The Cube. He had his hands full shutting down the entire complex, gardens and all. At least, I assumed that was the case. Or did he follow Maggie's ambulance wherever they shuttled her off to?

Just as I was about to call a taxi to pick up me and my thumb and take us home, an alert flashed on my phone, and all the phones in the lobby of The Cube buzzed at once, sounding like an orchestra tuning up.

Mayor Simon Duffy announces the Chatham Crossing's Independence Day celebration is rescheduled for Tuesday, July 6. The annual parade will start precisely at nine.

Folks simply looked around and shrugged. I heard someone say, "Sounds like a day off to me!"

I called Carole back. We needed to keep Oldies & Goodies open. If not for locals, certainly for the tourists swinging through town during Cape Cod's customary weekend turnover.

"Not to worry, Venus." She told *me* not to worry! Worry was my middle name. "Double C Signs is already making billboard ads to spread the word about the rescheduling."

"And that the town is open for business?"

"Yes, Venus. Cool your jets. Double C promised Simon a dozen signs will be up by two o'clock. So whether they're coming from or going to the Cape, they'll know there will be plenty to see and do here beyond checking out a crime scene."

"Sounds dark and creepy when you put it like that."

"It is what it is. Some people may stay away. I bet someone dying in the whaling museum won't stop those with morbid curiosity. After all, everything there is already dead."

"Too bad we don't have a new slogan yet for this holiday. Maybe some intriguing quip to bring people into town, at least for the parade," I pondered, still trying to figure out how I'd ever get home.

"How about *Sleuths On Parade? Come one, come all.*"

"You do recall, Carole, I'm the Grand Marshal, don't you? Wouldn't that make me a sleuth too?"

"Alright. How about *Murder, They Wrote?*"

"Carole!" I nearly broke my toe stamping my right foot. "You don't really think Maggie was murdered, do you?" I turned away from the patients in the waiting area.

"I don't. You're right. She may have fainted and hit her head."

"Or maybe she had a heart attack. Collapsed and died. You don't know. Let's keep the word murder to ourselves."

"Let's." Carole cleared her throat. I pictured her rolling her eyes as she liked to do most regularly when I expressed my opinion.

"Do you think she was dead when I tripped over her?" I whispered, hoping none of the folks in the waiting area at The Cube heard me.

I spied Tommy, my trusty ambulance driver, sweet-talking the sweet-young-thing at the check-in desk. She pointed in my direction where I was trying to instill a bit of privacy into my conversation with Carole.

"Look gotta go. I see my ride is here." I assumed I could convince him to take me home.

"I don't need an ambulance, Tommy, but—"

"Actually, I'm off duty for about an hour."

"Cool beans for both of us." I handed him my purse to carry, and looped my good hand through his left arm.

"Well, off life-saving duty, anyway. Detective Donovan asked me to swing by to see how you're doing. He really needs to talk to you as soon as possible."

"Is that so? If that's the case, why isn't he here in all his glory?" I accompanied Tommy through the sliding doors out of The Cube into an oven-like July day.

"It's about Margaret McGee."

"I just heard. Take me home, Tommy. I need a little nap. I'm feeling a bit delirious."

I looked around, half expecting Tommy's ambulance to be waiting. I was prepared to put up a fight about riding in it again. But it wasn't at the curb. Instead, Tommy directed me to his car. I stopped at Paul's old Jeep Wrangler that Tommy bought from me after Paul's death.

"Is this okay, Ms. B.? I should've thought …"

"Sure, Tommy. Just take me home."

CHAPTER FOURTEEN

Tommy and I rode in silence. He attempted to ask about my thumb, but every time he opened his mouth, I raised my thumb not just to show its splint, but to indicate I wasn't in a talking kind of mood. I spared him the shush I would've liked to send in his direction. Instead, with my good hand, I touched the dashboard I'd touched many times before. I breathed in the cool air, swearing Paul's cologne was still recycling through the vents. My imagination insisted on playing tricks on me.

Luckily, the drive to the Hilltop was short. When we pulled up to my house, I noticed Budd's car wasn't in our shared driveway. I wanted to ask Tommy whether he'd seen Budd in his comings and goings, but even that would've taken too much of my energy at the moment. Especially if he told me he'd seen Budd with Maggie after the fact, like at the hospital or the morgue.

I was perfectly capable of opening the passenger door with my right hand. So I just about flew out of my seatbelt when the door swung open. *Lookie here.* Who was the gentleman doing the honors? None other than Detective Oscar Donovan.

"Hope you haven't been waiting long," Tommy said.

"Whatever it takes," Oscar said.

"Takes for what?" I leaned against the car door, willing Paul's good karma to come to my aid.

"We need to talk."

"I'll leave you two." Tommy handed me my purse. With his slight wave, I interpreted his gentle suggestion to mean I should step away from the car so he could make haste and leave. He bowed his head affirmatively, climbed in Paul's car, I mean *his* car, and drove away.

"You've had a difficult day already, Venus." Oscar tilted his head toward the Jeep backing out of the driveway. "It wasn't supposed to be like this. Your party and all."

"Then don't make it worse." I made my way up the stone walk without inviting him to follow, but he did anyway.

With my good hand, I rifled through my purse to find my keys.

"Can I help you with that?"

My hand trembling a bit, I uttered, "Just hold the door, please."

Once inside, Oscar removed his hat and remained in the foyer with his hands crossed in front of him, waiting for a formal invitation.

I plopped my purse on the bench next to a stack of three-year-old *Dance* magazines I never opened or scanned. I kept renewing Paul's subscription, unwilling to let it expire even though he had.

"How about if I take those to the studio?" Oscar offered, pointing to the *25 to Watch* issue that sat prominently on top.

First Paul's car, now his favorite reading material. Would I finally accept he was gone once and for all? Was today the day Budd had been waiting for? Perhaps it was me that prevented our relationship from moving to the next level, not Maggie.

"Hold that thought. Come with me." I finally made a positive overture toward Oscar, realizing I needed his help to make some tea. Halfway down the hallway to the kitchen in the back of the house, I stopped and turned around. I cocked my head. He took the hint and followed me back to the foyer. Again, I fumbled through my purse.

"Phew. Here it is." I held up an amber pill bottle. "Nirvana," I announced, followed by a big sigh.

"One of my favorite bands of all time," he said.

Rolling my eyes, I headed back toward the kitchen with Oscar close on my heels. I was grateful he hadn't yet referred to me as the Song and Dance Lady. I gave him props for that, at least. Maybe he was just trying to break the ice or set the stage for divulging the real reason he was sitting at my kitchen table. I added the pills that Jeanne gave me for pain on the tray on the table alongside my vitamins and salt and pepper shakers.

Oscar, it seemed, liked coffee. Not that I held that against him. My Keurig was always at the ready. That he requested Nantucket blend was a different matter altogether. I knew it was in the tall pantry cabinet somewhere, but finding it with one functional appendage presented a bit of a challenge. Not sure why he didn't choose another flavor when he could have easily observed I was struggling to find his preference. As a detective, wasn't he supposed to solve problems, not create them?

"Here it is," I said, powering up the Keurig.

I probably should've arranged a plate of cookies to accompany our hot drinks, but truthfully, I had no intention of entertaining him any longer than absolutely necessary. Oldies & Goodies was waiting for me, and I was anxious to locate Budd. I couldn't do either with Oscar hanging out at my house. To my dismay, Oscar didn't seem in any rush to get what he came for and leave.

"Why are you here?" I asked, jump-starting the conversation. From where I sat, I had a clear view of the cottage. If Budd came home while Oscar was there, he'd recognize the detective's black car with town plates out front and come in to find out what was what.

"It's about Margaret McGee."

"No kidding. I couldn't have guessed. Not sure how I can help you."

"You can't be serious, Venus. You were the last one to see her alive."

"That's impossible. No one saw her since I saw her Friday morning?" I was totally baffled. Maggie was at the museum all day yesterday. She was not invisible. "Have you checked out the local pubs? Someone young and vibrant as Maggie certainly wouldn't sit home on Friday nights."

Oscar removed a pen from his breast pocket and opened the cover of his notebook. He flipped past four pages until one suited his needs. I wondered what was on those first pages.

"I'm not concerned about Friday morning. This morning, Venus. You were the last one to see her alive *this* morning."

I cursed to myself, my eyes blinked uncontrollably as I tried to concentrate on what he just uttered.

"Didn't we just have this conversation earlier at The Cube?"

"Well, only a bit of a conversation."

"Let me remind you then, detective. I told you I tripped over orange platform shoes. Oh, and for your information, I broke my thumb in the process." I held up my splint as if I was an elementary school student at the front of the class doing show and tell.

"Those shoes belonged to Margaret McGee. And she's dead."

I swallowed hard and then wet my whistle before responding. My tea was cooling way too fast, but I had no desire to zap it in the microwave or make another cup.

"Can we just call her Maggie?"

"Sure," he said, and he was off and running. "Here's what we know. Maggie's dead. You fell over her shoes. So, I need to ask you a few questions, especially while your memory is fresh."

I decided to humor him. "Go ahead. What do you want to know?" I tried to interlock my fingers on the table in front of me.

"Why did you go to the museum this morning?"

"Really, Oscar? You know why I went there. My party."

"Sorry, Venus. I'm a detective. It's my job to investigate. If you cooperate, I'll be out of your hair in a jiffy. Did you go there specifically to talk to Maggie?"

"Today? No, not specifically. She was involved in setting up for the party. So maybe indirectly I figured I'd be talking with her. But her name was not on my checklist for the day, if that's what you're asking?"

"Let's switch to the shoes. Did you know those were Marg ... I mean Maggie's shoes?"

"Yes."

"How did you know they were hers?"

"She wore them on Friday."

Oscar made another note. "Where did you see her wearing them?"

"At the museum. In the gift shop. Where she worked. But then you already know where she worked."

"So you saw Maggie on Friday?"

"Yes." I pinched my lips together. Was he really going to go there?

"What did you talk about?"

Oh, God. He went there.

"Let me think. Oh, I gave her some cookies from the store."

"You specifically brought *Maggie* cookies from the store?"

"That's not a crime, is it?"

Oscar shook his head. It was obvious he was going to continue that line of questioning. I explained I looked at the postcard rack and bought five for my niece in San Francisco.

"What else did you talk about?"

"She asked me if I'd come to the museum to see Budd. He works there."

Oscar shook his head again. "I hear you two are an item."

"Kind of." I crossed my right ankle over my left.

"Did you?"

"Did I what?"

"Go to the museum to see Budd?"

I shook my head.

"Or just to bring a gift to Maggie?"

"My party's tonight. Or it was supposed to be tonight. I went to the museum yesterday to check in with the people there that were responsible for ensuring it went off without a hitch. That would be people like Sadie Hawkins. The curator there. And yes, Maggie. Sadie had tapped her to be the garden party coordinator. Bumping into Budd would always be a bonus." I forced a sheepish grin.

"Did you bring Sadie cookies?"

"No, I did not."

Oscar jotted down something else.

"Let's move to today. What happened after you tripped?"

"I screamed."

"Why did you scream?"

"Because I was hurt."

"Not because you saw someone face down in the pachysandra?"

My eyes watered as the enormity of the situation weighed on me. He didn't give me a chance to respond. I was not even sure how to answer.

"Did you touch the body?"

I paused before answering. "Obviously, my feet touched her shoes, and I guess that means her feet as well. Other than that, no. I was also face down on the ground for your information. Be sure to make a note of *that*." I waggled my index finger three times at his notebook.

The kitchen's screen door whined … *rap, tap, tap* on the glass panes of the inside door. Praise the Lord. Budd.

Since Oscar sat nearest the door, like a gentleman, he got up and let him in.

"What's going on here?" Budd asked, after crossing the kitchen and kissing my cheek. "You, okay?"

I held up my splint, losing count how many times I'd unveiled my injury already.

"I'll bring you up to speed later." I patted him on the arm, reassuring him it wasn't as bad as it looked.

Budd asked Oscar why he was there. Shouldn't he be off hunting down whoever had it in for Maggie? Then he looked at me, and I tried not to make a face. Like me, sure as shootin' he remembered the argument we had only two nights ago ... involving Maggie. After our glorious make-up session upstairs last night, I hoped he considered it water under the bridge and not a bridge over troubled waters.

Oscar refrained from sitting down again. Rather, he shifted from one foot to another. "I'll be getting out of your way."

Not sure whose way he meant. Mine or Budd's?

I reached for the pill bottle. Something else to show Budd. "Time for my next pill," I said with a frown. Oh, pity me, I thought.

And then Oscar added, "For now."

Not expecting Budd to show the good detective out, I used my good hand for balance and got up.

The men allowed me to lead the way up the hall to the front door. I handed Oscar a stack of the magazines he offered to drop off at the dance studio. As I thanked him and turned to reach for the doorknob, I heard one of them clear his throat.

"One more question. Were you and Margaret McGee on good terms?"

CHAPTER FIFTEEN

Good terms? Of course I said yes! There was no reason for me to explain Maggie and I really weren't on any terms—good or bad. Since I hadn't told Budd about my conversation with Maggie the day before, he was none the wiser. Since she was dead and out of the picture, out of our lives, did it really matter whether Maggie and Budd were BFFs *or* FWBs? Still, the thought of sharing him at this point in my life curled my recently pedicured toes.

My response must have satisfied the good detective because he left without further ado. Budd and I turned on our heels and made our way back to the kitchen, the room in the house where more than meals were prepared and shared.

Neither of us pulled out a chair to take a load off. There was no thank-goodness-we're-alone-now embrace. Instead, we claimed our positions, standing opposite one another. Budd leaned against the stainless steel double sink, his arms behind him, his hands propping him up. He wore his work garb—khaki pants, a brown belt, and matching New Balance leather shoes. The shirt? As usual,

Oxford button down, the same green color as Maggie's smock, and long-sleeved to hide his tattoos.

Facing Budd, I leaned on the kitchen table. One palm flat down, the other angled to accommodate my injury. Barefoot, having slipped off my sandals earlier when I entered the house with Oscar, I'd give anything to change out of everything I was wearing before heading to the store. Suddenly, that presented a problem. Getting my shirt over my head would take some maneuvering. If the situation were different, I'd have asked Budd to do the honors. But I was in no mood. I suspected neither was he. Anyway, I needed to get the skinny on what happened to Maggie. But Budd had other ideas. And not the kind you're thinking.

"What did he ask you?" Budd asked eagerly. "Do you need a lawyer?"

"Hmph. What I need is for you to drive me to the store so I can check on things there."

Budd had already talked with Carole. She called him—such a good friend—after she and I talked, to give him a heads up that I was going home.

"She's at the store and wants me to give you a message."

"Is that so?"

"Carole says if you show your face at the store today, she'll break your other thumb."

First, I flashed Budd two thumbs up and then, somehow uncontrollably, the middle finger of my good hand whipped up in the air. He tsk tsked me.

Without my asking, he poured water from my Brita pitcher into my favorite Red Sox tumbler, grabbed my pain pills off the table, and nudged me toward the living room.

As soon I settled into my chaise lounge, deciding my legs needed a rest as much as my thumb, my stomach gurgled. I attempted to swing my legs back off the chair to go fix some lunch for both of us.

"Don't you move." Budd handed me the glass and one capsule. "I'll be right back. Then we need to talk."

I watched him leave the room, thankful whatever bad blood bubbled up between us two nights ago had vanished. I was perturbed, though, that everyone seemed to be hell-bent on talking with me. I assumed Budd's topic of conversation would not be too dissimilar to Detective Donovan's. But I could be wrong. We'd see. I tilted my head back and closed my eyes. Drifting, I heard the refrigerator door latching and the silverware drawer slamming a short distance away. Would a tuna salad sandwich on rye or peanut butter with four-berry jelly be in my future? On that thought, I dozed …

"What time is it?" I lifted my elbows and extended my arms out to the side, inhaling deeply. My mouth was dry as dust. I touched my face just below my lips. How embarrassing. My jaw must have drooped while I napped.

Budd rose off the couch, plunked whatever he'd been reading on the coffee table, and headed for the kitchen. "Just after two. I'll get your lunch."

I wiggled my toes to get my blood moving, whipped off the Red Sox throw Budd must have covered me with, and stretched my arms before hoisting myself off the chaise. A pit stop was essential before I ate. *Good choice*, I murmured as I saw he appropriated *Isaac's Storm* by Erik Larsen from the bookshelf that contained Paul's favorite books. That was the third memory of Paul that day alone. Was Paul trying to tell me something?

"I'll eat out there," I threw my voice in Budd's direction. I tucked away my thoughts of Paul. No reason to share them with Budd.

Back in the kitchen once more, I took a seat. So did he. I sensed I'd be doing more than eating a late lunch.

Budd looked ready to start an inquisition. I was not ready to indulge him.

I lifted my drink and raised it, as if toasting something. He must have made sun tea while I slept. It was still warm. He'd make someone a good wife someday. He reached across the table and stripped away the tinfoil covering the plate in front of me. Not my usual quick sandwich lunch, to be sure. I faced a healthy scoop of what just might be homemade chicken salad, large curd cottage cheese, three slices of red tomatoes, and a Kosher dill pickle. I transferred the pickle to a napkin and slid it over to him.

"I don't eat pickles."

"But, they're in …"

"Just for you."

Budd devoured the pickle in two bites and wiped his mouth with a fresh paper napkin. "So, Venus, what did Detective Donovan ask you?"

"Which time?"

"What do you mean, *which time?*" He pounded his fist on the table, sending the napkin he wadded up in a ball flying across the room.

"Excuse me?" This was not the Budd I'd come to care about. I'd much rather have the fellow who walked out the door when he was angry than the purple pickle-eater facing me right then.

"I'm sorry about that. It's just—" He got up, retrieved the paper ball, and tossed it in the trash can under the sink.

I realized I should apologize to Budd for my snarkyness. He couldn't have known Oscar followed my ambulance that morning.

"No, I'm sorry." I touched my chest. "Oscar and I talked twice today. Once while I was waiting to be seen at The Cube, and of course, you know the other time."

"Oh, I see. So, when were you going to tell me what he said?"

I approached my lunch in tiny bites. No need to get a chunk of chicken lodged in my throat and have to be rescued by Tommy twice in the same day. Of course, I would bet dollars to donuts Budd was trained on the Heimlich maneuver, given his vast caretaker experience.

"When did you learn the Heimlich maneuver? Was it in Maine?"

Budd glared at me, his eyes just about bulging. "What's that got to do with anything? Focus, Venus. Tell me why the police think you're a suspect."

I gently placed my fork on the placemat. "I'm not a suspect, am I? Do you think I need a lawyer?"

"How the hell would I know when you refuse to tell me what's going on?"

"I could say the same about you, Budd. While they carted me off with sirens blazing, you stayed behind at the museum with Maggie."

"With Maggie's body."

"I have an idea." I inhaled deeply, exhaling fully and loudly. "Let's start there."

CHAPTER SIXTEEN

Typically, on the Sunday of a holiday weekend, I'd bounce out of bed, shower, and get myself to the store ahead of Carole or any of the team, but that Sunday was far from typical. I took my last pain pill twelve hours ago. Clumsily, I propped my pillows against the headboard and contemplated my current level of discomfort.

"On a scale from one to ten," I said out loud, "how bad is your pain?" That's what Jeanne, the NP at The Cube, would ask. How would I rate it that would make any sense? Did a ten mean I should take the drugs before I did anything else? Did a one mean I was good doing whatever floated my boat? Or was it something in between?

A text message interrupted my health assessment: probably Budd checking in on how I slept. I patted the bed, searching for my phone (my bed partner when Budd was not, especially lately).

Oh, a message from the mayor! How nice!

FYI, parade moved to Tuesday. Will you still be able to be GM?

YES!

I already knew he rescheduled the parade, but that Simon thought to personally notify me made me smile like a schoolgirl. After we exchanged a few pleasantries, I slid the phone safely onto the nightstand, trading it for an unlit candle. Three little jars stood ready to enhance my mood. I selected the candle with a combination mint, nutmeg, and citrus and breathed in. It was one of my favorite scents, either to inhale to kick-start the day or, if it was lit, as a signal to Budd to light my fire.

Despite having all the windows closed and the air conditioning doing its thing, the creaky sound of a screen door slowly swinging open on its rusty hinges and the sudden sharp slap as it closed was more than enough cacophony to get me out of bed. I didn't have to pull back my sheer curtains to verify Budd was on his way to the museum even though it would be closed that day, but I did so anyway. If neighbors spotted me standing there looking out the window, they could easily mistake the spaghetti straps of my black silk nightgown for a tank top.

I was more interested in seeing whether Budd would glance up and catch me at the window. Would I wave? Throw him a kiss? Lift the window and shout down to him, "What's your favorite song today?" I couldn't remember the last time I asked him that.

If not the song, maybe I could invite him in for a wake and bake. He certainly wasn't in any mood to fool around last night. I wasn't either, but I liked to keep my options open just in case the situation presented itself. Which it did not.

I couldn't really blame Budd for not making the first move last evening, as he often did. He was still processing the events of yesterday morning. I didn't make it any easier on him, as I recalled. I wanted him to tell me every single little thing that happened after he handed me and my thumb off to Tommy.

I never finished my chicken salad, though it was yummy. There was something delectable in it that my taste buds couldn't identify. When Budd was in a better frame of mind, I'd ask him for his secret ingredient and then I'd tell Carole. I recalled her catering menu offered chicken salad as part of the summer buffet, and a new recipe could reinvigorate her selections. She was always looking for a spark to keep her clientele rebooking Carefree Catering for their events.

My appetite, however, went south as soon as Budd suggested the cops considered me a person of interest in Maggie's death. Why on earth did he say that? Why would they even think that?

"I only saw her shoes." I'd explained to him how limited my perspective on the incident really was. When I forgot myself and blurted, "If I hadn't seen her wearing them on Friday, I wouldn't have thought it was Maggie," Budd grabbed our drinks and shuffled us out to the front porch.

There. I'd gone and done it. Rather than Budd filling me in on what happened after they hauled me away from the museum, I'd opened my mouth and inserted my foot, revealing my conversation with Maggie, my very last conversation with Maggie, on Friday.

Budd slid his butt into one of the white Adirondack chairs. I paced. My brain worked better when I was in motion. Striding in one direction, I told him I brought Maggie cookies from the store. Turning around and re-tracing my steps, I described how I bought postcards to send to my niece Lexi, whom he hadn't met yet but really should someday soon.

"What else?"

"What else? Let me think." I chewed on my lip. I could've stopped at cookies and postcards, but it wouldn't make any sense for a cookie delivery and a postcard pur-chase to be the reasons I went into the gift shop to see Maggie. So, widening my eyes to appear innocent, I add-ed, "Oh, I asked if she'd seen you yet?"

"Why?"

I scratched my scalp with my good hand. Budd's short one and two word remarks reminded me of Paul. What was it with men? I'd read an article once that according to a survey a woman spoke nearly twice as many words in a day as a man did. The researchers should've asked me first. I could've saved them a boatload of money.

Taking a big gulp, I anticipated a little white lie was about to be born. I stopped crossing the porch back and forth and parked myself smack dab in front of Budd, our knees touching. I leaned in and kissed his forehead.

"I wanted to apologize for Thursday night."

When he rubbed the palm of his hands along my hips, I figured this line of questioning was finished, and he had something else on his mind. Boy, was I wrong.

"If you'd come to the museum to see me, why didn't you call or text me? Or ask whoever was at the informa-tion desk to page me? Why ask Maggie?"

"Because, I wanted to find out if you were more than just friends," I said, backing away and almost tripping on the pale green frog statue, sitting in a lotus position in the wrong place on the porch at the wrong time.

"Watch it."

Watch it? Did he mean the frog or my not-so-subtle allegation?

To substantiate I had ample reason to wonder about his relationship with Maggie, I was about to ask him how it was Maggie possessed the same identical Yeti bottle he'd given me? But I swallowed that question when his eyes filled with tears. I quickly decided I'd save it for another day.

Then it was Budd's turn to stand. He grabbed my arms and plunked me in the chair next to where he'd sat. The bluebirds and cardinals in the oak tree in the front yard sang out, and two squirrels chased one another around the wide tree trunk. For whatever Budd was about to say, a live audience had gathered.

"Get real, Venus. I heard you scream." I assumed he meant when I'd fallen in the museum gardens. "Well, I mean, I heard a scream. Fortunately, I was already on my way to the gardens. As I ran through the lobby, I passed Jeremy."

"The gardener Jeremy?"

"Right. I told him to call Security."

"Did I sound that bad?"

"Think about it, Venus. Most things in the museum are inanimate. Rarely, if ever, do they scream."

"You couldn't tell it was me?"

"No. You're more of a moaner than a screamer." A little twinkle replaced the tears in his eyes. "I didn't know who it was until I rushed in and saw you flat out on the walkway."

I played the scene out in my mind. If Budd didn't realize it was me, who else did he think was in distress?

"The gardens were closed to museum visitors because of the party. So, who did you think was in trouble?"

He wrinkled his nose and shrugged. "I had no idea. It could've been Sadie. She sits on one of the stone benches and meditates out there every morning."

"She does? On her own time, or the museum's?" Then I remembered her asking me for a mindfulness playlist after Paul's funeral.

"Aren't they the same thing?" He paused before continuing. "And then I thought of Maggie. She was responsible for setting up for the event, and I knew she was already doing her thing."

"Right. You told me you were heading in early specifically to open up for Maggie. And then I had my first medical disaster of the day." I pointed to my ear and narrowed my eyes.

Budd seemed to ignore me, choosing not to explore a subject he had yet to hear about.

"But it wasn't Maggie that cried out. It was you!"

And then the waterworks began: the sudden spurt of the lawn sprinklers interrupting his story. Though Budd and I jumped, the birds quieted, and the squirrels sought a new playground.

"Should we go inside?"

"No, I'm good right here, if you are," I said. I wanted him to continue telling me what happened—not get anymore distracted.

He pulled the vacant Adirondack chair so it faced me. My eyes followed the sound of wood scraping against wood, like nails on a chalkboard.

"Here's all I know," he said, settling in for what I thought would be a lengthy dissertation of how events unfolded.

"By the time I returned to the gardens after I knew you were safe and sound with Tommy, the police and the EMTs had arrived and roped off half the gardens. I couldn't get close enough to see a damn thing."

"What did they say?"

"Say?"

"Yes, Budd, what did they say?"

He bowed his head. "Better notify this woman's next of kin. She won't be home for dinner tonight."

Budd wasn't at my home for dinner that Saturday night either. My intense gaze at him Sunday morning as he walked to his car in the driveway apparently failed to trigger in him an eerie feeling that someone was staring at him. Was he preoccupied with something or someone other than me?

Determined to get my show on the road, I'd rated my pain threshold a two or three. So low, I swapped the hard drugs for Tylenol. I wished I could take off the splint. With nearly twenty-four hours under my belt, I appreciated the challenges of wearing it. But I did as I was told. "Three weeks," Jeanne had decreed. As I wrapped my hand in cellophane so I could shower, I faced an additional problem. The parade was in two days and my hair was in dire need of attention before I ascended to the perch on my float.

There was someone I needed to call.

CHAPTER SEVENTEEN

With the parade rescheduled, I had the option of going to the store Monday morning. I'd not been there since early Saturday, and I really needed take a pulse on what had been happening there in my absence.

As I walked through the back entry of Oldies & Goodies, I spotted *The Chatham Crossing Chronicle* sitting folded and undisturbed on the table in the backroom. Sonny and Cher greeted me with a happy mewl and warm rubs against and around my legs. I'd missed them, too, these past two days. I leaned down to give them a good morning scratch between the ears. That made them happy.

I could hear Hannah chuckling up front with two of the teenage girls who were scheduled for the first shift of the day. Not sure what they thought was so funny. Of course, they weren't suspects in a murder investigation. A male voice asked if they'd tried one of his cookies. I recognized the voice belonged to the new guy on the team. Would Carole approve of Roger P. Drake giving away the store for free?

With the daily newspaper in my right hand, I followed the sound of the fun.

"Oh, good morning, Ms. Bixby," Hannah said and then pierced her lips together as if I'd caught her with her hand in the cookie jar. The other girls chimed in with an identical greeting, just a half a beat behind her.

I acknowledged them and asked the only appropriate question for the moment. Not "What's so funny?" Or "Are we all set to sell, sell, sell on this holiday Monday?"

Instead, I asked, "What's your favorite song today?"

This stopped them cold, as if they were in shock. The girls looked at each other with half grins and their heavily tweezed and sculpted eyebrows raised almost to their hairline. Hannah, the leader of the pack, tried to save them. "Just give us a minute!" Evidently, I didn't train them as well as I thought I had, or their parents hadn't warned them that working there meant having a song title on the tip of their tongue each day.

While they were thinking, Roger P. Drake interjected. "Well, milady, 'A Pirate's Life for Me' is my favorite ditty today." Dressed all in black, with a white bandana around his neck, he bent over with a flourish and flashed an ear-to-ear grin. He handed me two of the cookies he'd been trying to palm off on the girls.

"Was this your contribution to my party? The party yet to be held?" I fondled what appeared to be square sugar cookies with black icing and the Jolly Roger skull and cross bones decorated in white.

"Most definitely. Fun, huh? There's plenty. Take all you want. Each of you."

I watched as the girls helped themselves to the trays Roger placed on top of the cookie display case, giggling as their waxed paper bags filled up.

"Don't you want to be sure you have plenty to sell today?" I directed my gaze at Roger.

"Oh, not to worry. I have plenty. On top of what's in the case, before I came in this morning, I picked up the trays I'd dropped off at the museum Saturday before all hell broke loose."

I wrapped my cookies twice in napkins and slipped them into the zippered section inside my purse for safe-keeping. Such an unusual treat. I wanted to show them to Budd before I sampled one. If he behaved, I might just share a cookie with him. Time would tell.

As I grabbed the newspaper and headed to the back room to brew some tea, one of the teenagers shouted out, "Only in America"!

"Brooks & Dunn," I replied, giving her a wink and an injured thumbs up.

Hannah high-fived her and shooed them all back to work.

Despite the news of Maggie's untimely demise spreading from Providence to all across the Cape, the store was open for what I hoped was another profitable day. I placed my hot tea on a rope coaster. Time I caught up on the local news.

I spread *The Chronicle* on the table. The initial words in the headline on the first page above the fold caught my eye. How would they not? "Song and Dance Lady." I expected to find an article about the incident, but I hardly expected I would be featured.

First, I scanned the article. Short enough to get the overall gist of it before picking it apart line by line, word for word.

My mouth suddenly became as dry as the Sahara desert. There was no saliva available to help me swallow. Thank goodness for my English breakfast tea.

I appreciated Daniel DaRosa, the reporter, mentioning Paul. I wondered, though, if the town would ever decouple us and simply recognize me for who and what I was? Would this reference to Paul annoy Budd? Reading further, though, it seemed Budd may have been right about one thing. The police suspected Maggie was murdered. How could they be so sure? Of course: an autopsy. I'd watched enough episodes of ER to learn that much. How long before those results were in, I wondered?

My index finger skidded to the next paragraph. The "news" there blew my mind. I read it three times. Someone in town implicated me as the last one to see Maggie alive. Not only did I doubt this was true, but who was this anonymous tipster? I chewed my lower lip. Besides the brief interaction with Detective Donovan, who I wouldn't characterize as my friend in this context, I'd only talked to two people about what happened Saturday: Budd and Carole. Budd would've told me if a reporter had contacted him. It must have been Carole. Either directly or through her husband, the mayor. Why would she do such a thing? Chances were *she* was one of the last people to see Maggie alive if she went to the museum that morning to be sure everything was set up for the event—not just the food, but tables, chairs, balloons, wine, and so forth.

Wait. Budd may have been the last one to see Maggie alive. He let her in to the museum that morning and certainly was helping her set up everything.

So, two friends of mine were more likely than me to have had an interaction with the victim on Saturday, and yet it was my name plastered on the front page of *The Chatham Crossing Chronicle*.

Something had to be done to change the narrative. Rumors surely were swirling throughout town like a tropical storm. If Carole and Budd wouldn't defend me, I needed to do it myself.

I pulled my phone out of my purse and sent a message and a link to a Brian Wilson song.

Waiting for a full statement from me, Detective Donovan? Wait no more.

Is now "The Right Time" to chat? Oscar texted back.

It will be after my hair appointment.

CHAPTER EIGHTEEN

The Chatham Crossing Chronicle
Obituary — Special Notice

By: Daniel DaRosa, Investigative Reporter

McGEE, Margaret (a.k.a. Maggie)
March 22, 1979 - July 3, 2010

With profound shock and sadness, Sandra Hawkins, curator of the Sofia Silva Whaling Museum (SSWM) announced the passing of Margaret McGee. The manager of the SSWM gift shop died suddenly on July 3, 2010, the second day of the much anticipated July 4th holiday weekend, as she prepared the gardens at the museum ahead of a major event planned for that evening.

Though nearly incoherent when asked to share her thoughts, Mrs. Hawkins said, "I hardly knew her. I don't know quite what to say. We're not accustomed to dealing with dead bodies at the museum. Except, of course, for the five whale skeletons that we proudly display in the Grand Hall."

When this reporter pressed for biographical details, Mrs. Hawkins shared that, according to her job application, Ms. McGee (a.k.a. Maggie) was divorced, no children, and moved here from a small town in Maine. She lived at the Chadborn estate where she was employed, attending to a myriad of administrative and secretarial duties. "Ms. McGee came highly recommended by Budd Nickerson, the caretaker at SSWM. I saw no need to request additional references."

By all accounts, Ms. McGee planned to settle for the long term in Chatham Crossing. Robin Ritchie, agent with Sailing Ships Realty, disclosed that Ms. McGee invested in the town's newest and exceedingly popular condominium complex, which would be ready for her in September had she not met with this unceremonious ending. Asked if that unit will be available for resale, Ms. Ritchie said, "That depends on what her next of kin decides."

When not fulfilling her duties at the museum's gift shop, Ms. McGee was spotted on most Friday nights at various pubs and restaurants in town. "When a new lassie arrives in these here parts," said Roger P. Drake, cook at the Tide Me Over Café, "most of the lads take notice. Let's just say, Maggie rarely bought her own drinks."

Margaret McGee will be sadly missed by the museum's staff and by those who were hoping to give her a warm welcome to the community.

A memorial service will be held at a later date.

Reporter's Note: As all of you regular readers are aware, it is unusual for me to cover the Obituary desk. But this is an unusual death notice. And despite the scarcity of details about Margaret McGee, the paper is determined to report on her death with the respect and reverence every Chatham Crossing resident deserves. It is true the investigation of Ms. McGee's sudden demise is well underway by the Chatham Crossing police. If you were at the SSWM Saturday morning or have information about Ms. McGee's background and/or personal history, please contact Daniel DaRosa, investigative reporter at this newspaper. All information will be held confidential, except for what investigators need and for notifying next of kin so they can arrange a proper farewell and disposition of her assets.

Print and digital editions.

CHAPTER NINETEEN

Gabby, short for Gabriela, was a godsend. Little did I know when she gave me her personal phone number a couple of years ago I'd ever need it. My hair appointments were scheduled every six weeks like clockwork. In between, I somehow managed the near chin length style myself. Until I stumbled.

After I successfully showered on Sunday morning without wrecking my wrapped hand, I called Bay Wash, Gabby's hair salon. Of course, I got the "we are closed" message. She was closed on Sundays and Mondays, whether or not it was a holiday weekend. Everyone deserved time off. But I needed her!

As I struggled with one hand to get dressed, I debated whether to call her cell phone. When I almost lost a fight with my bra, the decision was made for me.

"You know I'm closed on Monday?" Gabby felt compelled to remind me.

"Have I ever called and asked a favor before? My thumb made me do it."

"I gather. I heard it through the grapevine."

We both laughed at her song reference. "Kudos to you, Gabby! Now can you do me tomorrow?"

She explained she was hosting her family's holiday barbecue the next day, but if I could meet her at the salon at noon, she'd get me in and out before another group recorded and released that song again.

If Gabby ever tired of shampooing, I just might hire her myself for Oldies & Goodies.

Hold that thought.

Gabby was late for our Monday appointment. Okay, I was ten minutes early—a habit I adopted several years ago as a New Year's resolution. Routinely, I would always try to do one more thing before heading for any appointment—dentist, car maintenance, hair dresser—which resulted in my being late and having to apologize. I got tired of rolled eyes and hems and haws. So I decided to use the clock app on my phone to set alarms and timers. Worked like a charm. Yet, it seemed recently I was the one rolling my eyes and hemming and hawing.

Actually, I tapped my nine fingers on my steering wheel, sitting in the parking lot of the newest strip mall about a mile and a half away from my store and the historic district. This shopping area was another one of the Town Committee's big ideas. After they approved the Harbor View Cove condominiums, a developer—probably a relative of the condo builders—swooped in with a plan for a small row of stores to serve the expanding population of Chatham Crossing. Since the condos were up and away from the historic district, tourist traffic would be nearly non-existent. Of course, the Committee approved the stores.

Gabby saw dollar signs, moved her salon, which had been in the middle of the historic district on James Street, up to Buzzards Bay Boulevard and renamed it Bay Wash. In honor of the long-running television series with a similar sounding name, she tracked down a poster with lifeguards and surf boards and hung it near the shampoo sinks.

Grateful that she interrupted her holiday to make me beautiful for the ride on top of the parade float, I refrained from mentioning she'd kept me waiting for fifteen minutes.

"Are you sure you don't want a trim?" Gabby asked, as she tied a leopard print cape around my neck and pointed me toward the sink. "Your next cut is scheduled for Friday."

Quickly, I did a cost/benefit analysis of one appointment versus two, deciding the scale measuring both time and money tilted in my favor. I made two quick decisions. Yes, to the trim. And yes, I'd double her tip.

As my neck was hyper-extended at the sink, which was invented by someone much taller than me, I soaked in the shampoo's orange scent. Simultaneously, I tried not to swallow my tongue, which would trigger a third medical emergency in as many days. We chatted mainly about Gabby's plans for the afternoon. She reminded me how large her Portuguese family was (more cousins than she knew what to do with), most having lived in Chatham Crossing all their lives, dating well back to when the whaling industry reigned supreme. She could even trace her lineage to Sofia Silva, the woman for whom the museum was named.

"What the heck happened there Saturday?" she asked, toweling off my hair and gently sweeping a dry cape around my body. I tucked my hands underneath the cape, protecting my thumb from any accidental bumping as Gabby moved about me with a pair of shears in her hand.

"I fell and fractured my thumb."

"That's kind of obvious. But how did you fall?"

"Didn't you see the article and the obituary in *The Chronicle* this morning?"

"No, I was busy making my famous chorizo pasta salad for an army!"

That must have been why she was late, I surmised. I forgave her: if only I had an army to cook for. I closed my eyes thinking about my sister and her family out in San Francisco, as strands of hair fluttered down my face. I waited until Gabby blew them away before I opened my eyes and my mouth.

Rather than repeat word for word what Daniel DaRosa had to say in the paper, I shared what I knew about Maggie's demise. From time to time, Gabby stopped her shears and raised her eyebrows.

"Did you know Maggie McGee?" I asked, when I had nothing more to reveal. "Was she a client of yours, of the salon's?"

"I wish. She had gorgeous ginger red hair. I would've loved to get my mitts on her locks. But I did run into her occasionally."

"Really? When? Where?" I was all ears.

"Well, let's see. Of course, at the museum. When friends visit, my husband and I take them to the museum. During the February school vacation, we took a group of kids there. She was new in the gift shop then. So, I introduced myself on the chance she'd make Bay Wash her salon of choice. She didn't. I don't know where she went. Though, being a natural redhead with long locks, she may not have needed me or any stylist often."

I nodded slightly so as not to disturb Gabby's work or have a Van Gogh incident. I valued my ears as much as my fingers.

"Sometime later, I think it must have been in March, because our anniversary is in March; and we went to Whaler's Watch Pub for dinner," Gabby continued. "My brother, Louie, owns the place, so we get a terrific discount on our bill. And the food is great."

"You're right. I've been there many times. Mostly, with Paul." I felt Gabby squeeze my right shoulder. I urged her to go on with her story.

"Where was I? Oh, yes. After dinner, friends joined us for drinks. I remember Maggie was there. Not alone, of course."

"Did you speak to her?"

"Yes, briefly. Just long enough for her to introduce us to her date. My hubby was anxious to get me home. Our anniversary and all."

We shared another chuckle. My mind raced, scanning names and faces of the eligible bachelors of Chatham Crossing, including the gent living in my cottage. If Maggie was there with someone other than Budd, that could rule him out as more than a friend. So I said, "Oh? Anybody I'd know?" Goosebumps swept over me.

"Maggie's date? What was his name?" Gabby tipped the shears into the air slightly. "I'm sure you would know. That hunka hunka burning love Carole added to her team last Christmastime."

"Roger P. Drake, you mean?"

"That's him. Didn't he move here last fall? And Maggie a few months later? A coincidence maybe? Do you think they have a history?"

I couldn't answer Gabby's questions and didn't care to tell her Maggie and Budd had their own history from their time up in Maine. So I said, "I guess newbies are like magnets. They attract one another." I looked at myself in the mirror, hoping Gabby couldn't read the grin of relief on my face.

"You're probably right. Louie says they came in for dinner most Friday evenings. Even last Friday. And they always always always left together."

Gabby had no idea the gift she'd just given me. So, in turn, I gave her one. A one hundred dollar tip, and I booked shampoo and blow dry appointments for the next Friday, as well as the next three weeks. So much for my cost/benefit analysis.

"Your pain, my gain," Gabby laughed, as she shuffled me out the door. She was off to a family outing. I was off to clear my name.

CHAPTER TWENTY

Gabby was a miracle worker. I hoped to connect with Oscar after my hair appointment. Though I didn't get all dolled up for him, I had to admit I looked pretty damn good. Gabby applied a sufficient amount of hair spray to keep the style manageable and presentable for the parade on Tuesday.

Once in my car in the parking lot outside of Bay Wash, I checked the time. It was nearing two. I didn't think my hair would take so long. But of course, Gabby was late and then I opted to get a trim, and it took time to schedule out my next four appointments.

"You're late," Oscar said when he answered my call.

"Is that so? You'll be pleased my pain medication has worn off. I hear that's what you're waiting for."

I neglected to tell him I took two Tylenol before leaving Bay Wash. Extra strength. Prophylactically.

"Sure. But I can't meet now. Family picnic. You know how it goes."

"I see." *Was everyone at a family picnic, but me?*

I should've been relieved Oscar couldn't get together then, but I was kind of disappointed. Or maybe I was jealous that he, and Gabby for that matter, were spending the holiday afternoon with relatives. With my next of kin three thousand miles away, I wondered what my closest circle of friends was up to at the moment.

Budd was at the museum until at least five, or rather six. As the caretaker, he was usually the last to leave. And then there was Carole. She was either at the store or managing some major local catering event, which I was sure she told me about, but I couldn't remember.

Even over the phone, Oscar's finely tuned observation skills must have sensed my loneliness because he said, "Would you like to join us?"

I smiled and placed my right palm over my heart. "Do you normally invite murder suspects to your home?"

"No. But you're special, Venus. You know that."

"Thanks, Oscar. I think I'll pass." I was glad he couldn't see my eyes watering.

"Okay. But you're not off the hook just yet."

Damn it. He neither heard what I was thinking nor the gulp in my throat.

"Let's get together this evening," he said. "Will eight-ish work for you?"

I could've responded with six-ish, seven-ish, or that I had no plans. All of which would have been the truth. Instead I cooperated. "Sure. My place."

We disconnected. I waited there another moment before turning the car key. Jitter Bug's black interior had warmed up considerably, having sat in the sun for over two and a half hours.

What was on my agenda for the rest of the day? There was nowhere I had to be and no one to be nowhere with.

Swinging by the store was always an option. If I went there, though, would Hannah and the team misinterpret my visit and assume I was checking up on them? Not an impression I'd want to convey.

The museum had opened up again, just in time for the holiday tourist crowd. I considered swinging by there and showing Budd my fresh hairdo. Customarily, in the evenings following my hair appointments, Budd buried his head in my hair and then his face in my lap. Obviously, he could do the former, but not the latter, if I suddenly appeared at his place of work. I would've loved to take his hand and lead him into one of the museum's many storage rooms, but I couldn't do that either. Instead, I filed the image and fantasy to fulfill at a later time.

My stomach gurgled as I turned on the ignition. Not sure which sounded louder. I thought back. It had been hours since I finished my tea at the store. Time for lunch. Since my interrogation was postponed either for the worse or better, I needed to decide what to eat. I was in no mood to go home and scrounge for whatever was in the refrigerator.

As the car's air conditioning began to do its job, I also rolled down the windows to let some fresh air in. I pulled out of the parking lot and headed up Buzzards Bay Boulevard into the historic district, and then turned right toward the piers. Out-of-state cars, mostly SUVs, crowded Morgan Street. Families with baby buggies pushed their way past each other at crosswalks and sidewalks. As I passed my store on the right, I noticed a couple going in and a group of teenagers coming out. Probably locals, friends of the staff.

Obviously, neither the traffic light at the entrance to town nor an unsolved murder two days ago scared off visitors. Perhaps the intrigue of Maggie McGee even added to the attraction. Hmph. As if Chatham Crossing needed more appeal beyond Oldies & Goodies.

Nevertheless, I speculated the value of recommending one-way streets and sidewalks to the Town Committee. This should be a piece of cake to approve and implement once I'm voted in as a member.

Of course, I had to sit and wait for the red light at the intersection of Morgan Street and Wharf Way. The No Turn on Red signs hanging across Morgan and the one fixed on the side of the street reminded me to abide by the law. If anyone knew the rules around this light, it would be me. My stomach continued to talk to me, or at me.

Being this close to the bay, either sea water or the prospect of seafood made my mouth water. Either way, three snack bars along the piers beckoned me. Rather than drive up and down the street hoping to find a parking spot, I pulled into the lot designated for the apartment complex. I noticed a "for residents only" sign, but I also spotted five vacant visitor spaces. If anyone asked, I'd just point to the mini drug and convenience store on the corner and say my thumb made me do it. *Need to milk this thing for all it's worth.*

I walked past the first snack bar. Since it was the first of three from this direction, logically starving tourists stopped there. The line to place orders was dangerously close to spilling onto Wharf Way. Same was true for the third snack bar, since it was the first one people coming from the opposite direction encountered. I felt like Goldilocks and chose Captain's Catch. Just right … in the middle.

With the where-was-I-going-to-eat decision made, *what* I was going to eat became the most important decision of my day thus far. That is, if I didn't count letting Budd leave for work without stopping by for a quick tea and me or my decision to interrupt Gabby's holiday. Clearly, one lost out, the other benefitted.

Enough already. Food was of utmost importance at the moment. Not Budd. Not Gabby. Certainly not Oscar.

But that reminded me of his kind invitation to his family picnic. I wondered what was on the grill in his backyard? Burgers and hotdogs? I imagined cops kept things relatively simple, though I didn't have any experience to base that on. If I'm not in jail around Labor Day, perhaps I'd wrangle an invitation to his house then.

I knew Gabby was having some sort of salad and probably an array of grilled fish. She didn't invite me. But that was okay. She didn't know I was going to be alone. I didn't know it either. I expected to be at the store.

Letting a family of five go ahead of me in line, I stepped back enough so I could peruse the blackboard menu. There was the usual hamburger, foot-long hot dogs, clam rolls, and scallop dinners. But the lobster roll, sauteed in butter, spoke to me. I nodded yes for the coleslaw and no to the French fries. A bottle of water completed my order. With my receipt, I was handed the water and a black plastic chip with a number on it and directed to have a seat at one of the picnic tables alongside the shack.

I asked a man and a young boy if I could join their table. They nodded with their mouths full. I prayed my number would be called soon. The sight of their meals and the overpowering aroma of clams, calamari, and tartar sauce just about did me in. I took a swig of the water, hoping to tame my cravings. I heard "17" called over the loudspeaker. I turned my plastic chip face up, figuring it was too soon for my order to be ready.

My number was *22*.

Rather than believe Paul was following me, I decided to take it as an omen. A good omen. *Every little thing is gonna be alright.* At least for the rest of the day.

Six minutes later, I attacked my lunch without a care in the world, except for how to protect my thumb from the melted butter oozing out of my luscious lobster roll.

"Here, use these." The youngster sitting diagonally across from me offered, sliding his excess napkins as he and his father rose to leave. I'd thank them properly if my mouth wasn't full up, so I just bowed my head and gave them a non-splint thumbs up.

As I was about to take a forkful of creamy coleslaw, I noticed black Converse All Stars stepping over the bench opposite me. My eyes traveled up the lad clad all in black, except for a white bandana around his neck.

"Ahoy there, Ms. Bixby. Don't you just love coleslaw?"

"I do. I most certainly do, Roger."

"Mind if I join you?"

"Of course not, but shouldn't you be manning *Bixby's Dozen* along about now?"

"Been there, done that," Roger P. Drake said, flashing an ear-to-ear smile. He slid his tray onto the table and whipped out a mini bottle of Purell. As he squirted and rubbed the hand sanitizer on his palms, he added, "I've done my time today."

He made it sound as though he just got out of jail. Nearly finished with my lunch, rather than get up and leave, I decided to linger. My little chat with Gabby just a few hours earlier also lingered. Mr. Drake appeared more chipper than I thought one should be two days after the person they'd been having dinner with for months was supposedly killed. I hoped he didn't think this was the start of something new. No way would I replace Maggie as his dining companion. A cougar I was not.

Technically, as his boss, it was perfectly appropriate for me to ask him how business was going at the store. We spent a few minutes between bites and swigs of liquid—me water, him a soft drink of some variety—with Roger sharing great news about the steady stream of customers at the store.

"Seems like cookies and music go together. Like love and marriage."

"Admirable of you to do your shift today." I refrained from giving him the satisfaction of acknowledging his uttering a song title. That was my gig, not his.

"How so?"

"With Maggie …"

Putting down his cheeseburger with bacon he'd already half devoured, Roger asked to borrow one of my napkins. In all my life, I'd never understood why people asked to borrow things they had no intention or ability to return. Napkins being one of them. Scotch tape another.

As Roger busied himself wiping the ketchup off his lips, I recognized an opportunity when it dropped in my lap.

"Did you know her well?" I asked him, careful not to reveal Gabby gave me an inside scoop earlier.

"Well enough to know I'll think of her often."

Well, that tells me diddly squat.

"What about you? I hear you were the last one to see Maggie alive."

"Don't believe everything you read," I said, organizing my trash on my tray for easy disposal and then inching my way along the bench to leave. "Looks like we're done here."

Roger followed suit with his paper trash, gathered both of our trays, and headed to a not-yet-overflowing trash barrel.

I could've scooted without him noticing, but that wouldn't have been at all polite. Anyway, he had something I needed.

"Can I borrow some of your hand sanitizer?"

CHAPTER TWENTY-ONE

"What are your plans for the rest of the holiday?" Roger asked. Just like Paul—the gentleman that he was—Roger moved to my left, nudging me to the inside of the sidewalk along Wharf Way. I knew I was going to the parking lot to retrieve my car. Not sure where he was headed.

"Plans? Oh, I have places to go, people to see." I laughed, realizing only half of my response to Roger was accurate. No reason for me to tell him Officer Donovan would be interrogating me in about five hours.

"What about you?" I halted at the entrance to the lot, figuring we'd depart there.

"Me? I have some calls to make, maybe take a ride. Get to know the area better. Discover the fortunes of Chatham Crossing." His arm swept upward toward the historic district.

Sounded like we had something in common, but I chose not to appear sad and alone. Not a good look for Roger's boss to have.

I pointed across the lot to where Jitter Bug awaited. "This is my stop."

"Mine too."

Roger pointed to a candy apple red Mustang parked in the residents' section, just one lane over from where we stood. "That's my car."

Coincidentally, we had to walk past his car, which of course I recognized from all the buzz about it, to get to mine. So I asked the next obvious question as we stopped beside his vehicle, "You live here?" I slanted my head toward the building.

"I do."

My eyes caught something yellow billowing in the breeze on a door handle of an apartment on the second floor. "What do you think that's all about?"

"That's Maggie's apartment," he said, pressing his lips together.

"Neighbors?"

"Neighbors with benefits."

"I know how that goes," I said, an obvious slip of the tongue. My relationship with Budd flashed through my mind. I hoped Roger didn't say he'd heard all about us from his barber, the way I had heard about his relationship with Maggie from Gabby. I wondered how often he got his ponytail trimmed? Then, almost as if he read my mind, he reached behind his neck and swung his long ponytail over his left shoulder. *Such an unusual man.*

With the opening he just gave me, I was about to probe him more about Maggie when he lifted his sunglasses. So I held my tongue and instead followed his gaze. His eyes focused like a laser on someone standing in front of a door on a ground floor apartment.

"Excuse me, Ms. Bixby," he said, gently touching my left arm. He flipped his ponytail back where it belonged, untied the white bandana I noticed him wearing earlier, stuffed it in his rear pocket, and took long, sprightly strides toward the building.

"What a surprise," I heard him call out as he waved to the fellow waiting there. Heaven knows, Roger's visitor must have been new to the area. Was he wearing a New York Yankees jersey?

"As I live and breathe," I whispered. I hoped Roger had the presence of mind to buy the visitor a Red Sox T-shirt. I made a mental note to remind him Oldies & Goodies had a wide selection. I'd even offer him an "employee" discount.

Where to next? With my thumb injury, I'd taken to hanging my bag over my right shoulder, which was becoming weary from that unwise decision. As I switched it to the other shoulder, I walked behind Roger's car. His license plate captured my attention. *Jolly*. I chuckled, getting the joke or message I imagined he was trying to convey.

Jolly *Roger*.

I twirled back toward the apartment building expressly to soak in all of him. Dressed completely in black, he stood out against the white apartments. Roger appeared to be having an animated discussion with his guest—both arms outstretched toward the sky, then his hands on his hips. When he pointed to the NY initials on the fellow's shirt, I supposed I didn't have to school him after all.

Shaking my head, I wondered: who are you, Roger P. Drake? A cook, a baker, or perhaps a wannabe pirate? Aaaarrrrgggghhhh!

Feeling somewhat chipper after a yummy lunch and a hearty laugh, I hopped back into my car. *Think I'll give Carole a jingle. See how her day is going.*

"Hey, you just caught me," she said.

"How's that?"

"Just left the store. Business is much brisker than we expected it could be. Given the circumstances."

"You mean Maggie?"

"What else could I mean?"

Since she mentioned Maggie, I told her I'd be meeting with Officer Donovan at eight. "Which reminds me," I said, wishing I could see her face. "Are you the anonymous friend who gave Daniel the idea that I was the last one to see Maggie alive Saturday morning?"

Carole didn't answer. I checked my screen.

"You there, Carole? You did see *The Chronicle* this morning?"

"Um, yes, I'm here."

"Well, were you?"

"I think he misunderstood me, Venus. I'm so sorry."

"Oh blimey, Carole. I fell over her shoes! If she was upright, and we were having a conversation, I wouldn't have tripped over her. Now would I?"

"When you put it like that …"

"In fact, the last time I talked to Maggie was on Friday. In the museum gift shop."

"I saw her there Friday, too."

An image of Carole rushing through the museum on Friday raced through my mind. She was moving away from the gift shop. She must have just talked with Maggie.

"What was that about?" I asked.

"With Maggie?"

"Uh-huh."

"Not much. I was just, um, going over the details for the … party. Why?"

"Just wondering."

"What about you? I didn't know you were at the museum on Friday," Carole said.

"No big deal. Bought some postcards."

"The postcards at the store aren't good enough for you?"

Ignoring her snide remark, I laughed and tried to think fast, not wanting to let on that I was poking around about Maggie and Budd's supposed friendship. "Whales. We need more cards with whales and scrimshaw. Don't you agree?"

After Carole concurred with my suggestion, I switched topics. What was she doing the rest of the day?

"One more catering job. On my way there now. Let's talk later."

We clicked off. I looked at my splint. She never asked how I was feeling. What were friends for if not to utter a basic health question, especially after an emergency visit to The Cube?

I fired up Jitter Bug and reversed the course I followed when I left Bay Wash earlier. Turning left at the notorious traffic light, I drove up Morgan Street past the block where a line formed outside Oldies & Goodies. Carole was right about the store being busy. I took another left to get to the Hilltop. Briefly, I considered doing a uey and stopping at the store to lend a hand. But my thumb told me that was a bad idea. Time for some rest and quietude before spending time with anyone else, especially Officer Donovan.

As I pulled into my driveway, I spied a red roller bag sitting at the top of the steps on my front porch. I wasn't expecting company, especially not anyone who'd be carrying luggage. I parked, turned off the engine, and lifted myself out of the car.

"Hey there," I heard someone call from the back of the house. As I lived and breathed. I could name that voice in one word. Sister.

"Oh my God, Sherrie! What are you doing here and in the backyard?"

"You didn't answer the doorbell, so I thought I'd check the cottage. Though I didn't want to interrupt anything." She hooted, throwing her arms around me.

While I recognized her squeaky voice, I pondered whether I would have picked her out of a crowd. We're twins, just not identical. Neither in looks, nor in demeanor.

Neither of us had started the middle-age shrinking process, yet. I was surprised she'd let her bangs grow out and her hair fall carefree, about three inches below her shoulders. She should've gotten a dye job before flying East. Definitely, a more casual look than she had when last I saw her three years ago. But as a teacher, she'd probably wait until just before school started to handle things of that nature. Couldn't blame her. I didn't have the luxury of postponing salon appointments as an owner of two enterprises. I had an image to maintain.

I wrangled out of her embrace, covered my nose with my right palm, stifling a sneeze. Shalimar. Despite her hair, Sherrie really hadn't changed much.

"Budd is at work," I said, finagling with the keys on my carabiner until I found the right one. "And it's only three o'clock. I'm not like our father."

Oops! As soon as the words spilled out of my mouth, I knew I stepped in it. My goodness, nearly forty years had gone by since my sister and I walked in on our father doing the nasty deed with the neighbor lady one afternoon after school. Sherrie reacted differently than I. She wanted to squeal to our mother. Force him to fess up, face the consequences no matter what they were. I had a better idea. One that wouldn't start a family conflagration. I told him to put on his pants and find another hobby. The three of us agreed to pinky swear we'd keep his dalliance to ourselves. Which we did. But the act of keeping our mouths shut created a fissure between my sister and me that neither time nor distance had so far fully healed. To this day, our visits were rare; rather, we relied on Alexander Graham Bell's and Steve Jobs's inventions to keep the home fires alive.

So, her showing up on my doorstep without calling gave me the sneaking suspicion that something unpleasant was about to erupt.

My comment about our father stifled our hellos at least while we maneuvered her bags, yes plural, into the house through the front door. Once I climbed the steps, I spotted two more matching suitcases on the porch. One—a garment bag, slung across the back of one of the

Adirondack chairs. The other—a medium-sized duffel bag, which hid behind the roller bag.

Before showing her to the spare bedroom, which needed to be freshened up, I suggested something cold to drink. As I poured us both iced tea, I decided to bite the bullet, get the skinny on what Sherrie was doing here in the flesh on the fifth of July. After all, we just talked two mornings ago on our birthday.

"You sure got a lot of baggage. You headed somewhere on vacation, like Europe or something? Is this just a stopover?"

"Heck, no, Venus. I'm here to see you. Take care of you."

I tucked my left hand behind my back and inhaled as much air as my 50-year-old lungs could muster, allowing my mind to form a polite response.

"Do I look like I need to be taken care of?"

"Well, actually, no. You're looking well. Your hair looks divine—"

"Thanks. Just got it done this morning," I said, sweeping my fingers through my bangs. "I sense a *but* about to stream from your sweet red lips, Sherrie baby. So spill it."

"Well, it's kind of a long story."

"Go for it."

As she paced about the kitchen, Sherrie explained she hadn't intended to fly out here when we talked Saturday morning. In fact, she had a surprise waiting for me later that day if things had gone according to plan. Without my knowledge, Carole and Budd had contacted her a few weeks before the party and asked if she would be part of my birthday celebration. They'd make all the arrangements both on her end and at the museum for her to be piped in through live video feed when it was time to sing Happy Birthday. Carole and Budd would set up the screen in the gardens that morning and then power up the laptop in the evening.

My eyelids flapped like butterflies as I listened to Sherrie disclose their little secret. Given our childhood history, I knew she could keep quiet about something important, but I was astonished both Carole and Budd were able to do so.

"Well, that would've been lovely, Sherrie."

"Thanks. I'm glad you think so."

"But I'm surprised you all kept it so close to the vest. What's the proverb? A secret between two people is like a locked drawer, but among three people it's out the door?"

She chewed on that for about fifteen seconds, and then said, "The distance between us probably made it easier, don't you think? Just two here in town."

I furrowed my brow. Agreeing with my sister about something so soon after our unexpected reunion brought me unexpected joy. The question was, how long would it last? Sherrie still hadn't told me why she was here, but I was beginning to get the picture.

"Keep going," I said, waving my hand in circular fashion.

"Well, I don't have to tell you the party plans went down the tubes."

"That is true. How'd you find out?"

Budd called her.

"At first, I thought he was calling just to confirm the arrangements for that night. But when he told me they whisked you off in an ambulance, well, I just knew I had to pack my bags and get the hell out here. Party or no party."

"You could've checked with me first. Saved yourself some money. It's just my thumb." I held it up as if I was doing show and tell, again.

She told me she didn't care about the money.

"Budd was frantic. He was beside himself. He told me a friend of his died in the gardens where the party was going to be held."

"So you're here to support Budd. Because a friend of his died?" That made more sense to me than her sudden interest in little ol' me.

"No, Venus. Don't be ridiculous. Budd told me you're connected with his friend's death somehow. You might be in some kind of trouble. Are you in some kind of trouble, Venus?"

I made a mental note to have words with Budd about going behind my back to contact Sherrie. It was kind of him and Carole to try to do something nice for my birthday. But look where their little scheme landed: smack dab in my kitchen, stinking up the house with her perfume. My eyebrows found a new height. I slid out a kitchen chair so I could take a load off and waved my palm toward Sherrie, inviting her to do the same.

"Were you the last one to see … what's her name?"

"Maggie."

"Alive?"

"Is that what Budd said?"

She nodded.

I laughed because this was really becoming laughable. I knew for certain I didn't see Maggie alive on Saturday, but Budd and Carole did. And yet, they were pointing the finger at me. What were friends and lovers for, if not to defend rather than accuse?

"Well, Budd may want to think I'm in trouble. But —"

"So, you're not a suspect?"

"If the police think I am, that's about to change tonight. Now, let's get you settled upstairs. What you *can* help me with is putting clean sheets on the bed."

"What's happening tonight?"

"Let's go." Instead of answering, I pointed toward the ceiling. Together we rose.

Imagine that. I'm not alone this afternoon after all. Who knew?

CHAPTER TWENTY-TWO

Plumping the second of two pillows on the queen sized bed Sherrie would occupy for some yet undetermined amount of time, I gently suggested she might want to take a shower after her long trip from San Francisco.

She lifted her right arm over her head to assess her level of body odor. "Do I smell that bad? Truthfully."

Here was my chance. After decades, I could come clean. Should I?

"Can you handle the truth?" I snickered, giving myself time to decide what to say.

Sherrie raised her palms in the air as if to say, "What the …"

I rubbed my nose, giving her a hint. "It's your perfume, Sherrie. I can't believe you're still wearing that gosh forsaken Shalimar. I'm sure you love it. But it dates you and makes me want to retch."

"Excuse me? You've never complained before."

I tugged at my earlobe, at a loss for words for once.

"I wish you'd told me. I'd do anything for you. Change my perfume, fly cross-country …"

Well, that was easy. And touching.

Rather than saddle her with the old, ratty faded bath towels, I pulled a brand new set of white Egyptian cotton towels out of the linen closet. I'd been saving them for an unspecified special occasion. I guessed a breakthrough moment with my twin qualified.

"I'll be downstairs," I said, gulping back a potential teardrop.

"Do I pass muster?" Sherrie asked, interrupting my train of thought as I sat at the kitchen table, making some notes in anticipation of meeting with Officer Donovan in about four hours. I was trying to remember what happened Saturday morning. Why didn't I do this forty-eight hours ago? Oh yeah, my thumb got in the way.

My nose confirmed Sherrie arrived in the kitchen without her signature scent, and my eyes revealed she looked terrific. Seeing her then, as if for the first time in a long time, in sea green capris with a coordinated multi-colored three-quarter sleeve cotton shirt, she appeared at least ten pounds thinner than me. Consciously, I sucked in my stomach as I gave her both a nod and a smile.

We hadn't had a chance yet to talk about her visit. How long was she going to be in town? What would she like to do? Frankly, while I was happy to see my sister, I wasn't sure this was the most opportune time for her to visit. Conceivably, I could be spending a good deal of my time and energy expunging the notion by anyone interested—the police, townspeople, Daniel DaRosa at the paper—that I had anything to do with Maggie's death.

Thinking about it, I didn't even know how she died. I wrote *cause of death??* at the top of my note and folded the paper in half. I placed the napkin holder on top of it, saving it for later.

"Bet you're hungry," I said, more of a statement than a question.

Sherrie placed her hand on her stomach. If only I hadn't just had that yummy lobster roll.

"We'll need to go out. Obviously, I wasn't expecting you."

I hustled us out to the car. What would she feel like eating? What was open? Ah … back to the pier.

Driving down Morgan Street, I pointed out Oldies & Goodies. Of course, Sherrie remembered it, as well as Paul's dance studio across the street. The last time she was there was for his funeral three years ago.

"Did you sell the studio?"

"No, why?"

"The name …"

I explained why I changed the name.

"So you changed the name to remind you of Paul?"

"I did. That's a good thing, right?"

She grunted. "How does Budd feel about it?"

"Budd? He has nothing to do with it. We're really not that serious. Besides, we have our own histories. Our own baggage."

"Was Maggie his baggage? He sounded devastated when he called. I couldn't tell whether he was more concerned about you being hurt or Maggie. Now that she's gone …"

I gasped and asked what she was implying. As I pulled into the same lot I parked in earlier in the afternoon,

Sherrie waved me off as if what she'd said meant nothing. Luckily, there was still one narrow visitor spot available, as if it were made specifically for Jitter Bug.

Leading Sherrie out of the lot, I noticed the yellow tape still flapping in the breeze as well as the absence of one candy apple red Mustang. Hoping she wouldn't follow my eyes to the second floor of the building, I sought to distract her by mentioning I'd eaten there on the pier just a couple of hours ago. But that was okay. I'd probably just get a bottle of water or lemonade.

"So, tell me, sweet sister of mine. What's your favorite song today?"

"I can't believe you're still asking such a nonsensical question. I'm sure you think it's your brand. But I've heard it so often, it's bo-ring!" Sherrie said, emphasizing the last word.

"Fair enough. Now we're even." We strolled arm in arm toward Captain's Catch. Sherrie started her rendition of Carly Simon's *You're So Vain*. I reminded her, vain or not, I never got to walk into the party Saturday night.

"Which is why I'm here."

We grew quiet as she scanned the menu board. Without asking for a recommendation from me, Sherrie ordered the exact lunch I had just hours earlier. Of course she did. I refrained from stating the obvious so as not to bore her. I also saw no reason to tell her we were sitting at the same picnic table where Roger and I had our little chitchat. Roger meant nothing to her. Besides knowing Carole from her previous visit and talking with Budd by phone, Sherrie hadn't met many of my Chatham Crossing friends, for that matter.

"I can't wait to meet Budd in person," Sherrie said, reading my mind. "Will he come by tonight? I didn't tell him I was heading out here."

"Oh, I forgot you haven't met him in person. He didn't move into the cottage until after Paul died."

"How convenient," she said with a testy grin that sent a stream of melted butter over her bottom lip and down her chin. I handed her a napkin and rubbed my fingers across my chin in case she couldn't feel the grease.

"I'm sure you'll meet Budd while you're here. If not tonight, certainly tomorrow."

"Why not tonight?"

"Officer Donovan's coming by the house at eight. To get a statement from me about Saturday morning."

Sherrie glanced at her watch. "That's over three hours from now. What do you suggest we do in the meantime?"

This late in the day, the crowd at the Sofia Silva Whaling Museum typically thinned out, even on the Monday after Independence Day. Nearing dinner time, folks most likely were rushing off to picnics or to their favorite towns to scope out the best location to watch the fireworks displays being held that night, as they would be in Chatham Crossing.

We stopped by the ticket kiosk not to pay to enter, but just to be polite and to acknowledge I was bringing in a guest. I was a VIP after all. The on-duty ticket person recognized me, smiled, and made two marks on a sheet of paper, completing one set of hash marks. I wondered how many freebies they granted each day. How it impacted the museum's bottom line? So sue me. As a businesswoman, I obsessed over such things.

I recalled I'd brought Sherrie and several out-of-town friends there in the days following Paul's burial, so a formal tour for her was unnecessary. And we really didn't have enough time to check out all the historical documents, displays, and artifacts anyway. I'd brought her there that afternoon for one purpose and one purpose only.

To introduce her to Budd.

To get the inevitable out of the way. When that was done, I'd be able to check it off the list I'd been forming in my mind of things Sherrie would want to do before I drove her back to the airport. She just had a lobster roll, so check that off. New England clam chowder, baked beans, Boston cream pie. Those were all easily accessible and wouldn't take days to accommodate.

To my surprise, while she devoured her late lunch, she expressed a keen interest in taking a ferry ride over to one of the islands.

"I've never been to the Vineyard or Nantucket," she said.

I didn't commit exactly, as I was taken aback by her reference to Martha's Vineyard in a casual manner, usually reserved for locals. I merely replied, "We'll see," using the store as an excuse for being evasive.

"With this thumb, I've left the store to Carole and this weekend's temporary staff to manage. It's not fair of me to monopolize their summer—their best days."

She seemed to accept my frivolous explanation until a family of five sat at the picnic table next to us. They were all decked out in Red Sox gear. Hats, shirts. Even the tote bag hanging from the mother's shoulder.

"How about a Red Sox game?" Sherrie whispered. "You can make time for that, can't you?"

She had me there. I hadn't made a trip to Fenway yet this season—not sure why. I promised to check the schedule, half praying they were out of town. Normally, I'd know such things off the top of my head, but the events of the last few days had thrown me off my game. While I'd love to go to Fenway, spending nine innings having to explain balls and strikes to my sister was not high on my bucket list.

Maybe Sherrie would like to go shopping instead. We'd see what suited her fancy and my patience.

I looped my right arm through Sherrie's left and led us toward the main exhibit hall, expecting Sadie would be in her office surreptitiously overseeing the visitors' visits. But as we passed the gift shop just off the lobby, I heard, "That'll be twenty-two fifty, including tax." Sadie's throaty voice was unmistakable.

She must be filling in for the late Maggie McGee until she hires someone to fill her shoes. Oh, dear, I hope whoever she finds doesn't wear platforms.

With those thoughts, I nudged Sherrie toward the shop. We stepped in and busied ourselves with the postcard rack until the customers left.

Here was an opportunity to kill two birds with one stone. Sherrie hadn't met Sadie on her last trip East. I intended to make this quick.

"Oh, hi, Sadie. How's everything going today? Good, I bet. I'd love for you to meet my sister. Sherrie Moore, this is Sadie Hawkins, the museum's curator. Can you let Budd know I'm here?"

As she came from behind the counter, Sadie's mouth dropped as she extended her hand to Sherrie. "All the way from San Francisco?"

"Yes. How did you know?"

"Small town."

"So, you must be the Sadie who insisted on sharing part of my sister's birthday celebration?"

"Yes. How did you know?"

"Small world."

This wasn't going well. I brought Sherrie here specifically to meet Budd, not to fight my battles with Sadie Hawkins.

I inserted my body between them. "Could you please let Budd know I'm here? If you don't mind?"

"He is working, Venus, as am I." Sadie moved back to her station behind the counter.

I bit my lip and clenched my good fist. "I promise not to keep him tied up long."

Sherrie chuckled, turning away from Sadie so she couldn't hear her say, "How long do you usually keep him tied up?"

"Stop it." I smiled, my eyes twinkling. I gave her arm a love tap.

Just as I was about to repeat my request of Sadie, I was interrupted. Pleasantly.

"There you are."

I turned toward his familiar husky voice. Budd to the rescue.

"How'd you …?" I asked.

"Cecilia spotted you and texted me."

Flipping Sadie a quick wave, I dragged the three of us into the lobby. "Thank goodness for Cecilia. I'm not sure Sadie would've let me talk to you. What? Does she think this is high school?"

Budd just laughed at me. He'd grown accustomed to my skirmishes with Sadie.

"Don't tell me." Budd opened his muscular arms and enfolded them around Sherrie. "This is your sister! I'd recognize this beautiful face anywhere."

I tapped my foot one, two, three, four times. "Alright, you two. At least let me properly introduce you before I suggest you get a room."

Budd released his bear hug, but he grabbed Sherrie's hand and placed it on his chest.

Was the twin thing going too far? Next thing, he'd propose some kinky threesome. Another good reason to keep Sherrie's spontaneous visit short and sweet.

"Budd, this is indeed Sherrie Moore. My sister. Who I recently learned you've been talking to behind my back."

They were smiling at each other in a creepy sort of way. I raised my eyebrows and continued.

"Sherrie, this is Budd Nickerson. He's the caretaker here at the museum."

"You can call me Budd … or Buddy. Whatever your little heart desires."

"The museum caretaker? That's not all you take care of, I hear." Sherrie winked as she slapped his arm with her free hand.

This was not going as I would've imagined. Of course, I didn't, couldn't imagine this scene unfolding because I had no idea when I got up that morning that my sister would be inserting herself into my daily life.

Shifting from one foot to the other, I said, "Did I mention Sherrie's married? And has a daughter?"

Budd shook his head affirmatively. "Lighten up, Venus. I'm just kidding around."

"A little innocent flirting never hurt anyone," Sherrie added.

I was not so sure of that. My eyes caught Sadie flitting around the gift shop. I watched her fold T-shirts and then re-stock the carousel full of refrigerator magnets. Less than a week ago, Maggie was probably doing the same thing at this time of day. Did Budd take the same liberties with her? Hugs? Hand holding? Winks? Or more?

How well did I really know Budd Nickerson? Was his interaction with Sherrie a picture into his soul I hadn't yet seen? Being smart, handsome, proficient with a hammer and other unmentionable tools didn't necessarily qualify him as a keeper for the long term. Did it? Doubt produced goosebumps on my arms.

"Time to go," I said, pulling Sherrie away from Budd's grasp.

"So soon?" they asked virtually at the same time.

"Will you stop by later?" Sherrie asked him.

"About that." He turned his attention to me, finally. "An old friend of mine from Maine is in town just for a few days. We're thinking of hanging out together tonight. Catch up on old times."

I looked at Sherrie, then Budd. She'd turned the smile she had moments ago into an unflattering pout for a fifty-year-old woman. He widened his eyes, anticipating permission to have an evening with a friend.

"You'll have more time to spend with Sherrie," he said.

As if I needed his approval to hang with my sister. What he didn't know was that I'd be splitting my time that evening between Sherrie and Detective Donovan. What Budd didn't know wouldn't hurt him. After all, it was my statement about what happened Saturday the police were interested in. Not his. When the time was right, I'd get him to come clean about his relationship with Maggie. Why, for example, did Sherrie sense he was more devastated by her sudden demise than I believed he was?

Budd leaned down and gave me a quick peck on the cheek.

"Sounds good," I said, "have fun." For a brief moment, I thought he was back in my corner. Until …

He locked eyes with Sherrie and announced, "I've got the morning off tomorrow. I'll swing by the house at eight. We can go to the parade together."

CHAPTER TWENTY-THREE

I was in the kitchen retrieving two tall glasses for the sun tea I'd made when the doorbell rang. Before I could get there to answer it, I heard the front door open and the murmur of voices. I recognized both.

"You must be Officer Donovan."

"I am. And you are?"

"Can't you tell?" Sherrie said, twirling around, as I rushed to join them in the front hallway as fast as my bare feet would take me.

Other than the fact that I was expecting Officer Donovan at eight, I was surprised Sherrie assumed who he was. By the looks of him, he could've been a neighbor asking to borrow a bottle of ketchup. Wearing khaki cargo shorts and brown flip flop beach sandals, he obviously came directly from his family picnic. At least his navy Izod shirt had the name of the police department embroidered in white above the pocket. And since my sister and I were pretty casually attired ourselves, I couldn't hold Oscar's five o'clock shadow against him. He wore the stubble on his chin well, along with his lean and sunburned body. It was a summer holiday after all.

"Hi, Oscar. This is my sister, my twin sister, Sherrie Moore. She's here from San Francisco."

As introductions concluded, I prayed there wouldn't be a repeat flirting scene like I recently witnessed at the museum. Wanting to get this show on the road and over with, I waved toward the living room, which to me was the proper place for an inquisition at eight o'clock in the evening. As Oscar headed for one of the two overstuffed accent chairs, I asked him to give me a minute and turned toward the kitchen with Sherrie on my heels.

"He's cute, Venus. Is he married?" She teased.

Oh, God. Not again. My intuition was right. "You're kidding, Sherrie. He's our town's number one detective. And yes, he's married. Very married. Why do you ask such a thing?"

"Well, just in case things go south for you and dear ol' Budd."

"So all *this* is on my behalf? Why would things go bad for me and —" I waved my hands in the air.

"The Maggie/Budd connection is still not solved, is it?"

She had to remind me. I put the pitcher of sun tea and two glasses on a tray and turned toward the living room where Oscar was surely tapping his foot, waiting for me.

"Only two glasses?" Sherrie sulked. "What about me?"

I inhaled deeply and let out an audible sigh. "Precisely. What about you? This isn't about you. Not sure there's anything you can add."

Sherrie reached across the kitchen table, lifted the napkin holder, and retrieved the notes I'd made in anticipation of this meeting with Officer Donovan.

"Well, there is this." Sherrie waved it in my face. She must have snuck a peek at it when I wasn't looking.

With my hands full carrying the tray and shaking due to my injury, I conceded. Sherrie had me there. I directed her to the second drawer next to the stove, where she'd find a pen and notepad. "Oh, and get yourself a glass. In the cabinet to the right of the sink." While Sherrie made herself useful, I made my way to the living room.

Oscar stood when I entered. "Here, Venus, let me help you. You shouldn't have. But I'm glad you did. I'm a bit parched. Outside in this heat with my family's picnic this afternoon. And I love iced tea."

Was I imagining it? Was Oscar bumbling? Was he nervous? If I were guilty about something, shouldn't I be the one exhibiting signs of anxiety? Would I be able to balance a tray with a full pitcher of sun tea and two glasses without spilling? Nevertheless, I accepted his offer.

In what seemed an instant, Sherrie swept in behind me. "I'll pour," she said, as she handed me the pen, notepad, and my notes. "Here, you sit."

So, I sat in the center of the couch and spread my arms out across the cushions. Sherrie's only option after handing each of us a glass of tea was the other accent chair that floated with its back to the hallway. "A triangle," she said. "This is nice."

Not sure where she was going with this, but since Oscar seemed focused more on his beverage than starting the conversation, I hadn't much choice but to allow her the floor, so to speak.

"Our mother and father settled in California during the hippie movement. Did you know that, Officer Donovan?"

Enjoying his drink, the best he could muster was a grunt. At this rate, he'd need a refill before Sherrie enjoyed her first sip.

"My mother passed down to us some of the cultural symbols manifesting her life back then. I remember what she said about triangles. Do you, Venus?"

I reached across my body with my good hand and scratched my elbow. "No, but I'm sure you're about to educate us." Thankfully, we all laughed.

"Well, let me see. A triangle can mean many things, especially when it comes to religion. The obvious, of course, is the trinity."

Oscar and I both conceded that as Sherrie continued.

"But I prefer to think of a triangle as providing balance, harmony, and stability." Sherrie reiterated by pointing to each of us. "And I'm feeling each of those in this room right now." She let out a sigh, as if she was satisfied with her performance.

Oh, geez. Any minute now, Sherrie would have us singing "Kumbaya, My Lord." Here I thought *I* was the Song and Dance Lady.

"A triangle can also mean change, as in the Greek delta symbol." I offered my two cents.

"Or danger, like a traffic sign," Oscar piped in.

I swallowed my drink, gratified it cooled my throat which suddenly felt a tad distressed. I sensed an uneasy twist in the conversation. Clearly, Sherrie hadn't meant for that to happen. How did a simple seating pattern force a turn for the worse?

I decided to take the bull by the horns.

"Since you came here to talk to me about Saturday, Oscar, I trust you've made progress on the investigation, and I'm not a person of interest regarding Maggie McGee's death."

Sherrie visibly shifted in her chair, looking a bit out of balance. So much for her triangle theory. I, myself, was as stable as a Plimouth Rock.

"You know I can't share details with you, Venus. But I need a statement from you in order to fill in some blanks."

Some blanks? I had some blanks, as well. I unfolded the paper that was under the napkin holder in the kitchen and placed it on my lap.

"I'll be glad to answer any question you have, but I have one of my own."

"Shoot," Oscar said, followed by, "Sorry, my bad." He tapped his right hand over his heart three times.

"How did Maggie die? I mean, what was the cause of death?"

Oscar bowed his head, as if in deference to Maggie. Or in deference to me … and Sherrie? Seemingly uncomfortable that he had to talk about such things to us.

"Was an autopsy performed?" Sherrie spoke up out of turn. I glared at her, trying to decide whether to give her a thumbs up or to toss a throw pillow in her direction. Instead, I looked at Oscar for an answer.

"Blunt force trauma to the head," he blurted out, touching his left temple with his fingers. "According to the medical examiner that was on the scene," he said, answering both of our questions. "We'll have to wait for the autopsy results."

With that news, the three of us sat in silence for what seemed like an eternity. Not sure we knew quite what to say. How should you respond when you hear such horrible news? I decided I better say something before Sherrie did.

I got up and walked behind her chair, resting my good hand on her shoulder. Perhaps some of Sherrie's strength and energy would rise and enter my body, which suddenly felt drained, as if I'd experienced some unexpected trauma as well.

"How can I help you?" I whispered and took my seat on the couch again.

Officer Donovan reached into his pants pocket and pulled out a palm-sized notebook similar to the one I saw him write in when he was there on Saturday. As he flipped page after page after page, I gathered I was right. He asked, "Where did we leave off?"

I tried to remember where we were. The words *good terms* came to mind. I recalled telling him Maggie and I weren't on bad terms. She'd only moved to Chatham Crossing in January. Knowing someone for six months was hardly enough time to be on any kind of terms. My interactions with her primarily centered on when I'd see her at the museum gift shop or when she'd come into Oldies & Goodies for one thing or another. We didn't share social circles.

Oscar listed off what he learned from me the other day. "You say you couldn't have been the last one to see Ms. McGee alive? She was already down on the ground when you entered the gardens?"

"Correct. I fell over her shoes."

"Orange platform shoes," he said, "which afterward you associated with her because she was wearing similar shoes on Friday when you brought cookies to her at the museum."

I nodded, acknowledging everything so far.

"You screamed because you fell."

"Makes sense," Sherrie offered in support, interlacing her fingers and resting her elbows on the arms of the chair.

"You told me you went to the museum Saturday morning to check on the arrangements for the party. No other reason?"

"None."

"Venus, can you think back? Maybe close your eyes. What did you see when you entered the gardens?"

I did as he asked. Initially, I closed both of my eyes, but then lifted my right one to see what my sister was up to. This clearly felt right up her alley. "Close them," she said, shaking her finger at me.

"I don't see anyone when I enter the gardens." I paused, almost about to say *ooooh* as if I'd seen a ghost, but I thought better of it. Instead, I reminded myself this was no laughing matter. "I walk past two, no three groups of white folding chairs. I'm heading to the opposite side of the gardens where tables are assembled to hold the food that Carole and her team will be setting up later in the day for the event."

"Carole?" Oscar asked.

"Carole Duffy, the mayor's wife."

"She's a caterer." Sherrie apparently thought she was telling the detective something he didn't know.

I still had my eyes closed, trying to concentrate on what was on the tables.

"It's too early in the day to set out anything perishable. So there's not much on the tables yet besides dinnerware, glasses, napkins, salt and pepper. Things like that."

Oscar told me I was doing good, encouraging me to keep going.

"Oh, but there are platters, multiple platters, of cookies covered with clear packaging like the grocery stores use with fruits, vegetables, prepared foods. Polyethylene terephthalate." An internal grin warmed the cockles of my heart. *Okay, Oscar, what are going to do with that little piece of information? Perhaps look it up in your* Funk & Wagnalls?

"Poly what?" he said.

I opened my eyes and pointed to his notebook. "Just write down PET."

His eyebrows lifted and then quickly returned to their normal position. "Close your eyes. What else do you see?"

"As I'm walking next to the food tables, I notice a projection screen sitting all by its lonesome ahead of me. It's already set up on its tripod, as if waiting for a movie to start. I immediately think it must be there for the special reveal Sadie has been touting all week."

"That's not why the screen was there, Venus. Remember, I told you earlier?"

I ignored Sherrie because I wanted to finish my story and get this over with. "And that's when I trip. I almost fall on my face, but my arm and thumb save me. I must have screamed when I fell. I turn my head to the right, wanting to see what the heck caused me to lose my balance. I'm usually pretty good on my feet. That's when I see the orange platform shoes. Then, all hell breaks loose."

"Maybe you screamed when you saw Maggie spread eagle in the brush?" Sherrie added.

"Perhaps," Oscar said. "I'm not sure it matters when you screamed, Venus, but that you did. What happened next could be important."

"Oh, wow! What happened next, Venus?" Sherrie inched her bottom to the edge of her seat, all eyes and ears.

I opened my eyes. Oscar didn't seem to mind. "I remember Budd kneeling down next to me, helping me to a sitting position. I was glad I wasn't wearing a skirt."

Both Oscar and Sherrie nodded in agreement.

"So, Budd is the first one on the scene?" Oscar asked. "Anyone else?"

"Why yes, now that you mention it. Jeremy was standing there next to the table with the cookie trays. And then I heard Sadie."

"Sadie, the museum curator?" Sherrie asked.

"Yes, that Sadie," Oscar replied.

"You've spoken to her?" I said, my eyes wide opened.

"Yes, but that's all I can report."

"And Jeremy, who's—?" My sister continued with her questions.

I explained Jeremy Roserun was the museum's gardener, probably there early not only to tend to the gardens but also to ensure no one damaged his pride and joy. "And then Maggie goes and does a face plant in his pachysandra."

Again, the living room quieted, except for the sound of the air conditioner kicking on and humming.

"Officer Donovan, what do you think happened?" Sherrie broke the silence. "Maybe it was an accident?"

"She could've fainted, or maybe she tripped on those damn shoes. I warned her …"

CHAPTER TWENTY-FOUR

Oscar accepted, at least for the time being, my explanation for how I'd warned Maggie on Friday that wearing those platform shoes could be dangerous to her health. It was a friendly warning. As it turned out, her shoes were more dangerous to me.

Oscar's initial theory of the case was that it was no accident. Maggie was indeed found face down in Jeremy Roserun's award-winning gardens. Had she fainted, fallen and hit her head—say on the table her body was found next to—the injury to her head would've been on the opposite side than it was. And, for that matter, the dinnerware etcetera arranged neatly on the tables would've been disturbed to some extent, maybe even scattered to the ground. But he believed the photos showed the only thing disrupted on the tables was one of those PET covers protecting the cookies. Sitting askew, it had obviously been opened and several items taken.

"Well, that's a clue." Sherrie excitedly suggested fingerprints could finger Maggie's attacker.

"Wish it were," the good detective said. "It seems the sweets were too attractive to leave untouched. Both the emergency and museum crews admitted to sneaking at least one treat while they roped off the scene and carted Ms. McGee's body away."

"So, where were you, Officer Donovan, while this evidence was being tampered with?" My sister's inquiring mind wanted answers.

Like a puppy dog caught with a box of Milk-Bones, Oscar lowered his head toward his chest, interlaced his fingers, and said exactly what I knew he'd say. "I was following the ambulance your sister was in."

So before he left my house, I gave the following statement to Detective Donovan in person and then, later Monday night, I emailed it to Daniel DaRosa at the paper:

Just like all Chatham Crossing residents, I am saddened by Margaret McGee's untimely death. I didn't know her well when I tripped over her feet in the Sofia Silva Whaling Museum's gardens after she'd fallen for some unknown reason. I have faith this unfortunate mystery will be solved by our esteemed police force, and in short order, Chatham Crossing will be humming along nicely once again.

Oscar completed his inquisition in just under an hour. Sherrie accompanied me onto the front porch as I bade him so long, farewell auf Wiedersehen, adieu. Almost as an afterthought, he apologized for his attire, especially the sandals, saying meeting with me was more important than taking the time to change. I suggested Bay Wash as a great place to get a pedicure, pointing to and wiggling my toes.

"Message well taken." He shook my hand and gave a tip of an imaginary hat to Sherrie.

I should be proud and pleased my sister brought out the gentlemen in friends of mine. Who knew?

Just as we turned to go back inside, an explosion erupted, forcing us to face the direction the sound came from. Buzzard's Bay. At first, we mistook it for the sound of a gunshot, but we were relieved to see firsthand the one-day-late Fourth of July fireworks celebration was underway. There was no better spot in all of Chatham Crossing to take it all in than my porch on the Hilltop.

Sherrie and I settled into the Adirondack chairs for an hour of stunning color, dazzling bursts of rockets' red glare, and the twinkling of lights as they fell from the sky into the black water. As the lights from the fireworks descended, they shone a light upon the Happy Whaler, a schooner anchored safely nearby. I pointed it out to Sherrie, explaining that it was a replica of one pictured at the museum and how it provided a learning environment for teenagers interested in nautical history and enriching their seafaring skills.

"Simply amazing," Sherrie exclaimed, clapping her hands and stamping her feet like a five-year-old. "Totally worth this trip."

"Paul knew what he was doing when he settled us here, don't you think?"

"I do. But do you think he predicted his replacement would end up living in the guest house?"

Rocking my chair, I let a few minutes pass before answering her. I could share my thoughts as she was sitting right next to me, or I could change the subject.

"About Budd," I started to say. "He's not Paul's replacement. No one could …"

"I know. I'm sorry. But he's kind of great, isn't he? Can you see yourself spending the rest of your life with him? Moving him out of the cottage and in here permanently?"

Once inside, before heading upstairs for the night, I gazed out the kitchen window. The cottage was dark. The outside light wasn't even on. Budd's car wasn't in the driveway. I had no idea who this old friend was he was hanging out with so late. I had no clue if it was a man or a woman. Thinking back, did he use a pronoun when he said he'd be going out? He or she? Her or him? My mind blanked.

"Too soon to consider such a life sentence. Ask me in a year or two or three," I said, turning off the lights in the living room and pointing Sherrie toward the stairs.

"Fair enough. What's this about a parade?"

"Wake up!"

Expecting to hear the smoke alarm blaring, I bolted upright, preparing to pull back my covers and sprint out of the house in my nightgown. But alas, it was just Sherrie sitting at the foot of my bed. She grabbed my left foot through the comforter, shook it, and repeated her rude command.

"Wake up! How can you sleep?"

Two emotions overwhelmed me simultaneously. Confusion and reminiscence. What time was it? Memories of our childhood flooded my mind. She always got up first, whether it was a school day or the weekend. Whenever she'd say, "The early bird gets the worm," I took for granted I was in for a long day.

"How can you sleep, Venus?" she repeated.

I lifted my phone that sat on my nightstand and clicked it to life. "What the devil, Sherrie, it's five-twenty-five. It's sunrise, not Venus-rise!" I fell back on one pillow and pulled the other one over my face. I tried to explain I didn't have to get up until six. I could get ready in less than an hour and be out the door in plenty of time to get to the Stop 'n Shop parking lot where the parade floats and marchers would be gathering.

"We need to talk, Venus. To strategize."

Strategize? This was a new side of Sherrie. Where had it been hiding all these years? But then again, I recalled she'd been in cahoots with Carole and Budd about my birthday celebration and kept that a secret.

"About what?" was all I could muster at that ungodly hour. Though well-honed, my strategic skills didn't normally kick in until after my first cup of tea, preferably English breakfast.

"If you're not a suspect in Maggie's death, who is?"

I slung the pillow covering my face across the room. It barely missed a vase I'd made at Whale Craft Pottery the holiday season after Paul passed. Therapy, Carole had suggested. It would be good for me to squish my fingers in wet clay and wrap my hands around a pottery wheel. "Imagine you're Demi Moore, and Patrick Swayze is …" she'd said. She didn't need to fill in the blank. My broken heart took care of that.

Succumbing to Carole's advice, I walked into the pottery studio carrying an unhealthy attitude of skepticism and left with my cottage rented to the gentleman who Sadie had recommended to me. She was right, I had to give her that. With Paul gone, I could utilize this fellow's handyman skills to keep both the main house, as well as the cottage, in good repair. On closer inspection, during the month after he moved in, I discovered there was more to Budd than his ability to drive in a screw. He could mix a great cocktail and cook a splendid meal. A man after my own heart. Blessed with many talents, Budd Nickerson charmed and reinvigorated the woman in me faster than *The Chronicle* posted breaking news.

I hopped out of bed, relieved the vase had escaped my high-risk pillow toss. "Great question, sister of mine. Let me shower. I'll meet you in the kitchen in thirty minutes."

Sherrie, too, jumped off the bed, did a happy dance, and exited the room singing "Oh, what a beautiful morning!" And here she called me boring.

"What's all this?" I asked, entering the kitchen. Sherrie wore white capris and a light gray T-shirt with an American flag, obviously in celebration of the day. Her hair was tied back in a low ponytail, and her make-up flawless, except for lip gloss, which I assumed she'd apply after we finished the breakfast she was fixing.

"You'll need energy to wave to your fans high above your float, Ms. Grand Marshal," Sherrie teased, as she delivered a plate with two pieces of lightly buttered whole wheat toast and two eggs over easy, onto a placemat already holding a small glass of cranberry grape juice.

Rather than criticize her for using one of my favorite, and rarely used, plates from the first set of china Paul and I had chosen together, I replaced that thought with a positive comment. "You remember how I take my eggs?" I was beginning to regret how annoyed I was when she showed up in my yard the day before. If Sherrie was going to be there for any length of time, I'd need to give her a tour of the kitchen and the linen closet. Give her the lay of the land, as it were.

She joined me at the table and slid a purple college ruled legal pad in my direction. Apparently, she was industrious enough to rifle through my desk and find what she needed with little help from me.

"Write," she mumbled while chewing the corner of her toast, pointing to the black felt-tip pen and then to my Plimoth Plantation mug of hot tea. "They spelled it wrong. Is it a knock-off?"

"No," I explained briefly I'd gotten the white mug the year before at the plantation itself. "See all these names in blue? They all came over on the Mayflower."

"Anybody we know?"

I pierced my lips and tapped the pen on the table. Another tour we could squeeze in during her visit. Perhaps.

Moving on, I asked her what I should write?

"If you're not a suspect, isn't everyone that was at the museum that morning under suspicion?"

My first reaction was to agree with her, but then I realized the possible culprits were all, or mostly all, people who were close to me or at least acquaintances of mine. Would I really finger someone I knew?

"Maybe I shouldn't get involved." I twirled the pen in a circle on the pad, considering my options.

"You're already involved. Even if you weren't the last one to see Maggie alive, you did discover her body. That's being involved if you ask me."

I yanked off the top of the pen. "Where do I start?"

CHAPTER TWENTY-FIVE

Sherrie's insistence I create a profile of suspects in Maggie's death consumed more time than I expected or wanted. I startled when the alert on my phone signaled seven-thirty, indicating I should be walking out the door.

"Crapola," I declared, closing up the pen. I slid my chair back, intending to take my empty dishes to the sink.

"Let me—" Sherrie grabbed the plate, utensils, and the Plimouth Plantation mug off my hands. She rotated the mug, checking out the names.

"Thanks, breakfast was great. I owe you one."

I snatched the pad containing three pages of notes and jogged upstairs to freshen up and finish dressing. The notes found their way into the bottom drawer of my bureau where I stored folders of important receipts, warranties, and instruction booklets that I never referenced but kept just in case. The last thing I wanted was for Budd to catch a glimpse of his name at the top of the suspect list.

After brushing my teeth—not enough time to floss—I slipped into the white sleeveless midi-sheath I'd hung on the back of my closet door. Why white? Because ... I'd be wearing a Grand Marshal sash, of course. Not sure of the color, but I expected it to be red, white, and blue with some stars and glitter accents. So, a basic white dress was the only logical choice. A brisk check of the make-up I applied over two hours ago, a brush through my hair, and a quick swipe of my favorite plum lip gloss, and I was good to go. *Lookin' good*, if I said so myself.

At the bottom of the stairs, I selected one of the half dozen or so hats on the free-standing wrought iron rack and plopped it on my head. I checked it out in the small mirror with the image of a yellow tabby painted on its blue frame, conveniently placed nearby. Clearly, the hat's brim was not wide enough to protect me from the morning sun I'd be battling on the float. I swapped it for another hat, an actual sun hat, which was my favorite anyway. It matched my white dress and had a large, flexible brim that could do it all—protect my face, ears, and neck—when I needed it to, and was easily flipped up when I'd want to check out the waving spectators along the parade route.

Carrying my keys, purse, and hat, I threw wide the front door just as I heard a knock on the kitchen door. An indication that it was eight o'clock, and I was late. Such was not the case for the man who lived in the cottage. Punctual as usual, Budd had arrived to gather Sherrie.

Holding the screen door open, I leaned back toward the kitchen and paused, hoping to overhear what Budd had to say.

"You ready?"

"Just let me finish up here."

"Is Venus still home? Shouldn't she be …"

I pulled the front door shut, not with a bang, but with enough force to rattle the doorknob bells I knew from experience could be heard in the kitchen. Fearing any interaction with Budd because of where it could lead or that such a face-to-face would have only made me later than I already was, I descended the front steps faster than usual and made haste to my car. Rather than taking the time to open the passenger door and place my belongings on the seat there, I slid into the driver's seat and tossed my stuff over the gearshift onto the passenger seat. In the time it took to count to ten, I made it out of the house and was backing out of the driveway.

I didn't look back to witness Budd holding Sherrie's hand, guiding her as she stepped out through the kitchen door or as he opened his car door for her. What I didn't see wouldn't hurt me. I admit I was more than a little curious how Sherrie would handle things since less than an hour before we'd labeled Budd number one on the suspect list. It pained me to do so. But since I knew he went to the museum early Saturday morning specifically to open up for Maggie, and he was the first to come to my rescue, I had to agree with Sherrie that, if nothing else, Budd should be the first person we check out and then quickly eliminate.

If only we'd taken more time to truly strategize.

As I pulled into the Stop 'n Shop parking lot, a man wearing a yellow vest waved at me to stop.

"Ms. Bixby, where have you been?"

"Busy morning," I answered, not able to return the courtesy of addressing him by name. Did he really recognize me or had someone alerted him to be on the lookout for Jitter Bug?

He pointed me in the direction I should park my car.

Since the parade didn't start until nine, I was confident there was plenty of time for me to park; run into the grocery store to buy some wrapped candy to toss to the crowd; and maneuver my way around and through the various excessively red, white, and blue decorated floats; the three marching bands tuning up their instruments; the Boy Scouts and Girl Scouts; and the veteran's groups.

But before exiting my vehicle, I called Hannah, figuring she was at the store. Earlier, the kitty painted on the mirror at the foot of the stairs in my hallway had reminded me how much I missed Sonny and Cher. Hannah assured me the kitties were doing fine, especially enjoying the attention from the steady flow of tourists shopping at the store.

"Good news for a change," I said.

"Yes, right on. Whatever happened at the museum the other day hasn't put a damper on business, for sure."

"Curiosity seekers unable to pass up a good scandal, I guess."

"So it seems. I hear your sister's in town."

If Hannah was insinuating something about Sherrie by that remark, I bet Sadie had put the idea in her head. Leave it to her mother to start a conspiracy theory. Of course, I wondered if Sherrie would've made the trip out here if Budd hadn't implicated me in Maggie's death. Be that as it may, I'd handle Sadie at the appropriate time. My priority right then was to get my rear in gear and out of the car.

"Yes, Sherrie arrived yesterday. I'll bring her by this afternoon to meet Sonny and Cher. See ya'." I clicked off.

Stepping out of the icy air of Stop 'n Shop, I could tell it would be a scorcher of a day. Good thing the parade would finish up early. Otherwise, spectators might jump into the Crescent River along the route for some relief and miss seeing my float.

I spotted Detective Donovan even though he was dressed just like the other policemen he'd be marching with. I recognized the way he stood confidently with his thumbs looped inside his waistband. Though he appeared deep in conversation, I moseyed up alongside of him.

"Oh, Ms. Bixby." I assumed he addressed me this way in front of the other policemen so as not to reveal we really were on a first name basis. So, I followed his lead.

"Good morning, Officer Donovan." I inclined my head to the left, indicating I needed to have a word with him.

"What's up?"

"We need to talk."

He removed his aviator sunglasses and squinted. "What? We just talked … what, twelve hours ago?"

I dipped my head, affirming I was well aware of that. "Not now," I said. "Later." With my right hand I gave him the *call me* sign. "Perhaps we can cooperate in areas of mutual interest," I added. His jaw dropped, obviously wanting more of what I was not prepared to give him in front of half of the Chatham Crossing police force. Stepping aside, I turned and pranced away in search of my pumpkin disguised as a float.

"There you are!"

Holding my hat, I saw Carole rushing toward me. "Where have you been?"

"Why are you here, Carole? I thought you'd be at the store?"

"It's Simon. He called me, so I rushed over. He's on the verge of apoplexy. He's on the float with you, you know. I was afraid you had another medical emergency."

Not sure if Carole was joking, I let her remark pass. No one told me I'd be sharing my ride with Simon, but it made sense since he was the mayor. Initially, I thought as Grand Marshal, this was my fifteen minutes of fame. Yet, with everything that had happened over the last few days, being in the limelight was not high on my agenda.

"We need to talk, Carole," I said, gritting my teeth, trusting after all these years she'd realize I was not kidding.

"Not now," she said, clutching my elbow and guiding me to wherever I needed to be.

She was probably right. That was not the time to tell her she was number four on the SLS (a.k.a. the Sisters' List of Suspects, which I just cleverly coined). For that matter, I hadn't figured out the best way to ask about her whereabouts on Saturday morning. She'd probably be highly insulted by my inference, given our long-time friendship and mutually profitable business relationship. Nevertheless, I had to give her a heads up before Officer Donovan knocked at her door and asked if she and Maggie were on good terms.

After all, what were friends for?

My hat slipped out of my hand as Carole said, "Here she is, Simon," pointing upward to the top of one of the most magnificently adorned floats I'd ever seen in a Chatham Crossing parade. And I'd seen quite a few over the three decades living here. The float was long, maybe as much as the fifty feet restrictions allowed. It was decked out in red, white, and blue streamers, as one would expect given the holiday.

When I bent down to retrieve my hat, my eyes soaked in the greenery that decorated the float.

"Are you okay?" Carole asked. Maybe she thought I was about to faint. She wouldn't be too far off as I was overwhelmed by the grandeur of my carriage.

"You … you like it?" A voice approached me from behind. I recognized it before I turned around.

"Oh, hi, Jeremy. Yes, it's splendid."

"Thank you. The parade's de-delay gave me ex-extra time to work on it."

I should have recognized this work of art belonged to Jeremy Roserun. His horticulture skills transcended beyond what he'd been able to achieve in the museum's gardens. He had a reputation of creating breathtaking, colorful floral displays even at the expense of his allergies.

"Jeremy, your arms!"

"What? This?" He swept his palms up his arms. "Don't wor-ry, I have pills and ointment for this."

"Thank goodness. I do love what you've done here."

All by itself, Jeremy's smile would light up all of Fenway Park.

I was reluctant to put a damper on his moment of joy, but I recognized this as an opportunity to have a chitchat with the second suspect on the SLS. It would only take a couple of minutes for me to rule him out. After all, why would he want to harm Maggie?

CHAPTER TWENTY-SIX

"We were so-so worried you wouldn't sh-show up, Ms. Bix-bixby," Jeremy said.

I'd grown weary of so much attention to my tardiness. Everyone was well aware of my reputation for promptness. Instead, my neighbors and friends should've concerned themselves with the first murder in the town in over twenty years.

"Well, I'm here, Jeremy, and I need a word with you. Now, if you don't mind."

He followed me around to the opposite side of the float, which abutted a row of shade trees.

"What's up? Something wrong?"

Not with the float, I assured him he'd outdone himself. Jeremy beamed.

"I need to ask you about Saturday. Okay?"

He nodded, leaning toward me, most likely needing to hear me over the rumble of pickup trucks starting their engines. "Parade's getting underway," he said, waving a thumb toward the float.

"I'll make this quick, then. Jeremy. How well did you know Maggie?"

He shrugged, adding he only knew her through their interaction at the museum. "We were coworkers. Nothing more."

Since my hands were full, with no easy access to my iPhone, I had nothing on which to record his answers. So, I made a mental note. Was this really any way to conduct an investigation? Probably not, but I persisted … because I had a reputation for persistence as well as for punctuality.

"When did you first see Maggie on Saturday? Do you remember what time it was?"

Jeremy chewed his bottom lip and bent his head in thought. He raised his head and looked me straight in the eyes. "About eight o'clock, I'd guess, give or take a few minutes. She was setting things up in the ga-garden for the party. I brought in two ped-pedestals and set them up."

"Pedestals?" I didn't remember seeing pedestals and couldn't recall them being on the list of things Carole and I had requested for my birthday party. "What did you put on the pedestals?"

"Nothing. That's not-not my job. You'll have to ask Mrs. Hawkins."

Indeed, I would. Yet still wishing I could make note of it so I didn't forget. But I needed to move on. I bit my lip ahead of the next question.

"Jeremy, did you see Budd Nickerson Saturday morning?" I whispered, even though there was no one nearby to overhear our conversation.

"Of course, we were helping Mag-Maggie set up the tables in the gardens. He offered to help me get the pedestals out of the gar-garden's storage closet. Many hands …"

"Make light work," I filled in the rest of the saying.

"I was glad he was there. I'd left my keys to the back door in my car."

"What back door? There's another entrance besides the doors from the lobby?" I'd never noticed another entrance or exit. Then again, why would I?

Jeremy explained when the gardens were expanded a few years before, a storage closet was added as well. The only way to get to it was through a door which went to the outside.

"Yes. And the door has a deadbolt that needs a key to open it."

"I see." I tried to picture both the door and the pedestals without much success.

"As it turned out, I didn't need my k-keys."

"Why not?"

"The door was already un-unlocked. The ta-tables were delivered through the back door instead of through the fr-front of the museum."

I rocked back and forth on my heels, trying to ingest all the details Jeremy provided.

"What about the storage closet? Was that unlocked too?"

"No. Budd di-did the honors."

"Of course, he did," I said, fresh out of questions for Jeremy at the moment.

"I think you'd better get going. We can't start without you." Jeremy leaned toward the float.

He was right, of course. I followed Jeremy to the other side of the vehicle. My hands were full, so he held the bag with the candy, then offered me his hand so I could safely climb the ladder to the main level of the float. Then it hit me. I should ask him what Oscar asked me.

"One last question." I hesitated as I stepped on the top rung of the ladder, lowering my eyes onto his. "Were you and Maggie on good terms?"

"I told you. We were co-coworkers. So good terms?" Handing me the candy bag, he said, "Mostly, except—"

I felt the mayor's hand on my wrist as he assisted me off the ladder to a more stable landing.

Looking down toward Jeremy, I shouted down to him, "Thank you so much, Jeremy, you've made my day."

Biting my lip again, I had no clue why those words escaped my mouth. Most likely, it was me being polite, considering all the work he did to create a stunning float. My day, though, was far from made or complete.

Once safely off the ladder onto the float, I was about to mentally cross Jeremy's name off the SLS, except …

CHAPTER TWENTY-SEVEN

Everyone loves a parade. Everyone, except Sadie Hawkins. It didn't matter to her whether the town's Independence Day parade was held on the fourth or the sixth of July. She had no intention of lining up along the parade route to watch the pageantry or observe spectators cheer for this year's Grand Marshal.

Sadie was where she was happiest—at the Sofia Silva Whaling Museum among the whale skeletons, scrimshaw exhibits, and artifacts that even the highly trained and licensed had difficulty assigning value to. She arrived much earlier than she needed to Tuesday morning. With the parade starting at nine, Sadie delayed opening the museum until noon. That way all the employees could go and enjoy seeing their kids and other relatives march, twirl, and toot their horns. They'd have a much better time, she admitted to herself, without their boss hovering, so she declined their invitation to join them. She knew they were only being polite.

Sadie and her daughter, Hannah, walked out of the house at the same time. Seven-thirty. Hannah offered to drop her off at the museum before she went to Oldies &

Goodies, but Sadie turned down the offer. Her reasons for taking her own car were thinly veiled. She couldn't predict when she'd be done at the end of the day. And on top of that, she'd need to make a grocery run. No reason to make Hannah late for her date that evening.

Of course, Hannah dating Detective Donovan's son, Jesse, had its perks. Sadie often learned the town's scuttlebutt from her daughter even before it made *The Chronicle*.

"You going to the parade?" Hannah had asked her. "Bet you'll run into Venus's sister there."

"Already met her yesterday."

And with that, Hannah shrugged and climbed into her car, leaving Sadie alone with her thoughts. If only Hannah knew what was occupying Sadie's mind. What she'd been hiding for three days from her family, from her staff, from the media: the truth, the whole truth of what happened Saturday, according to what mattered most to Sadie.

The incident with Maggie was just half of what threw Sadie's life in a tizzy, causing her migraines to kick into high gear. Why'd Maggie have to go ahead and die? Sadie had given her a major responsibility, just what she'd been bugging Sadie for. But Maggie tripped up big time, and Sadie was left to clean up her mess.

The big event planned for Saturday night was supposed to propel her to prominence not just in the town, but also within the National Organization of Museum Curators (NOMC). Sadie could kiss her dreams goodbye. The death of an employee, coupled with a burglary of a valuable museum piece, screwed everything up.

Now, sitting alone at her desk at the museum, she slipped on a pair of protective gloves, unlocked the bottom drawer, and gently lifted out the treasure she'd brought down from the storage room Friday morning. She unwrapped the bubble wrap, resisting the temptation to pop the air-filled plastic.

Nearly a year had passed since a generous donor from Pennsylvania contacted Sadie. She had an extremely valuable piece of art that might be more appropriate sitting in the Sofia Silva Whaling Museum than in the curio cabinet of a historic home where few visitors could appreciate its beauty.

Sadie had received similar offers in the past. Fortunately, the NOMC provided guidance on how to handle such overtures so member museums were protected from fraud and grift. After Sadie had the organization conduct their due diligence, verify its authenticity, including its age, maker, and condition of the piece, Sadie moved with great haste to acquire it.

Why did the donor choose Sofia Silva Whaling Museum from among the thousands of museums around the world?

Because of Poseidon, of course.

On its main floor, SSWM already owned and displayed one of the most famous antique bronze statues of the god of the sea. The museum's most prized possession. Without a doubt, visitors to the museum consistently asked the docents where Poseidon was located. A trip to SSWM would not be complete without getting a gander, or a photo, of the god that was revered by all seafarers—sailors, whalers, and pirates, alike.

It was about time, the Pennsylvania donor had explained, that Amphitrite assumed her rightful place alongside her husband in Chatham Crossing. She had only one request. Well, according to Sadie, it was more like a demand: when the statue of Amphitrite was revealed, a proper celebration suitable for a goddess must be held, and she must be placed stage right of Poseidon during the event. Like her husband, at only a foot tall and less than ten pounds in weight, the coveted statue of Amphitrite could easily be a target for a thief interested in making a quick million or more. Naturally, Sadie assured the donor she would be well secured and protected in a locked glass cabinet afterward.

As Sadie held Amphitrite in her gloved hands, she gulped. Her eyes moistened as she contemplated her predicament. Poseidon was gone. Maggie was gone.

The weight of the situation was getting to her. She realized she hadn't enjoyed her customary meditation in the museum's gardens since early Saturday morning. Not her fault. The police had cordoned off the gardens for over twenty-four hours, and since then, she needed to manage the gift shop without Maggie around to do so. Logically, Sadie's mindfulness practice had taken a back seat.

Inhaling deeply, Sadie gently re-wrapped Amphitrite, placed her in the bottom drawer of her desk, and locked it.

She listened. Silence. The only sound was a low hum of the museum's cooling system. No better time than the present to take advantage of being totally alone. But she was not totally alone. As she opened the door to the gardens, birds chirped their hellos. She looked around. Not one parrot among them to squeal on her if given the chance. She gazed up at the cameras that should be fixed tomorrow. Now, it was just Sadie, the magnificent gardens, the birds, and her thumping heart.

Sitting on a bench on the opposite side of the gardens from where Maggie was found, Sadie realized she left her phone on the desk so she couldn't access her meditation music. She didn't let that stop her. Instead she closed her eyes and started the deep breathing exercises she knew as well as her ABCs. She hoped somehow twenty minutes of peace would calm her throbbing head.

Not so quick, though. Perhaps if she prioritized what bothered her, she could settle her mind, and figure out how to control the narrative with the powers that be.

She started with the board of directors. For museum curators, like herself, money wasn't the issue that it was for the board of directors. Nevertheless, Sadie knew she'd be making a lot of disclosures in the very near future.

Certainly, she'd notify the board that Poseidon was missing.

Then, of course, there was the insurance company. Most likely, the board would rely on her to manage that interaction. It's why they hired her. But never in her career had she made a claim to a museum's insurance company.

What will they want to know?

With her palms up resting comfortably on her thighs, she let her fingers count off questions as they came to her.

Will they accuse her of carelessness?

Who handled the piece besides her?

Why did she remove Poseidon from the display and hand it to a staff member hours before the event?

Where was the museum's security staff that morning?

Had she arranged extra security for the event?
Who was the last to see Poseidon?

Sadie's thoughts came fast and furious. Her breathing did the opposite of what she intended ... accelerating to the point of distraction.

She switched gears from the insurance company to the donor. At some point she'd need to notify the woman who donated Amphitrite that the big reveal never happened. Thankfully, she wasn't stolen along with her husband. Would she want her back? Could the museum staff be trusted to keep her safe and sound?

The staff. Damn it. Sadie chastised herself for letting over three days go by without questioning the staff herself. She assumed the police would investigate a burglary at the museum. Normally, a robbery at the museum would be headline news. But no, they were more interested in Maggie than the disappearance of the god of the sea.

On Saturday, when she pulled aside the police officer who was roping off the gardens with yellow crime scene tape to alert him Poseidon was missing, he'd mumbled something to the effect that a human life was more important than a hunk of clay. Of course, Poseidon wasn't just any old hunk of clay. But Sadie let him take a back seat to Maggie, which was her first mistake. When she raised the issue with Detective Donovan when he returned to the scene late Saturday morning, he, too, brushed her off.

"Later, Mrs. Hawkins. Priorities ..."

Her animosity toward Venus led to her second mistake. She'd overheard the good detective say all signs pointed to Venus Bixby. Not that she'd harmed Maggie, but that she was the last person to see Maggie alive was enough to consider her a person of interest. That, Sadie figured, could work in her favor with both the board and the Town Committee. At least until it was proven untrue, as Sadie was certain it would be. While Venus was Sadie's forever rival, she knew she wouldn't have deliberately hurt Maggie. Even if she didn't like Maggie's favorite song that day, she wouldn't hold it against her, literally. Thinking back, she could have defended Venus with the police. But she didn't.

Because, on one hand, Sadie derived pleasure in the negative attention being directed toward Venus. Anything that tarnished Venus's reputation was a good thing in Sadie's mind. On the other hand, the robbery clouded her thoughts. How could the police ask her specifically not to announce the robbery? Would they take care of it appropriately when the time was right? And when would that be?

Giving up on having a meaningful meditation, Sadie left the gardens and headed back to her office. She'd waited long enough. She had to do something to shine the light on the theft; take control of the situation. She needed to show the board and the insurance company she was as proactive as she could be. She considered calling the police, then figured most of them would be marching in the parade or doing crowd control.

She looked at her phone: time was of the essence. Within the hour, the parade would wind down and the staff would clock in for their shifts.

Sadie refused to be rebuffed by the police again. She would not make a third mistake. Someone had to listen to her.

She scrolled through her phone.

"Good morning, *Chatham Crossing Chronicle*. How may I direct your call?"

"Daniel DaRosa, please."

"I'm sorry. Mr. DaRosa is out on assignment. Care to leave a message?"

CHAPTER TWENTY-EIGHT

The Chatham Crossing Chronicle
A Body in the River

By: Daniel DaRosa, Investigative Reporter

BREAKING NEWS! **Tuesday, July 6, 2010, 1:15 p.m.** Shortly after 10:30 a.m. this morning, a bloated body was spotted by a resident of Chatham Crossing floating in the Crescent River during the town's Independence Day parade, according to local police.

Just as the Chatham Crossing high school band marched over Morgan's Bridge to the majestic and dramatic theme of "Pirates of the Caribbean," the mother of one of the snare drummers saw something floating in the river. Though unrecognizable from a distance, the body was thought to be of a man.

"See that white tank top?" an onlooker said, pointing at the corpse. "Definitely a wife beater."

Emergency crews monitored the subject and waited until the parade passed them by, since only the police and their horses were left in the procession. Then, they cordoned off the area and recovered the body.

They hauled the remains off to Providence, Rhode Island, for an autopsy to determine the cause of death.

The incident remains under investigation, as does the death of Margaret McGee, who died suddenly Saturday.

Two suspicious and unsolved deaths in a matter of days have historically safe and secure Chatham Crossing in uncharted waters. Could there be a connection?

Perhaps we'll find out during the press conference scheduled for five o'clock in front of police headquarters.

If you have any information that would help the investigation, the police ask you to contact them directly.

Print and digital editions.

CHAPTER TWENTY-NINE

In all honesty, being the parade's Grand Marshal sucked more out of my sails than I expected it would. Constantly having to smile and greet the crowd with a royal wave with my non-injured hand was more than enough exercise for me. Or maybe the events of the last few days, or the energy I was expending in an attempt to heal my thumb, or entertaining my unexpected house guest, were what really drained me. Maybe one or a combination were to blame. Whatever.

My fifteen minutes of fame morphed into one hour. I should've enjoyed it more than I did. As soon as my float reached the end of the parade route and Simon Duffy graciously helped me down the ladder, I texted Sherrie to let her know I was heading home.

No need for u and Budd to leave on my acct. May nap.

I wished I could take back my message. I shuttered to think Sherrie might interpret my words as giving her permission to get to know Budd better. But then, what would be wrong with that? Unless, of course, Budd was somehow connected to Maggie's death. I tried to shake off that thought as I kicked off my shoes in the front hallway, aligned them with others sitting there, and climbed the stairs to the bedrooms.

A delicate, sweet floral smell greeted me at the top. I peeked into Sherrie's room, scanned the premises, and spotted an unlit candle sitting on the nightstand. *Where'd that come from?* She must have brought it with her and lit it last night. How had I not smelled it earlier? Tiptoeing into her room, I lifted the candle and inhaled deeply, thankful for the calming benefit of candles even after extinguished. Who knew she liked lavender as much as me? A twin thing, I conceded, and then sneezed as I left Sherrie's room otherwise untouched.

I headed to my room for a Kleenex, fully expecting a second sneeze. And, of course, I was right about that.

I stripped, intending to take a power nap before planning the rest of the day. Just after ten-thirty, so I assumed I had an hour before Budd dropped off Sherrie and then headed to the museum. Lunch and a trip to Oldies & Goodies were definitely on the agenda for the afternoon. Where I'd fit in a conversation with Oscar remained to be seen.

Despite the windows being closed to keep the heat out and the cool air in, I detected sirens in the distance. I never quite understood the role emergency vehicles played in a parade, and why their drivers insisted on blasting their horns. Perhaps it was a competitive thing—fire department versus police—which gorilla could pound its chest harder.

The sirens reminded me of Oscar, which reminded me of the Sisters' List of Suspects I'd safely tucked away in my bureau. I got it out and climbed on top of my bed, with a power nap still on my mind.

"Wake up, Venus!"

I lifted my left eyelid and then closed it hoping I was dreaming and Sherrie wasn't standing at the foot of my bed, again.

"Wake up, sister!"

Raising my right eyelid sent a not-this-again message to my brain. At first, I panicked. Was it was already Wednesday morning? Had I slept all Tuesday afternoon and through the night? But then, there was no way Sherrie would allow that to happen, and she was still wearing the white capris and the gray T-shirt with an American flag over her left boob she had on when she left for the parade with Budd.

"Oh, God, what time is it?" I lifted myself onto my elbows.

"Time for you to get your rear in gear and get downstairs."

I pulled myself to a full sitting position, ready to ask *why* when Sherrie grabbed the pad with the list off my bed.

"Number four is downstairs. You can talk with her now."

Still trying to shake out the cobwebs, I attempted to understand her blathering. *Her? Who? Number four?*

Sherrie knew me well enough to read the look on my face.

"Carole. Number four." Sherrie waved four fingers in front of me. "Now get up."

As I did as I was told, Sherrie explained she hitched a ride home from Carole since Budd had to hotfoot it to the museum. That made sense, but I was clueless what Sherrie expected me to ask Carole that would exonerate her without letting on we thought she had something to do with Maggie's death.

"Gimme five." I shooed Sherrie out of my bedroom. "Leave that here." I snatched our notes from her, shut my door, and shoved the pad back in the drawer.

Think, I ordered the reflection in my bathroom mirror as I brushed my teeth. *Carole's your BFF and loyal business partner. Could she really be a person of interest? Well, at least she's not number one.*

Budd is.

I spat out the mouthwash and gripped the countertop with both hands as best as I could. I rationalized my mind skipped so quickly to Budd because, of the four persons we identified as suspects, he'd known Maggie the longest. So what? Just because they worked together in Maine, wasn't a motive to harm her, was it? Just because he helped her Saturday morning, did that mean he did her in?

Focus, Venus. Carole was downstairs, not Budd. One suspect at a time.

By the time I made it downstairs, Sherrie had set out three glasses of iced tea on a tray on the kitchen table. Not my favorite so soon after mint mouthwash, but I was a bit hungry. Hopefully, the tea would quiet my stomach until Carole left, and Sherrie and I could get some lunch.

After exchanging some pleasantries about the parade and how much I enjoyed sharing the float with her husband, I simply added, "Hey, thanks for bringing Sherrie home."

Carole replied it was no problem. She just wanted to stop by and say hello, check on how my thumb was really doing, inquire when I might be back at the store. I translated that as, "Enough already. When will you be back to work?"

I glanced at Sherrie, hoping Carole would get the message I wanted to spend time with my sister while she was in town rather than at the store.

"Hannah's got things under control, doesn't she?"

"For the short term, I'm afraid," Carole said.

"Afraid? Of what?" I asked.

"It's possible Sadie may need her at the museum?"

"What for? She's not a trained docent."

"The gift shop. Sadie's been manning it with Maggie gone …"

I sensed Sherrie's eyeballs pierce my brain. Carole opened the door for me to walk through, if I chose to do so. Sherrie's fingernails tapping on the table warned me I better go for it, or she would.

"The gift shop," I mumbled, simultaneously rubbing the back of my fingers across my eyelids for effect. "That's the last place I saw Maggie alive. We had a pleasant conversation." A white lie never hurt anyone, right?

Carole shifted her butt in the chair with such force I could swear it moved to the left six inches. Probably my imagination, but she grunted lightly and certainly offered nothing to further my unsophisticated, yet potentially significant, investigation. Of course, she didn't realize what I was up to.

I looked at Sherrie, who I bet was trying to communicate telepathically with me. How should I broach Carole delicately? I thought back to all the detective shows I'd consumed for the right words.

"Isn't that the question Columbo always asks?" I said.

"What question?" Carole said.

"Oh, you know," I said with a sly grin. "Who was the last person to see the victim alive?"

"I think you mean Jessica Fletcher," Sherrie said, enlightening us. We all chuckled: two of us somewhat nervously. Thank you, sister, for inserting a little humor about *Murder, She Wrote* to relieve what for me was excruciatingly stressful.

"Well, I was in San Francisco and never met Maggie, that I can swear to." Sherrie clapped her hands and tapped her palms on the table, clearing her of any involvement.

"What about you, Carole?" I bit the inside of my mouth. "You saw Maggie that morning, right?"

"Friday?" Carole affixed her eyes on the glass of iced tea.

"No, Saturday," I clarified.

"Yes, who do you think set up all the serving stations? It's my job. Maggie didn't have a clue …"

"By any chance, did you see Budd while you were there?" I was quickly getting into the sleuthing groove, realizing this question would kill two birds with one stone. Perhaps it would distract Carole, make her think I was more concerned about Budd than I was with her. And determine if she had been alone with Maggie?

"Why, yes—"

My phone buzzed. A text from Oscar. He was on his way.

Investigation interruptus.

CHAPTER THIRTY

Indeed, Detective Oscar Donovan pulled into my driveway just after Carole backed out. On her way out the door, Sherrie thanked her again for the ride. Carole hoped to see us at the store later. I hustled upstairs to get the Sisters' List of Suspects. After all, that was why Oscar came to visit. Because … when I saw him at the parade, I told him we needed to talk.

If Sherrie weren't there, I'd invite Oscar to sit on the porch. But since there were only two Adirondack chairs, it would be too awkward to drag out a chair from inside. So, once he hit the top step, we headed indoors. Oscar, Sherrie, then me.

As if we were in high school or college, we chose the same seats we had the last time we gathered. Humans were such creatures of habit. Like comfort food, I guessed.

Oscar was still in his uniform, the one he wore for the parade. His light blue shirt had seen better days. His anti-perspirant seemed to have failed him. I'd changed into a floral blue sleeveless midi dress, taken a power nap, had some iced tea, and re-energized my "little grey cells." I was ready to solve Maggie's murder. Seriously.

"How about some iced tea, detective?" Sherrie graciously offered. I wasn't sure if she purposely left the two of us alone, or if she noticed, as I had, the good detective looked as though he could use something to drink—iced tea or perhaps something stronger. After all, it was five o'clock somewhere.

He quickly considered her offer, mumbled his thanks, and raked his fingers through his hair. And here I thought the parade took a toll on me!

Sherrie didn't ask if I wanted anything to drink. Was it possible she remembered I had a sensitive stomach? Too much iced tea and I'd spend the rest of the day indisposed. This was one trait I was sure she was grateful we didn't have in common. My issue was the consequence of a ruptured appendix when we were seventeen. I never understood how or why hers remained intact.

Once we were all seated, I started. "Oscar, I've put together—"

"*We've* put together," Sherrie corrected.

"Right. *We've* put together a list of suspects in Maggie's murder." I waved the pad in the air. Sherrie gave me a thumbs up. Despite her support, my stomach churned, knowing Budd was at the top of the list. A major part of me believed he'd be ruled out faster than I tossed the candy at the parade that morning.

"That's why you asked me here?" Oscar sprang to his feet and attempted to swipe the pad from me.

I wasn't quite ready to relinquish it and pulled it close into my chest.

"Yes, and to offer my help. I've already begun questioning two of the four suspects. I'll fill you in on what I know, and you can follow up with them."

Oscar said nothing. How could he? His jaw dropped to his knees.

"Cool, huh?" I said proudly.

I noticed him take in Sherrie's smug grin before reverting his gaze to me. "Wait a minute, Venus," he said, raising his voice louder than I'd ever known him to do. "Not cool. You have no idea what you're doing. What danger you could put yourself in."

"Danger? I know these four people. They'd never hurt me. I'm not even convinced Maggie was murdered. Maybe it was an accident?"

"Not an accident, Venus. I think I told you that."

"So, you have the autopsy?"

"Not yet, but I will. And that's only the half of it." He stared at the Oriental rug.

I looked quickly at Sherrie, who shrugged. She knew about as much as I did.

"Half? What's the other half? Spill it, Oscar."

Over the next few minutes, Oscar previewed for us news that was about to rattle the entire town. They found a body floating in the Crescent River just before the parade ended.

"Sirens. I heard sirens."

"I'm sure," he said.

"Do you know who …"

He claimed he did, but he was not at liberty to say.

"Cut the—" I said, springing to my feet and pacing around the living room. "Two unexplained deaths in four days!"

Oscar wrung his hands and let out a sigh so deep from inside of himself I wondered if his lungs collapsed.

"Well, it'll be public knowledge after the press conference this afternoon, so I guess there's no harm."

"Now you're talkin'," I said, with a modified clap just missing my thumb.

"The deceased is a man named Brian McGee."

An abnormally long silence hung over the room. The wheels in my mind flipped like a Roladex card file and then came to an abrupt halt.

"McGee? Any relation …"

"Her husband. Margaret McGee's husband."

"Ex-husband," I offered.

"Apparently not divorced," Oscar said. "Our investigation into Mrs. McGee's background revealed she was not divorced as she claimed. Looks like she may have left her husband back in Maine."

"Do you expect foul play?" I asked. "Maybe he was drunk? Maybe *he* tripped and fell?"

"You mean like Maggie?" Sherrie added.

I glared at her, although I knew she was just trying to be helpful.

"Until we know more, I can't say for certain. But, yes, we expect the post mortem to confirm Mr. McGee's death was a homicide."

"Maybe he was mugged?" Sherrie continued interrogating the detective.

"Not likely. Not with his car keys and wallet still in his pockets. That's how we were able to identify him so quickly."

I returned to my assigned seat, my legs feeling as though they might give out any second. I lowered my face in my palms.

"And that's not all …" Oscar started, giving me no time to compose myself. "There's more."

"More dead bodies?" Sherrie piped in.

"No, thank God," he said. "But serious all the same. Poseidon is missing."

"Who's Poseidon? Someone's dog?" Sherrie asked, her eyes blinking in double time. Could it be she was enjoying all this drama?

My shoulders drooped. I explained to my wide-eyed sister that Poseidon was the most prized treasure in the museum.

"Stolen, it seems on Saturday," Oscar added.

How could that happen? That statue was protected behind anti-reflective glass under lock and key. My thoughts swung from Maggie's husband to Sadie. She must have been frantic. No wonder I didn't see her at the parade. Not much for her to celebrate these days. I choked back any potential antagonistic remarks I customarily made about her. Thinking about my past behavior, I felt a bit ashamed, to be honest. I wouldn't trade places with her at the moment. Between the Town Committee and the museum board, her career was most definitely in jeopardy.

"This is serious," I muttered.

"No kidding. Two deaths and a burglary," Oscar said.

"Can they be related to each other?" Sherrie interjected with the next logical question.

"Ya think?" Oscar groaned. "Too much of a coincidence, wouldn't you say?"

After fumbling through the end table drawer, I located a red felt-tip pen. I flicked through the first three pages of notes until I got to an empty page.

"What are you doing?" Sherrie asked.

"Number five. Brian McGee." I flipped the pad around and showed them my handiwork, including the huge exclamation point under the newest suspect's name.

Oscar rolled his eyes. He challenged my latest theory of the case: that Brian killed his wife. What was his motive? Then who killed him? And why? Where does Poseidon fit into all of this?

I moaned, slapping the pad on my lap. "Don't confuse me with the facts, Oscar. I'm just trying to help."

He appreciated that, or so he claimed. I had a hunch he was humoring me. What he didn't realize was that I'd do anything to free Budd of any suspicion. At that point, I believed the more persons of interest there were, the better.

Oscar finished his drink and appeared to be getting ready to leave.

"The other four, Venus?"

"What?"

"Who are your four suspects? Those people you say you know so well." Oscar pulled out his handy-dandy notebook and pen, and started scribbling. He reminded me of Detective Columbo. All he needed was a crumpled raincoat. But it was July … hot, sunny, and definitely not raining.

I looked to Sherrie for strength, but at a time when I needed her, she remained close mouthed. I couldn't blame her. If the situation were reversed, I'd have confidence in her ability to handle it however she deemed appropriate.

What seemed like a good idea to both of us that morning suddenly sounded like trouble to me, double trouble. Could one of these folks have committed two heinous crimes? And be a thief on top of it all?

Suddenly, I wished I had something to drink. Even a glass of water would have allowed me to pause, give me time to think before I spoke. And it would moisten my mouth and throat, both of which were bone dry.

After a pointless gulp, I explained to Oscar that the list we compiled contained the names of those I believed interacted with Maggie Saturday morning. Any of them could've been the last one to see her alive.

Of course, there was Carole Duffy. I began with her because I'd known her the longest of the four suspects and couldn't believe she'd physically hurt anyone.

"I saw her leave here as I arrived. Did you question her?" Oscar winced.

"I simply confirmed she was at the museum Saturday morning. Setting up for the event," I said in her defense. "Mostly we talked about the store. I haven't been there for a few days." I held up my thumb and shifted my head toward Sherrie.

I pinched my lips and glanced at my notepad as I chose who to finger next.

"Naturally, Jeremy Roserun saw Maggie that morning."

"Why naturally?" Sherrie asked, re-engaged in the conversation.

"He's the museum's gardener, right?" Oscar offered his expert knowledge.

I nodded, adding how I ran into Jeremy at the parade. Straightening my back, I shared two pieces of information that were new to me, and perhaps would be new to Oscar as well.

"There's kind of a back door to the gardens."

"Yes, we know the door."

"Well, I didn't. Maybe important?"

Oscar shrugged and raised his glass. An obvious request for a refill. Sherrie jumped out of her chair and scurried off to the kitchen. Since I hadn't the chance to fill her in on my chat with Jeremy, I waited until she returned to tell Oscar the rest of the story.

"Pedestals," I finally said. "Jeremy said he set up two pedestals. I don't remember seeing one pedestal, let alone two. Do you, Oscar?"

"You can't expect to remember everything, Venus." Sherrie came to my rescue as my intention of offering up new clues flew out the window.

"But pedestals?" I continued, still hanging on and hoping I was adding valuable information. "We—Carole and I—didn't request pedestals. Jeremy said I'd have to ask Sadie about them. Which I haven't had a chance to do yet. But—"

"Forget about it. Mr. Roserun was correct. There were two pedestals. They found one on the ground, tipped on its side. The other was still upright when we arrived on the scene."

Exasperated and impatient, I blurted out I still didn't understand what they were doing there to begin with.

"That's easy. Mrs. Hawkins already explained to one of my officers who met with her earlier this afternoon. One was for Poseidon, the other for whatever she intended to unveil that night."

I stared up at the ceiling. While logical, it still didn't explain how or why someone ripped off Poseidon. I filed that for later.

"Who's next?" Oscar asked, eager to move along.

"Oh, Sadie. Sadie Hawkins. As I mentioned, I haven't had a chance to talk with her, but I gather she has a habit of arriving before almost everyone else at the museum. So I'm assuming—"

Oscar asked me why I'd assume Sadie saw Maggie on that particular Saturday morning? I simply informed him I'd heard it from several people: her daughter Hannah— who works at the store—and the museum's caretaker.

"The caretaker? Budd Nickerson?"

"Yes," I whispered.

"Your Budd?"

"Yes."

"I gather Budd is the fourth person on your list?" Oscar looked me straight in the eyes.

There was no way for me to lie, so I nodded. I neglected to share with him we ranked Budd the number one suspect.

"It's his responsibility to get to the museum early, especially on Saturdays which are always the busiest day of the week, and unlock or open up all the things that need to be—the gardens, the gift shop—and to check with Sadie to be sure his list of things to do for the day matches her list of all things she needs for him to do." I stopped, drew in a breath. "It's his job." I interlaced my fingers and placed my hands, which a moment ago were flailing in the air, on my lap.

"I get it," Oscar said. "What was his relationship with Margaret McGee?"

My eyes watered. I blinked, hoping to stem an impending tide. Not sure if I was helping or hurting Budd. "You'll have to ask him."

"Well, Detective Donovan," Sherrie piped in, "there you have our four, plus your one, makes five."

"A caterer, gardener, curator, caretaker, and a husband. Quite a menagerie. Four out of the five somehow connected to the museum." Oscar tapped his pen on his notebook as he labeled each suspect.

"Menagerie? Perhaps. More like a whale of a mystery, if you ask me," Sherrie said, proud of herself.

"Not funny," I said, trying to stifle my sister.

"Your sister is right, Venus. Quite a conundrum. A mess. Not sure where we should go from here." Oscar flipped his notebook closed and slipped it and his pen in his damp shirt pocket, his anxiety having traveled from his armpits. He got up, intending to leave.

"Wait, don't go," I commanded, as Sherrie and I both stood.

"I have an idea," my twin and I blurted out simultaneously.

CHAPTER THIRTY-ONE

"**B**etter change this shirt before the press conference," I suggested, patting Oscar on his back as he hustled down the front steps.

"You noticed? Sorry," he turned back and shouted. The three of us chuckled, welcoming a little comic relief even if it was at the detective's expense.

Once he started his car, I signaled to Sherrie to get a move on. If we wanted to get both Sadie and Carole on board with the plan the three of us just cooked up on my porch, we needed to start by getting to the museum ASAP.

We agreed in order to get Sadie's buy-in, we'd have to be upfront with her about Brian McGee, and in turn, she'd need to come clean about Poseidon, as well as the big reveal she'd kept secret.

Similarly, when we talked with Carole, we'd need to put a name to the body she probably already heard about either from her husband (the mayor) or via the press conference. If we were first able to meet Sadie, we should be able to share with Carole what we learn about the burglary, as well.

With my keys and our purses in hand, we hustled ourselves into Jitter Bug. A half hour ago, we were shocked as we faced the reality that we were suddenly living in a multi-crime city. My mind worked overtime imagining what Daniel DaRosa's headlines could be.

Crime Spree Curdles Chatham Crossing Character, or *Mystery Careens Beyond Whaling Museum,* or simply *Crime Center — CC's New Brand?*

Before starting the car, I texted Carole and told her we'd be at the store in about an hour. Could she please not leave until we got there? We needed to talk.

While I was texting Carole, Sherrie hummed as she scrolled through her phone.

"Sister, dear," she teased. "How is this for your favorite song today?"

A nanosecond passed. I could name that song in one note, or maybe I'd take three.

"Magical Mystery Tour," I slapped my palm on the steering wheel. Not surprised Sherrie would make lemonade out of lemons and put the first real smile on my face since the parade. Unfortunately, my smile lasted only about a block until I rolled up to the first stop sign.

"What if we run into Budd at the museum?" Sherrie quickly brought me back to the task at hand.

"I'll just tell him I need to see Cecilia about something."

"Cecilia? Who's Cecilia?"

"Oh, one of the docents, but she's also one of Carole's cookie bakers."

"Think he'll buy that?"

"Probably not. But I'll cross that bridge ..."

"If you're worried Budd's involved in all of this, why don't you just ask him?"

I kept my eyes on the road. Sherrie couldn't see them rolling. "Easier said than done, don't ya think? If he's murdered two people, who's next? Me? You?"

Sherrie sighed. "I get your point."

Since it was late afternoon, only a handful of tourists mulled around the museum's lobby, scoping out the floor plan to be sure they missed nothing. I wondered how many asked about Poseidon and what excuse was being offered?

I grabbed hold of Sherrie with my good hand and gave the host at the ticket counter a wave with my not-so-good one. She returned the wave and passed us through. I kept my eyes open for Budd. So far the coast was clear.

As we neared the gift shop, I overheard Sadie talking to a customer. "Great choice," she said. "Kids love these pirate puzzles. How about an eye-patch or two to go with it?" I didn't realize she was such a formidable sales person.

Leading Sherrie into the gift shop, I was trying to figure out how to get Sadie out of there and into her office where we'd have privacy.

"Just be honest," Sherrie whispered in my ear. Okay. Now that was weird. How'd she read my mind? Did the hesitant look on my face or the clammy hand she held give me away?

Sadie finished with the customer and diverted her attention to us. "Hello, Venus. What brings you in here today?"

Thank you, Sadie, for making this easy.

"Can we talk? In private?" I looked around the store. Empty. At least for the moment. It was small; a museum gift shop after all. If I owned it, I'd expand and make it a sizable profit center for the museum. But my mind digressed.

Sadie appeared instantly shaken by my request. Her eyes scanned the store. No customers there needing her help.

"I can't leave the shop unattended."

"Maybe close it?" Sherrie suggested.

"No can do. Near closing time. People tend to buy on their way out."

Of course, knowing retail the way I do, that made perfect sense to me.

"Maybe get someone else to cover?" Sherrie was on a roll. Where did all of my sister's assertiveness suddenly come from?

"It's that important?"

I nodded.

"Alright. I'll call Budd. He can handle everything."

Sherrie's eyes locked with mine. *Think quick, Venus.* What was the risk? The trade-off?

"Great," I said. "We'll meet you at your office, okay? Ten minutes." I looped my arm through Sherrie's, and we skedaddled out of the store, back through the lobby, and into the main exhibit hall. I crossed my fingers Budd wasn't heading toward us from the opposite direction.

It was impossible not to notice Poseidon's glass display was vacant. I pointed to the clear case and nudged Sherrie so she'd move toward it. I wanted to read the card affixed to the glass.

Poseidon's on a seafaring mission! Be back soon!

"Clever," Sherrie said.

"Optimistic."

I urged Sherrie to step into the half-scale model of the whaling ship that sat in the middle of the enormous hall, not for a quick lesson, but to hide from Budd should he walk by. She didn't argue, perhaps understanding my motivation. I directed her attention to the galley and the variety of knives and casks on board without saying a word.

As I played docent, Sherrie coughed and pointed to something outside of the ship. She mouthed, "Budd." I peeked overboard as he passed by. *Phew.* I turned Sherrie around. Coast was clear. Time we disembarked and waited for Sadie outside her office.

"Hey, ladies. Glad I found you."

Budd was halfway up the steps. He leaned up toward me as if to plant a kiss on my cheek. Contrary to my normal instincts around him, like a cat sensing danger, I retreated a step back onto the ship. The hair on my neck even reacted. For once, I was tongue-tied.

Sherrie picked up my vibes and the slack. "Found us? How'd you know …"

Apparently, Sadie didn't just ask him to cover for her, she also told him why: I was there with my sister.

"Come on, Venus. I knew you were nearby, most likely in the ship. Everyone loves it. I recognized your perfume. I could pick you out of a crowd or from a crew of whalers." Budd laughed alone at his joke. I considered changing my fragrance.

"That's nice," I quipped, hoping to curtail further discussion about how I smelled.

"You gonna tell me why you need to see Sadie?"

"Of course, I will. Later, okay?" I stepped down to where he blocked us. This time, I leaned in and kissed his cheek. "Now go." I shooed him away.

"That was close," Sherrie whispered, even though he was no longer within earshot.

"I know."

"How do you know?" Sadie said, squirming in her chair. Sadie positioned her desk and chair so she had a bird's eye view of the main exhibit hall. After directing us to the two extra side chairs, she swirled around so we kind of formed a circle, our knees less than a foot away from touching.

Her office looked like you'd imagine a museum curator's would. Organized chaos. Magazines and journals stacked haphazardly everywhere. A pale green yoga mat sat rolled up in a corner. A super-sized jar of extra strength pain reliever rested next to the phone. The current SSWM calendar hung on a wall above a two-shelf bookcase. I couldn't help but notice a red star filled the square marking Saturday, July 3. My eyes wandered, locking on three Yeti bottles of various colors decorating the room. Two on the desk. One under it. More than vaguely familiar.

"Pardon my office. A lot going on lately." Evidently Sadie read my mind.

"Looks like mine," my sister chuckled. Somehow I didn't believe that. Not my sister.

I explained we *knew* about her loss because Detective Donovan told us he planned to hold a press conference soon.

"If it's about Poseidon, I should be there." Sadie grabbed her phone, scrolled her photos, then showed us the last two pictures she had of Poseidon.

"It's not mainly about Poseidon. More about Brian McGee." I opted to lead with the latest homicide in Chatham Crossing, leaving Poseidon and the real reason Sherrie and I were there for last.

"Brian McGee?" Sadie perked up. "Any relation?" She got up and moved to a three-drawer oak finished file cabinet. Fumbling with her keys until she located the one she was looking for, she didn't wait for my response. "I thought—"

"Maggie's husband," I said.

Sadie flipped through the Pendaflex files in the middle drawer until she found the right one. Sitting back in her chair, she opened it. "Ex-husband. Look. Right here in Maggie's application." She rotated the file toward me and confirmed Maggie had checked the box *Divorced*. "What about him?"

"They found his body floating in the Crescent River this morning," I explained.

"Hell of a way to end a parade, don't you think?" As always, I could count on Sherrie to provide color commentary.

"That must be where Daniel DaRosa was when I called to tell him about Poseidon."

"So, you've talked to *The Chronicle*?"

"Yes, about the robbery. And to the police. Daniel insisted I do that. The paper and law enforcement work hand in hand. But neither mentioned anything about another untimely death in town."

With Maggie's job application in plain view on Sadie's lap and facing me, my eyes swept to the bottom. The words *Referred by Budd Nickerson* made the hair on my arms stand on end. Sadie slapped the folder shut, curtailing anymore sleuthing on my part.

Suddenly, I felt as though I was playing "Let's Make a Deal." There were three doors to choose from to get to my raison d'être at the moment. Which direction should I choose to take this conversation that would result in the outcome we needed: Maggie's death in the museum's gardens? Maggie's estranged husband's demise? Or the disappearance of the god of the sea?

Decision made. "Tell us about the robbery," I encouraged Sadie as she returned Maggie's folder to safekeeping.

Flustered, Sadie told us her story, probably for the third time that day. I told her our idea. "Sounds like a plan. A good one. I might not need these anymore," she said, shaking the bottle of pain relievers and smiling somewhat optimistically.

CHAPTER THIRTY-TWO

"You didn't drill her about Maggie," Sherrie started on me when we were ten feet from my car. "Why not? I was on pins and needles. Almost jumped in myself. But I waited to see where you were headed."

"Really? Sherrie?" I turned on the ignition. "After hearing how devastated she is about Poseidon, do you really think she had anything to do with Maggie's death? Be honest. Let's leave it to Oscar to interrogate her."

"I guess you're right. But those pictures. Kind of eerie, if you ask me."

I didn't ask her, but the pictures were the reasons I believed Sadie was no longer a suspect.

"If you're about to knock off someone, you don't ask them to pose for a picture alongside the museum's most prized possession. The date stamp on that picture proves Maggie was alive at 9:21 a.m., standing next to a pedestal with Poseidon perched safely on top. The second photo, two minutes later with Sadie and the god of the sea, taken by Maggie, is further evidence. And you don't show them to anyone if you're guilty of something nefarious. That photo of Maggie may be the last one of her alive. So, yes, I agree. Kind of eerie."

We reached the parking lot in back of Oldies & Goodies in less than five minutes. At near five o'clock on a Tuesday evening, traffic was thinning for sure.

"One down, one to go," I said, as we headed into the store through the back door. Sonny and Cher scampered to greet me but stopped in their tracks when they caught sight of Sherrie: a stranger. I bent down, picking up Sonny for a quick scratch between his ears and assurances that Sherrie was my sister, just like Cher was his. Cher twisted around my right leg, awaiting her turn. She nuzzled into my neck, purring. She got the message.

Sherrie offered her open palm to Sonny, who sniffed and strutted away. "I love how you've kept Dad's legacy alive in naming these two. Maybe if I sing 'I Got You Babe' they'd accept me." Unlike her brother, Cher approved of Sherrie with a soft swipe of her paw, friendly-like.

I made my way to the front of the store. While closing time was in about an hour and no customers were milling about, I gave the teen staff members the rest of the day off … with pay. I assured Hannah I'd take care of the cats.

Carole didn't stop me. Though she owned her own catering business and managed the *Bixby's Dozen* half of the store, she always left it to me to decide when to open and close. So, after the staff happily departed, she flipped over the Open sign and locked the front door. Together, we retreated to the back room. I looked over my shoulder, expecting Sherrie on my heels. But she hung back, her fingers walking through a rack of Motown records.

"What's this all about, Venus? Sending everyone home? Closing shop early? If I didn't know any better, I'd think you were about to fire me."

My head whipsawed, my eyes blinking rapidly. Where did that come from? Lingering guilt, perhaps, about her anonymous comment to the reporter?

"Like that's ever gonna happen. At least not today. But we need to talk." I pulled out a chair and waved my hand toward another, inviting Carole to join me.

I quickly rolled the tape back in my head to where we left off earlier at my house. Carole had admitted she'd seen Maggie in the museum gardens Saturday morning, and then I chickened out and switched the topic to Budd. Now was not the time to continue going in that direction when my immediate goal was to get Carole to buy into the latest plan to identify Maggie's assailant.

"You heard what happened?" I started.

"The man in the water, you mean?"

"Maggie's husband."

Carole covered her mouth with her hand, stifling a sudden gasp. "You're kidding."

She knew I'd never kid about a dead man in the water, whoever he may be, so I filled in the blanks.

"As we speak, Detective Donovan is holding a press conference at police headquarters. It'll be all over the news. They're treating it as a homicide, just like Maggie."

"I'm sure Simon is there. I bet he's going out of his mind. It's been years since we've had one murder in Chatham Crossing, let alone two."

"And there's more," I said, mimicking Oscar's piece-meal method of delivering bad news.

Carole leaned forward, propped her elbows on the table, and rested her forehead in her hands. "How can there possibly be more?"

"Anything's possible. And that's where you and *Bixby's Dozen* come in."

Over the next ten minutes, I filled her in on Poseidon. Carole had virtually nothing to add except to agree with me: Sadie's future was in trouble.

"Which is why we need your help this weekend."

"This weekend?" Carole slumped in her chair. "I'm sorry. Saturday's out. I have a big event to cater. It's on the Cape. A wedding."

I was afraid of that, so I played the ace in my pocket. "How about Friday, then?"

Carole raised her body and stared up at the overhead light, her eyes squinting. She was thinking about it. "Friday? That might work. In fact, it might work really well. It's National Sugar Cookie Day, so the staff is already in full baking mode."

She's in. I texted Sadie and announced to Sherrie, as she joined us with Sonny cradled in her arms.

CHAPTER THIRTY-THREE

The Chatham Crossing Chronicle
SSWM's Poseidon Adventure

By: Daniel DaRosa, Investigative Reporter

BREAKING NEWS! **Tuesday, July 6, 2010, 6 p.m**. Sandra Hawkins, esteemed curator of the Sofia Silva Whaling Museum (SSWM), reported today that its most precious treasure, Poseidon, was stolen three days ago on Saturday, July 3, 2010.

Why the delay in reporting this crime? In all likelihood, the Chatham Crossing police prioritized the death of Margaret McGee at the museum that occurred on the same day over the disappearance of the god of the sea.

What a disaster for our town! Over the last few days, Chatham Crossing experienced a series of incidents that can only be described as a tsunami. Will tourists continue to be drawn here even if only out of curiosity? Or will all of this turmoil reduce the numbers of vacationers who normally overcrowd our enclave, thereby managing traffic flow in a manner the Town Committee had hoped the traffic light would?

Needless to say, efforts to recover the priceless statue are underway. Besides cooperating with local law enforcement, Mrs. Hawkins informed this reporter that the museum's board of directors and the insurance company have pooled resources with the goal of having Poseidon returned unharmed.

"Bottom line, we want Poseidon back," Mrs. Hawkins said. "To whoever pirated Poseidon, if you return him uninjured and without a scratch to the Sofia Silva Whaling Museum, we are offering a $25,000 reward."

To bring our own Poseidon Adventure to a mutually beneficial conclusion, contact either Sandra Hawkins at SSWM or this reporter immediately.

Follow updates to this story online or through our print edition.

Digital edition.

CHAPTER THIRTY-FOUR

A feeling of running on empty rose from my stomach and registered in my brain. All of this drama had caused my blood sugar to plunge. I needed to eat something fast.

"Let's pick up something for dinner on our way home," I said to Sherrie as I reached into the *Bixby's Dozen* glass case to swipe a sample. My eyes passed over the tray displaying the Jolly Roger cookies. I flashbacked to the napkin in my purse.

I grabbed two of Helen Davis's famous cookies. One for me. One for Sherrie.

"Where's mine?" Carole asked.

I laughed as I pilfered a total of three. "At this rate, you'll need to charge me!"

"You're so right. Helen is so possessive about her merchandise. She tracks how many cookies she brings in and how many are sold. A true businesswoman!"

"Speaking of Helen," I said. "Did she find her precious binder yet? She was frantic the last time I saw her."

Carole shrugged, saying she hadn't heard one way or the other.

Before leaving, I set out fresh kibble and water for Sonny and Cher. Carole removed the cash and receipts out of the register. That was not unusual. We took turns making deposits. She'd been handling this task on her own since I'd not been in the store much lately. It occurred to me that if I trusted her with our money, I should trust she wasn't involved in Maggie's demise. Following a checklist we established years ago, Carole checked the lights we left on overnight. Finally, the three of us exited through the back door, and Carole locked it.

We agreed to connect by noon on Wednesday. Sadie, Carole, and I had our assignments. Sadie—in charge of props. Carole—all about cookies, of course. And me? I guess I was the general contractor. From then on, it was all about implementation.

But first, food!

Sherrie suggested soup and salad. "I can't come all the way to New England and not have chowder, right?"

Worked for me. We stopped at Say It Louda for Chowda, the best place to get chowder this side of Cape Cod.

Back in the kitchen at the house, I heard the glass doors of the hutch in the dining room rattle, the clatter of dishes, and the click of the doors closing. I gathered we'd be eating on our mother's good china that night.

I retrieved a chilled bottle of chardonnay and handed it and the antique brass corkscrew to Sherrie. "I don't trust myself." I held up my thumb.

She ignored me. No quick comeback. I assumed she was tired of hearing about the constraints imposed by my thumb. If truth be told, I was tired of it too. Nevertheless, I did what I could and got out the wineglasses.

We could've sat in the kitchen and enjoyed our dinner, but Sherrie found placemats, the cloth kind that I rarely used since they required washing rather than wiping. She set us up in the dining room. Nice.

Just as I lifted the soup spoon to my mouth, Sherrie decided to ask, "Do you trust Budd?"

"Trust? In what way?"

Waving a hunk of Tuscan bread in the air, she asked, "Is he faithful to you? How much do you *really* know about his relationship with Maggie?"

"You saw his name at the bottom of her application?"

Sherrie slurped her chowder and nodded. "You know, you're going to have get to the bottom of it before …"

In my heart of hearts, I knew Sherrie was right. Before closing the museum that evening, Sadie would've already met with Budd and given him his marching orders for Friday. After all, he was the museum's caretaker. We couldn't move forward without his involvement.

"Maggie is not the only issue I need to resolve with him."

"Really? What else?"

"Where was he last night? Who was he with?" My voice elevated with each question.

Sherrie tried to bring me down the best way she knew how. First, she ignored my questions even though she'd brought up the subject of Budd. Then she dropped the dishes in the sink for later, uncorked a fresh bottle of wine, and grabbed a bag of popcorn from the pantry.

"Follow me, sis," she said.

I knew what she was up to, and I was all in. Definitely the distraction I needed. The next two days just might be the longest of my life. But it was movie marathon night. Starting with *He's Just Not That Into You*—Sherrie's choice; something to lighten the mood. Ending with *Sherlock Holmes*—because I needed inspiration and practice in crime solving, even if it was only make-believe.

CHAPTER THIRTY-FIVE

But it wasn't make-believe. And since it was already Wednesday morning, there were two days to kill before we exposed the real life whodunit.

As I descended from my upstairs bedroom, having slept in a bit for a change, I caught a glimpse of Sherrie already comfy cozy on one of the Adirondack chairs on the porch. Lord only knew what book she'd stuck her nose into. Considering the two movies that kept us up way past my bedtime last night, I figured she'd chosen either a romantic comedy or a mystery from my overflowing bookshelves. There was plenty of historical fiction there, as well, but my guess was that any of those would be way too intense for either of us to journey through while we tried to be crime solvers that week.

Rather than disturb Sherrie, I headed to the kitchen to fix something easy for breakfast. I opted for Cheerios with bananas and, of course, a small glass of cranberry grape juice. A nutritious and easy breakfast to clean up after. Just my style.

In between bites, I texted Hannah to check on Sonny and Cher. I missed their customary morning greeting at the store and thanked the heavens above that Hannah was there to shower them with the TLC I'd been unable to provide, considering the past week's insanity.

Speaking of insanity. How was I going to occupy my sister? It was already too late to hop a ferry to one of the islands. Maybe a good alternative for Thursday.

While my tea brewed, I checked the Red Sox schedule prominently displayed on a magnet on the refrigerator. Usually I knew their schedule, but I didn't—not this week anyway. *Forgive me. I've been otherwise engaged.*

Drat. They were out of town. *Figures.* We could drive up to Boston anyway, walk the Freedom Trail and all that jazz. But it was a hike to get there, and frankly I was in no mood to be closeted in Jitter Bug with my sister for a three-hour round-trip excursion. And parking in Beantown could be its own nightmare.

I scrolled through my phone, praying I'd find something to entertain Sherrie for the day. The front door slammed.

"How about Newport?" she said, arriving in the kitchen with Stephen King's *Under the Dome* under her arm. I should've known. Another thing we had in common: our favorite authors.

"Good morning," I said, "and good choice."

"Which? Newport or our mutual pal Stephen?"

"Both. But I'm focused right now, as you've so astutely noticed, on finding something to occupy our minds today. I'm already getting antsy about Friday."

"Shopping and a sumptuous meal should do the trick. Wouldn't you agree?"

Within the hour, Jitter Bug was gassed up, and we were heading west on I-195 toward Newport, Rhode Island.

"Hump day is the perfect day for a visit to Newport in the summer," I remarked, passing the time nonsensically.

"Oh? Why is that?"

"Fewer tourists."

"Aren't we tourists?" Sherrie asked.

I grunted. She had a point, but I didn't award her one.

Over the next half hour, I owned the conversation, babbling on about the history of the area and recommending some good books on the topic, if the spirit moved her.

When we were stuck in traffic less than ten minutes before we reached our destination, I raised my palm toward her and uttered, "Don't say a thing."

It was her time to grunt. I allowed her that.

I suggested we tour a mansion first, then shop, then dine. Sherrie liked that agenda.

"How about Rosecliff?" she said. "I read *The Great Gatsby* was filmed there."

"I see you've done your homework. Let's do it."

In the mansion's visitor parking lot, I texted Sadie and Carole, telling them we were in Newport and that I was just checking to be sure everything was still a go for Friday. Both replied with a thumbs up. Not much else. Their emojis were sufficient for me.

As we began our self-guided tour of this stunning home and its luscious gardens, I slipped my sister a hard candy to suppress any hunger pains I assumed she might be having since I was already battling them. When we left the tour and returned to the car, she handed me a mini bottle of water and a granola bar.

"Here. If we're going to shop, you'll need something more than a sucker to tide you over until dinner." Leave it to Sherrie to think she needed to take good care of me, just like when she arrived in Chatham Crossing unexpectedly on Monday.

With so many stores to choose from, I asked my sister if there was something in particular she'd like to take back with her to commemorate her trip?

"You mean other than a receipt from the bail bondsman that I nearly—"

"Not even close, my dear, not even close. Oscar never had grounds to arrest me."

Sherrie grasped my hand and hustled me into an art gallery. We spent a good hour in there fawning over original paintings by local artists. She kept circling back to one depicting Rosecliff Manor, finally settling on a print costing several hundred dollars. Wouldn't you know? The smiling store owner gladly offered to ship it back to San Francisco. No problem.

Walking out of the gallery arm in arm, I whispered, "We were just there! You could've bought a postcard for a dollar!"

"But this I will frame and think of you every day."

It was my turn to shop. I dragged her into one of those general stores that had everything. If you couldn't find what you wanted there, it probably didn't exist. What I wanted was black and white. A white long-sleeved T-shirt with Newport imprinted in large black letters that I'd add to my collection of white long-sleeved T-shirts with town names imprinted in large black letters.

"For just $29.95, when I wear this, I'll think of you. Not every day, of course." We looped our arms, laughed, and made tracks to The Black Pearl.

Since we were ahead of the dinner rush, they ushered us to a not-yet-reserved corner table: a perfect setting. I decided not to order a cocktail since I was driving. Just water for me. Sherrie ordered a Cosmopolitan and offered me a sip, as she noticed me eyeing the yummy pink liquid. I declined and gave myself an imaginary atta-girl.

"Suit yourself," she said.

Actually, it was my sister who suited herself. While I ordered the shrimp and scallops combo, she went hog wild and ordered a lobster dinner with all the trimmings. Between the Cosmo and the meal, I was confident she'd sleep most of the way home.

But as we devoured our salads (seems our little snacks didn't tide us over as well as predicted), I sensed Sherrie had something on her mind. I was right: Budd was on her mind. Again.

"I know we talked about Budd briefly, but Venus, how well do you know this man? Is it possible …"

I didn't really want to go there. I preferred to eat my dinner and talk about *The Great Gatsby* or Robert Redford. But like a healing scab, Sherrie continued to pick at the subject until I caved.

"He's a good man, Sherrie. He works hard, not just at the museum. He's quite handy."

When she raised one eyebrow at that remark, I slapped the back of her hand, causing her fork to flip to the floor.

I paused my defense of Budd until the server brought a clean fork, and then I said, "It's one reason I rented the cottage to him. After Paul died, I knew the house would be too much for me to keep up on my own. You know I'm all thumbs."

She tilted her head toward my left hand.

"Well, you know what I mean. I'm not joking. Having Budd on site has saved me a bundle in maintenance and repairs."

"Is that enough reason to invite him into your bedroom?"

"For some, that's all it would take. But now that you've met him face to face, can't you see how attractive he is? In some ways, he reminds me of Paul. Tall, good looking, confident, debonair. Kind of like Jay Gatsby." I winked.

"You watch too many movies," she said. "He's not Paul. Didn't you tell me he doesn't dance?"

I threw my head back with a laugh. "He dances, certainly not like Paul, but it's not his favorite thing to do. You don't expect me to hold that against him, do you?"

Any further conversation on this topic was scuttled by the server bringing the check. To my surprise, Sherrie placed her credit card on top of it. "My treat," she offered as she led me out of the dining room and into the restaurant's shop.

This time, we were both drawn to black T-shirts with The Black Pearl imprinted in white. She held up one to inspect it. "It's a deal," she said to the salesperson. "We'll take two."

On the walk back to the car carrying three T-shirts as evidence of our day in Newport, Sherrie suddenly stopped in her tracks.

"Wait a minute. The Black Pearl. Wasn't that Johnny Depp's ship in *Pirates of the Caribbean*?"

"If you mean Jack Sparrow's ship? Yes."

"What is it with you Yankees and your obsession with pirates?"

"It goes with the territory, I guess. And don't call me a Yankee."

Unlike the day before, Thursday morning we were both up at the crack of dawn. We gobbled a quick breakfast of carbs and fruit. We each swallowed a Dramamine prophylactically, with me assuring Sherrie it was just for good measure. With bottles of water, a few granola bars (evidently my sister's go-to snack), hats, and sunglasses, we set our sights on Nantucket Island. We drove down to the docks and hopped the first ferry. We arrived at Steamboat Wharf in less than an hour.

Having learned a lesson yesterday, we turned our agenda upside down. Eat first, take a little tour of the island, and then shop. Our plan worked like a charm.

Neither of us were in the mood for another big meal like we had in Newport. So, we snagged a picnic table at a café just a couple of blocks from the dock. I opted for the lobster roll. After all, it'd been four days since my last one. And Sherrie ordered a Fenway frank and fries.

"Hey, it's the closest I'll get to the Red Sox on this trip, so what the heck!"

After lunch, I flagged down a taxi that was all too happy to give us a private tour around the island for a fee that seemed rather exorbitant to Sherrie, but I accepted the fellow's offer, because what the heck!

The driver gave us his gold tour—stopping at two of the most beautiful beaches I'd ever seen so we could put our toes in the sand; pointing out where celebrities (including ex-Presidents and sports team owners) hid out during the summer; and entertaining us with the history of this vacation paradise. He became most animated when he shared tales of shipwrecks, the rise and fall of the whaling industry, and notorious pirates.

Though I needn't do so, I shot a glance at Sherrie, expecting a reaction. She didn't disappoint. Even as she gazed out the window, I heard her murmur, "Pirates. Of course. Pirates."

He dropped us off back near the ferry dock, where he assured us there was plenty of shopping. Just what we needed: more T-shirts.

But on this trip, we avoided the general stores and instead made haste straight into a jewelry store. Because who could have too much bling? Not us!

Running my fingers lightly over the glass display cases, I couldn't help but admire the jewelry handmade by local artisans. Much of it was symbolic of Nantucket, with the Island's trademark basket incorporated into the designs of bracelets, earrings, necklaces.

"You're in the right place if you're looking for something authentically Nantucket," I said to Sherrie.

She asked to take a closer look at several whale tail charms. "What do you think?" she asked me.

"Lovely," I said. *Whatever.*

"I'll take two gold charms and one silver," she instructed the salesperson.

"Three charms?" I asked.

"Silver for Lexi. And gold for you and me. Something to keep us connected. We deserve it."

I slid my arm around her waist and gave her a squeeze. For the first time in our lives, Sherrie felt more like a girlfriend than my sister. Pulling away, I turned my head so she wouldn't notice the tear or two I sensed forming in my right eye. A tray of rings sitting freely on top of a display case on the opposite side of the store saved me from having to explain my sudden emotions. I moved there to take a gander at the rings while Sherrie checked out.

"Hey Venus, there's a bonus!" she said, moments later as she joined me at the ring counter. "Look. Tiny packages. No shipping required. Whatcha lookin' at?"

"Can I show you something?" The salesperson who just rang up Sherrie's purchase smelled another sweet sale in the offing.

My sister touched my arm. "I'll be over there," she whispered, retreating to a different display that caught her attention.

"This one," I said to the salesperson, picking up a ring that looked familiar to me, but I couldn't put my finger on why (no pun intended). "Tell me about this one."

She placed the ring on a red velvet cloth. "Legend has it a very famous pirate wore one just like it. These titanium replicas are quite popular with men, especially those thinking ahead to Halloween. You know how men like to dress up and play make believe," she said with a wink.

I didn't encourage her, but she droned on. "It's an easy costume to create. All black. A diamond earring. An eye patch. A pirate ring."

"Really?" Totally intrigued with the ring, I picked it up and tilted it up toward the ceiling light. "A famous pirate, you say? Which one?"

"Drake, of course."

"You don't say." I dropped the ring on the cloth, half expecting it to burst into flames if I held it much longer.

I spun away from the counter, hustled over to Sherrie, who had the ear of another salesperson. Lord only knew what she'd buy next if I didn't stop her. "Let's go." I grabbed her by the elbow. "Our ferry awaits."

It really didn't. Boarding time wasn't for another half hour. In the meantime, I bought two bottles of water for us at a stand near the docks. We sat on a bench, soaking in the sun and enjoying a few minutes of people watching.

"What happened back there? In the jewelry store?" Sherrie asked. "You kind of freaked me out."

"Just another pirate story. It wouldn't interest you."

"You got that right. How about some whale tales?" She waved the small gift tote bag in the air. "It's a joke."

"Ah. Tails and tales, I get it."

"Aaaarrrrgggghhhh," we said together.

CHAPTER THIRTY-SIX

The alarm on my iPhone buzzed way too early. The sun was just peeking through the curtains. Five more minutes. Just give me five more minutes. And then reality crashed around me. It was Friday. D-day. One way or another, all would be revealed.

If one plus one really equaled two, we would solve both of the recent murders. And Poseidon would find his way back to the museum.

The plan should expose the culprit, at least whoever was responsible for Maggie's death and the theft. Given the timing and proximity of those crimes, Detective Donovan and I were confident they were linked. Even still, that morning there was a dotted line between them, and we hadn't figured out the Brian McGee connection. Who would want to kill Maggie's husband?

Over the last two days, Oscar kept insisting I back off. "Don't interfere with this investigation," he pleaded with me.

Without Oscar saying so, I feared his number one suspect was Budd, which was why he wanted me to bug off.

"Fat chance, Oscar. Whatever the outcome, I'm all in. Promise me you'll get me Maggie's autopsy report," I'd said.

Maggie's husband's cause of death seemed pretty straightforward. Strangulation and then an involuntary midnight swim. I could see no reason to read his autopsy.

It was nearly six o'clock when I arrived in the kitchen, still unaccustomed to having Sherrie there, let alone ahead of me. Two pieces of French toast, four strawberries, a small glass of cranberry grape juice, and a cup of hot tea greeted me. I could get used to this.

"You ready for today?"

"I will be after this. Thanks, sis."

My phone pinged as soon as I sat at the table across from Sherrie and sipped my juice.

"A text from Oscar." I wiped my mouth with the back of my hand. Sherrie tossed me a napkin. "Thanks, mom." We laughed at our shared childhood memories.

My eyes widened as I opened the email he directed me to. "Get my laptop. Upstairs. On my bed. Quick. And turn on the printer in the sunroom."

In the forty-five seconds Sherrie was away, I slid my placemat to my left, giving me plenty of room for my computer. I savored a strawberry and thought *This is it.* If this exonerated Budd, my prayers would be answered.

"Why was this on your bed?" She set the laptop down on the table in front of me.

"Because …" I just let that hang. I preferred not to tell her I stayed up late analyzing each of our suspects along the lines of motive and opportunity.

Sherrie hung over my shoulder as I opened the attachment Oscar had sent. I shook my left hand, pointing upward, forgetting all about my thumb. "I printed it out. Get it."

"Please?" she rebuked me.

"Please." I minded my manners even while I was sure my blood pressure was spiking.

In a flash, Sherrie was gone and back again, waving in the air three copies of the autopsy of Margaret McGee.

"Why three?"

"One for me, one for you, and one for safekeeping."

"An old habit of yours. I'd forgotten." Sherrie grabbed her copy and plopped down onto her chair.

The wonderful breakfast she made cooled as we read silently.

"Not much new here, is there?" Sherrie said, interrupting my second read through.

"Cause of death, blunt force trauma," I whispered, still trying to ferret out a clue that would expose whodunit. Something, anything that would absolve Budd of any involvement in the horrific tragedy that enshrouded Chatham Crossing over the past week.

I let my index finger do the walking through the subsections of the post mortem. I glazed over the descriptions of the external and internal examinations, as well as the heart, endocrine system, and genitourinary system (whatever that was!). My art history major was no help.

Then, buried within the gastrointestinal system section, a sentence I could understand caught my inquiring eyes.

"Get my purse," I shouted to Sherrie, even though she was sitting two feet away from me. Her chair screeched. She rescued her juice glass before it tipped over.

"Where?" she said, after swallowing a forkful of French toast.

"On the hallway bench."

I re-read the words again to myself.

"Why?" Sherrie asked, handing my bag to me.

"Not sure. Maybe nothing. Get me yesterday's paper." I barked at my sister. I couldn't help but notice she inclined her head, lifting her eyes as if to say, "I'm not your servant."

As she hustled out of the kitchen, I rifled through my purse. I pushed aside my Vera Bradley wallet, hair brush, small pack of Kleenex, lip gloss, two pens, and a tiny tin of Altoids. (Don't judge! What's in your handbag?) And then I found what I was looking for in the zippered compartment.

"On the coffee table," I shouted, answering the question she'd not yet asked. I re-wrapped the cookies for safe-keeping and slid them back into my purse.

Then, I accessed *The Chronicle*'s website and found yesterday's digital version of the paper. When this was all behind us, I vowed to nominate Daniel DaRosa for a journalism award for his work over the past week. His article about the town's own Poseidon Adventure was at the top of the feed, so I didn't have to scroll far down to confirm my suspicion.

Sadie's quote in the fifth paragraph provoked an uneasy, funny feeling.

I snatched the paper out of Sherrie's hand. Daniel's print article, "A Body in the River," logically appeared above the fold, without photos, of course. But it was the onlooker's observation that triggered a memory too coincidental to be ignored.

"What's going on?" my sister begged.

"Call Oscar. Tell him to meet us at the store. Pronto." I slid my phone across the table toward her. "Under W for Wiener." She furrowed her brow, I clutched my quivering hands.

CHAPTER THIRTY-SEVEN

The impromptu meeting with Oscar at Oldies & Goodies caused me to almost blow the first step in our plan.

Nevertheless, with all systems *Go*, at precisely 7:30 a.m., I arrived at the front door of the Sofia Silva Whaling Museum. Out of habit, I tried to open it. I was not surprised it was locked. That was the plan after all. Although I knew Sadie was already inside, I didn't knock or rattle the glass door to get her attention so she could let me in.

Instead, I waited. For Budd.

It wouldn't be long until he arrived, so I cooled my jets, shifting my weight from one foot to another. Like clockwork, Budd showed up, with keys in hand, whistling *"Don't Worry Be Happy."* My mind spun almost like a Rolodex until it stopped at Bobby McFerrin. Glad Budd wasn't worried.

"Hey, what are you doing here?" he asked, pulling up sharply to a standstill. "The party's not until tonight." He didn't lean in to kiss me good morning. Good thing. If he had, I may have pulled back away from him. While I was optimistic he'd be cleared of any wrongdoing soon, there was always the chance I'd misjudged him all along.

His role in the plan was to do exactly what he was doing. Show up and unlock the door, just as he did last Saturday. Then get to work setting up for the event. The major differences were that I was there to greet him, not Maggie, and the event was scheduled for this morning, not that night.

He was full of questions. Under the circumstances, I think perhaps that should've been my role. What really was his relationship with Maggie when they worked together in Maine? Did she know some deep, dark secret about him he'd hidden from me? Who did he meet and have dinner with Monday night?

I ignored his question about my presence at the museum, thankful he didn't press me further. When he asked why I left the house before he did, I merely shrugged and said, "It's a busy day."

After that, we hung around the lobby making small talk. Mostly about Sherrie, of course. When he asked where she was, I swallowed hard. I couldn't tell him she was shadowing Oscar. Staying close to the action, but out of harm's way. Seemed Sherrie still infatuated Budd. Perhaps he'd had threesome fantasies all week. I'd never know; I'd never ask.

Thankfully, Jeremy showed up ten minutes later. On time. In his denim overalls and light gray T-shirt, he was ready to work as well. All that Sadie told the museum's caretaker and gardener was that my birthday party, including the museum's big reveal, was back on schedule for that evening.

"Good-good morning, Ms. Bixby," Jeremy said. I corrected him for what seemed like the tenth time since we'd known each other. "Just call me Venus."

"Shall we get started?" Budd said, as he turned to head down a hallway, Jeremy close on his heels; both in the opposite direction of my destination. I assumed they were off to punch a clock wherever the staff did such a thing.

I passed the gift shop, which was gated and locked, and entered the gardens through the glass doors. I was immediately struck by the earthy smell and sensed a change in humidity from the fresh, cool air of the museum to the morning's dewy dampness of the gardens. Butterflies flitted around the white snakeroot that Jeremy expertly planted in the four corners. The dozen or so skylights in the domed ceiling provided more than enough sunlight to keep both the plants and Jeremy happy.

I observed Sadie sitting on a bench looking calm, cool, and collected. Her eyes closed, her ears most likely indulging in her meditation app of choice. Who knew? Perhaps she was relaxing to the playlist I gave her after Paul passed.

Relaxing? God bless her if she could. I rubbed the palms of my hands. The gardens weren't the only thing clammy that morning.

Without my interrupting, Sadie sprung to life. Did I stir up the air she was breathing when I entered? Or maybe I shut the door with too much force that the earth under her feet wobbled a bit, announcing my arrival? *Whatever.* She gave me a quick hello with a flick of her wrist. My inclination was to signal her not to quit her practice on my account. But then I remembered, this was all part of the plan.

As if on cue, Budd and Jeremy joined us. Not much was said beyond a good morning to Sadie and a *hey* to me. They had their marching orders from Sadie. Budd searched through his key ring as he headed for the door on the far side of the gardens: the door I had no idea existed. Jeremy dutifully followed. They were deep in conversation, so I couldn't hear them. I imagined they could be saying, *Here we go again.*

I noticed how easily the two fellows worked together. For example, they knew the proper sequence to haul out and set up the tables Carole would use to arrange her wares, the chairs for guests, and finally the two pedestals.

While they did that, Sadie cocked her head toward the exit. She was off to do the next thing on her checklist.

So far, everything was going according to plan.

"Ms. Bixby, I mean Venus, will this do?" Jeremy waved his arm across the set up.

I nodded and thanked him. He and Budd walked around the sidewalk. Jeremy stopped and pointed to several shrubs along the path. I could only assume they were discussing some gardening task needing attention. Weeding, pruning, or God forbid, pest control.

Just as Budd reached the exit, he turned and caught my eye. "See ya," he said and blew me a kiss. "Later," I responded loud enough for both of the fellows to hear. I could see Jeremy grin as he patted Budd on his back. Neither of them was aware of what was going to go down that morning. If all went well, I'd be able to give Budd more than an air-kiss. Fingers crossed.

At that point, though, his innocence was my bliss. Yet, even assuming he was innocent, I was more than a little concerned he'd never forgive me for not trusting him enough to include him in the objective of that day's scheme. Especially when he found out Carole was in on it.

Waiting for Carole to arrive, I sat on the bench Sadie had recently occupied. Taking a page from Sadie's routine, I closed my eyes. My heart pumped so hard I could feel it pounding through my eyes and my ears. I placed my hand on my chest. *Thump. Thump, thump.* I took a deep breath and exhaled. And then another. And then three more. *Calm down, Venus. You've got this.*

Less than an hour before at the store, Oscar was still trying to convince me to butt out. He said *he* had this.

Needless to say, I persisted. Protesting, I reminded him I was the one helping to put the puzzle pieces together for him. I had every right to see this through to its conclusion. Of course, I had an ulterior motive: I needed to clear Budd's name.

Oscar saw right through me. "Venus, I'm aware of your motivation. But you only presented one theory of the case. Unfortunately, everyone … including Budd … is still a suspect."

"Even me?" Carole had raised her voice, inserting herself into the discussion. "Maggie and I may have exchanged words on Friday, but that's as far as it went."

I was about to ask *what words* but Oscar beat me to it … kind of.

"You see, we have to execute each step of the plan in order to rule each person out," Oscar said.

"And that's why you need my sister to do that," Sherrie said, offering her two cents.

"I give up." Oscar rolled his eyes and shrugged, grudgingly accepting we outnumbered him.

Suddenly, Carole interrupted my train of thought as she arrived in the gardens. "Hey, you! You gonna give me a hand here? Maggie did."

I cringed at the mention of Maggie and lifted myself off the bench. I had to admit, having my eyes closed for five minutes did my blood pressure some good. Sadie had something there. Indeed, I was refreshed and ready to go.

"You think this is gonna work?" Carole asked as we straightened out the white linen tablecloths.

"It has to. Think about it. Even though you had an opportunity to off Maggie, you had no motive, right?"

Carole didn't answer my question and instead appeared to leap at the chance to deflect my attention on her. "Same with Sadie," she said. "Sadie had an opportunity."

"Shh! Keep your voice down." I tilted my head up toward one of the security monitors and did a side glance, hoping Carole got the message that Sadie may have already turned on the cameras that were repaired the day before.

We turned our backs away from spying eyes. "It makes no sense she'd be involved," I said, realizing I was defending Sadie for a change. "She entrusted Maggie with Poseidon. Why would she kill her or her husband?"

"Unless Sadie stole Poseidon herself. Did you ever think of that?"

While I stacked plates and arranged forks and spoons, I had to admit I had never thought of that scenario. "What? To get the reward?"

"It's one possibility."

"Maybe it's a good thing we only asked her to implement key elements of the murder scene. We'll see how she responds." I scratched a spot behind my right ear. I couldn't wait until all of this was over.

Carole inched close to me, a stack of red napkins separating us. "I don't think Jeremy's involved. Do you, really? This garden is his life." Carole turned away, making a sweeping motion with her right hand. More than a few napkins fluttered to the pavement.

We both stooped down to retrieve them, our heads even closer. "That kind of narrows things down, if we exclude Sadie," Carole whispered.

"It just can't be Budd. It just can't be."

Carole squeezed my arm as she pulled me in for a sympathetic hug. "What do you really know about him? Just because he's filled a hole in your heart—"

"Only partially filled," I said as I separated myself from Carole and touched the Two to Tango necklace. *Be with me today, Paul.*

"I think I'm done here for now," Carole picked up her bag and started to leave. "Be careful, ya hear? Two down. I don't want you to make it three." She headed out, reminding me she needed to check in at the store and would be back shortly.

For the moment, I was alone. I ran my fingers across the table, touching the accoutrements. Without a doubt, though I never really doubted it, Carole was a catering phenomenon. Everything looked inviting, festive, and innocent as it should have been last Saturday. No one would suspect all this effort—this reenactment—was designed to nail the person who committed such heinous crimes in Chatham Crossing.

I was about to check the time on my phone when Sadie returned, carrying something wrapped in bubble wrap. I met her by one of the pedestals. When she unwrapped it, my eyes widened as she displayed a stunning bronze statue.

At first, Sadie held it in front of herself, admiring it up close. Then, she lifted her arm above her head in Statue of Liberty fashion. A stream of light from above bounced off of it. I stepped back, instinctively raising my right arm as a shield between us. *Is she about to whack me? Maybe Carole has something there.*

Sadie lowered her arm. Turned the statue to face me, like a mother might her newborn. "Venus, meet Amphitrite. Greek goddess of the sea. Wife of Poseidon."

I reached out to touch the magnificent statue.

"Don't touch." Sadie waved a gloved hand in the air. "It's priceless." She gently positioned it onto one pedestal. "I think I'm done here for now." She pressed two fingers to her lips, touched the pedestal, and then stepped backward away from the treasure that would finally be revealed, even if it wasn't sitting next to Poseidon.

"Don't worry, Sadie, this one isn't going anywhere."

Alone again, I inhaled the sweet smell of gardenias and gazed up and around the periphery of this little piece of heaven. *Those cameras just better be working.*

As if he was reading my mind, I heard three knocks coming from the side door. Oscar was there and in position.

My mouth was parched, probably dry from anxiety. My thumb throbbed, reminding me why I'd put myself in the middle of a murder investigation to begin with.

The main double glass doors to the gardens opened simultaneously. At first, all I saw was a tall and lean body dressed in a black T-shirt and black jeans pushing through. Then, I noticed the ponytail and a black backpack with a white Sofia Silva Whaling Museum logo emblazoned on it. Roger P. Drake turned into the gardens, balancing a stack of cookie trays.

"Can I give you a hand with that?" I shouted, taking three steps toward him. I noticed his white bandana hanging out of his pocket.

"Sure can," he said, flashing me a big grin. "Wasn't expecting to see the guest of honor here so early, but since you are …"

I reached him halfway between the doorway and the tables waiting for *Bixby's Dozen*'s baked goods. Lifting the top tray off the stack, I saw his Jolly Roger cookies. As I turned to head toward the tables, my knees weakened ever so slightly. *Breathe. You can do this.*

"Nice of you to bring all of this over, Roger. I wasn't sure you'd be ready to return so soon to where we lost Maggie."

He didn't respond to my nudge. He just went about his business arranging the cookie trays on the tables. Obviously, he'd worked with Carole enough to know precisely how she wanted the cookies displayed so the foods she'd provide were featured center-stage.

"What's this?" Roger stepped toward Amphitrite.

"Don't touch!"

"Never fear!" He raised both palms and waved them in the air. He was wearing latex gloves. Black, of course.

"Still. Please don't."

"Why not? It's just a statue."

"Not just any statue," I said. This time I did the introductions. "Amphitrite, meet Roger P. Drake."

"Amphitrite! Blow me down! She's Poseidon's wife. Goddess of the sea."

"You sure know your Greek mythology."

"Of course I do. Especially anything to do with ships and the sea. I'm a pirate, after all."

I released a polite snicker. Did he really believe he was a pirate? Or was he delusional?

"Drake?" I murmured, my eyes lifting toward one of the skylights.

"Sir Francis. A relative of mine," he said, standing straighter, his chest puffed out.

"That explains your cookie theme."

Smiling, Roger popped the clear plastic cover off of one of the trays. "How about a cookie, milady?"

My body tilted away from him and the pavement. I stumbled. Trying to get my balance, my shoes sunk into something soft, like soil. The moist pachysandra enveloped my ankles. I was going down.

"Not again!"

CHAPTER THIRTY-EIGHT

Not exactly as last Saturday, and certainly not exactly part of the plan. Thankfully, I neither performed a face plant on the pavement nor buried my face in the ground cover. But I lost my balance, nonetheless.

Logically, *help* was the first and only word I cried out as I began an unladylike descent.

Roger grabbed my left arm, breaking my fall, preventing me from embarrassing myself. Total disaster thwarted. "Ms. Bixby!" he yelped. "Careful!"

"Oh, my God! Thank you!" I gathered myself and tried to regain my composure. "What did you say?"

Standing with his black-gloved hands on his hips, Roger said, "Careful? I think I said *careful.*"

"Before that." I twirled my right hand in a *before-that* motion.

He shook his head, shrugged. "That I'm related to Sir Francis Drake?"

I squinted my eyes. I knew things happened fast, but I swore he said *not again.* How far should I go to get him to admit he said that and to explain what he meant by it?

Before I could go down that path, Roger bent over and came up with my thumb splint in his hand.

"You dropped something," he said, handing it to me.

I lifted my left hand and stared at it as if it was a new appendage: something I'd never seen before. Obviously, the splint loosened and slipped off when Roger reached for me and saved me from falling. I quickly assessed the state of the splint. It'd seen better days. Could I just slide it back on? Would I have to make a trip to The Cube to get a new one?

This was bonkers. The foundation of our plan was to reconstruct the events of last Saturday. Most of the events, not everything. Certainly nothing involving my thumb and a visit to the ER!

"Are you okay, Ms. Bixby?"

I held the splint and stared speechless at Roger. Unable to control either my immediate emotions or my underlying fear for Budd, my eyes swelled with tears. I turned toward the doors. Not fight or flight. Rather fear and flight.

"Give me a few minutes," I mumbled.

"You got it. I'll get the—" he said, but I was out of the gardens before he finished his sentence.

"Feet don't fail me now," I whispered, as I hustled to the ladies' room. With the splint in my left hand, I used my right hand to retrieve the phone from my pocket. My shoulder pushed open the door. My reflection in the mirror wasn't pretty; my hair was disheveled (frankly, the humidity in the gardens didn't help); and my cheeks were streaked with mascara.

Ladies room. Get here now. I texted Sherrie.

No sooner had I pressed *Send,* then the door whooshed open.

"I think it's Budd," I said to my sister as I leaned against the marble counter. "Roger's too nice. He reads to young kids and just now he saved me from a repeat fiasco. And he thinks he's a pirate, for goodness' sake."

"Don't give up on Budd so soon. He's nice too. And don't pirates attack and rob treasure?"

I grunted, admitting she may have something there. Praying she had something there.

"What's this?" Sherrie picked the splint up off the counter and showed me what was left of it.

I held my thumb in the air. Sherrie got a load of the fracture for the first time.

"Not again," she said.

"No! Not again …" I swiped the splint she was holding and mimicked how it should slide onto my thumb.

With a paper towel, she tried to blot my cheeks. "You look raccoonish. You can't go out there like that." I stepped back, the left side of my lips curled, and my eyes grew as wide as dinner plates when she asked if I needed to go to the ER.

"That's it!"

"What is?"

"What Roger said when I fell. Well, almost fell."

CHAPTER THIRTY-NINE

There was no way for me to get to Oscar without exposing our plan to others. I could tell Sherrie what I was thinking and let her convey it to him, but I decided to keep my hunch to myself.

"Let Oscar know I'm okay. We're good to go." I gave Sherrie a little push toward the main lobby door she needed to exit through in order to make her way around the building to get to the side door where Oscar was camped out.

I swung by Sadie's office, opening the door only enough to poke my head in. She was perched in her chair staring at the CCTV feed. One of Chatham Crossing's finest peered over her shoulder.

"Give me ten minutes," I said. Keeping her eyes on the screen, Sadie gave me a thumbs up with one hand and fingers crossed with the other. The smile she added stirred a warm feeling inside of me. Reciprocating, I smiled, wondering if something positive between us would ultimately come from all of this.

I was careful not to open the garden doors with my left hand. With the cumbersome splint gone, at least temporarily, I should've experienced some sense of free-dom—that everything was back to normal. Clearly, that was not the case. I could see that. I could feel that. Another trip to The Cube was most definitely in my future.

But there was something else I needed to do. I swallowed hard. The time had come to face the music. *Think, Venus.* I came up empty. No song rescued me from the various scenarios swirling in my mind. *You have to do this.*

"Hey, Roger," I said, approaching him near the tables fully displaying four trays of cookies. His back was to me.

He swung toward me with a cat-who-ate-the-canary grin on his face. And then I saw what was in his hands.

Amphitrite.

"What do you not understand about *Do Not Touch?*" I bet I sounded like either his mother, his aunt, or one of his elementary school teachers.

"But it's mine," he whispered through perfectly straight, pearly white teeth I noticed for the first time.

Distracted, part of me wanted to ask him if he had braces growing up. But the adult in me knew that would be totally inappropriate given the situation.

Like a child, he cuddled the statue close to his chest and kissed the top of her head.

"Yours? *Blimey!*" Kudos to me for coming up with a word a pirate like Roger P. Drake would fancy and snap him back into reality. He must be kidding that the statue was his. But I was game to keep playing. "That *booty* belongs to the museum … not you!" My own personal pride in my newly found sleuthing talent clouded my senses, interfering with my ability to grasp what was really happening.

He pushed past me and reached for his backpack that was perched on one of the dozen folding chairs Budd and Jeremy had set up for the reenactment. Then, it dawned on me. *I should've had a V8!* Roger was bloody serious.

"We'll see about that. She belongs with Poseidon," he said, huffing and puffing.

"Poseidon? You know where Poseidon is?"

Instinctively, I reached for Amphitrite before he unzipped his pack. "Give it here."

Before I knew it, he raised the arm that held Amphitrite over his head, reminiscent of what Sadie did shortly before.

And then all hell broke loose.

"What do you think you're doing?" Budd charged past me, twisting Roger's free arm behind his back. "I warned you!"

Oscar sprinted in from the side door. No guns were drawn, thankfully. That would've really freaked me out.

Gracious! With this flurry of alpha male activity in the close confines of the gardens, my body wobbled. My legs flew out from under me and my derrière kissed the pavement. I was not totally flat out or face down, but more than my pride was bruised, just the same.

"Jeremy, take the statue," Oscar hollered, directing the gardener. "Budd, let him go. Move aside. Both of you, stand right where you are!"

From behind, familiar hands looped under my armpits. Sherrie lifted me to an upright position. "That was close," she said, rubbing my back while I rubbed my rear end.

"Sit down," Sherrie commanded. "Let me look at you." I acquiesced and gingerly sidestepped toward a folding chair next to where Roger's backpack rested undisturbed. When my bottom met the cold, hard seat, I cringed. First my thumb, then my bum. No one ever told me turning half a century would be so painful. And here I thought menopause would be my only impending nemesis. My sister lifted my chin, kissed the tip of my nose, and wiped tears off my cheeks that I hadn't had time yet to notice were wet.

"What happened?" I looked left, over the backpack, and saw Roger sitting, slumped forward. In the seat next to him was Budd, straight up, arms crossed, breathing heavily. Oscar straddled the area between Roger and Budd, his knees nearly touching theirs, forming a makeshift blockade. They weren't going anywhere, anytime soon.

"The statue?" I almost screamed, coming to my senses.

"You mean statues," Sadie said, forcing her way past Carole, who arrived on the scene and was already checking out the banquet tables. Jeremy directed everyone's eyes to the pedestal where he'd returned Amphitrite.

"Don't step on …" Jeremy clearly warned Sadie and all of us not to trounce on his shrubs. Or, God forbid, pick his flowers. As if doing so was on anyone's mind at the moment.

"Leave it there, Sadie. Take a seat, everyone," Oscar said in his detective voice. "Let this garden party begin. It's time to test Ms. Bixby's theory."

CHAPTER FORTY

Sherrie plopped herself in a chair to my right and held my hand. Sadie situated herself in a seat behind the chair housing Roger's backpack. Jeremy sat behind Roger, then leaned slightly to his left, resting his hand on Budd's shoulder.

Making a bit of a racket, Carole dragged one of the folding chairs onto the pavement, avoiding Jeremy's prized ground cover, and secured her spot near the table where Roger stacked the cookie trays. Frankly, I was at a loss as to whether she was guarding the cookies, was aiming to swipe one or two for her own pleasure with no one noticing, or was planning to offer refreshments at the conclusion of this proceeding. One never knew Carole's true intentions.

I, for one, could feel the earth move under my feet. Figuratively, not literally. But I wasn't in a mood to sing the song, nor to dance. My future depended on what happened next.

I raised my hand, like when I was in school. "Detective Donovan, can I get some water, please?" While I *was* parched, I was really trying to distract and delay the inevitable. It was fairly obvious Roger was somehow connected to the disappearance of Poseidon, given how he coveted Amphitrite. He just as much as admitted he had the god of the sea in his possession somewhere. But that didn't mean he had anything to do with the deaths of Mr. and Mrs. McGee. Budd could still be in the crosshairs where that was concerned. Was there a connection between Budd and Roger? Was that why Oscar instructed Budd to sit right next to him? Only time would tell.

The ball was in Oscar's court. I had done all I could to bring his investigation to this juncture, to help him solve these crimes.

Carole handed me a bottle of water so cold the garden's mugginess caused it to perspire. After one swig, I held the bottle next to my face, which I was sure was pink and flushed.

"It's not just Venus's theory." Sherrie was the first to speak once everyone settled down. "Excuse me, Detective Donovan, remember it's the *Sisters'* List of Suspects." I gave her palm a little pinch, and mouthed *shh*. Too late: all eyes riveted on my twin.

"Ah, yes. The list. And you are all on it." Oscar reached for his back hip pocket and pulled out the purple paper that appeared to be folded in half and then half again.

I heard a collective gasp followed by exclamations of "Not me. Impossible. You've got to be kidding." This must be some sort of detective ploy. Give the heebie-jeebies to the entire gang. Make them sweat. I knew not everyone surrounding me was on the list. But I decided to stay mum and let this play itself out.

"Well, all of you except for Ms. Moore, who wasn't even in Chatham Crossing last Saturday."

Good for you, Oscar. As if anyone would ever suspect my sister.

Sherrie shifted in her chair and touched the palm of her right hand to her chest in gratitude to Oscar for singling her out in such a positive manner. "And Venus, too, is in the clear. Right?"

"That's right. Gimme a chance. I was just getting to that."

I swallowed hard and glanced around from person to person. When my eyes reached Budd, he looked downward, not receiving my gaze. What did he know that I didn't? What did he mean when he said he warned Roger? What was that all about? Or maybe he was already angry at me for including him on the list? I wished I could telepathically send him a message that I was sorry, but he was not Paul who could uniquely read my mind from across a crowded room.

Bringing myself back to the scene at hand, I wondered who Oscar would start with? Excluding my sister and me, he had five potential offenders to consider. Would he go alphabetically? Budd, Carole, Jeremy, Roger, Sadie? That would make no sense. No one noticed me shaking my head.

Oscar paced the garden path. Back and forth. Five steps forward, then he turned. Five steps back. He mapped out his platform, staying safely away from Jeremy's greenery. He bowed his head, as if there were a teleprompter embedded in the concrete that would guide him through a prepared script. The nearest thing to a script was the Sisters' List of Suspects.

But that couldn't be all the evidence available to him. And the list really wasn't evidence. It was just an inventory of opportunity and motives for people who more than likely interacted with Maggie that fateful morning. It didn't even address the other two crimes Oscar was intent on solving that day. Chatham Crossing rarely encountered robberies or murders. A combination such as this was preposterous on any level and would be a test of Detective Oscar Donovan's mettle.

I'd done my best to prime the pump for him. I could only hope my observations served him … and all of us … well.

He stopped pacing in front of me, of all people. That would not be how I would play this. He got my attention.

"Last weekend, the Fourth of July weekend, was supposed to be a time of celebration here in Chatham Crossing. More so than our usual annual festivities."

Heads nodded, a few joined me in a low affirmative grunt.

"But things didn't go quite as planned. Why not? Let's review what we know. Fact is, right here," he lifted his head and waved his hand around the gardens. "Right here in the beautiful Gardens of the Sofia Silva Whaling Museum, we were all invited to bestow good cheer on Ms. Bixby as she marked her fiftieth birthday."

I gulped. He made me sound *so* old.

"And," he continued, "to witness the unveiling of a newly acquired treasure by the museum."

I turned slightly toward Sadie, who was nodding.

"But not everyone who was in the gardens that morning was, in fact, invited to the big affair last Saturday night."

Heads turned toward each other. Shoulders shrugged.

It was my turn to pat my sister's arm. "It's okay," I whispered, "he doesn't mean you." Sherrie sighed, *Phew*, and wiped her forehead with the back of her hand.

By process of elimination, I easily figured out where Oscar was heading.

One by one, he set his gaze on each of us for no more than a couple of seconds.

"Oh, come on," Budd said, "get on with it. Why all the drama?"

Budd's comment gave me a glimmer of faith that he was not involved in any of this; otherwise he wouldn't be encouraging Oscar to move along.

"Did you all know Margaret McGee never received an invitation to the party? And yet she died in the process of setting the stage for all of us to enjoy that night. Oh, the irony."

Budd groaned. From my vantage point I could see him rub the palms of his hands on his work pants. Whatever hope I had quickly faded.

"That was my mistake," Sadie offered. "I tried to make it up to her."

"Thank you, Mrs. Hawkins, we'll get to that."

I noticed Oscar addressed each of us by our surnames even though he'd known most of us for years. Just doing his job, I guessed. Or maybe he was just playing to the cameras.

"But that was not the only crime that occurred six days ago, right where we are today. No siree. A major theft occurred right under the nose of the museum's curator."

"If I might, Detective Donovan," Sadie interrupted. "Not quite under my nose. The cameras were not operating that day."

"Thank you, Mrs. Hawkins, we'll get to that."

All chins lifted upward, all eyes circling around the four corners of the gardens. Sadie and I knew the closed circuit television was restored during the week and was capturing the whole gathering.

"If that weren't bad enough," Oscar continued, "much more *drama* occurred than we want Chatham Crossing to be known for, wouldn't you agree?" He glared at Budd.

Almost everyone uttered some version of *right on, of course, to be sure*, except Roger, who remained close-mouthed, still folded onto himself.

"Three days after Ms. McGee's demise, her husband Brian McGee turns up face down, floating in the Crescent River at the conclusion of the town's annual parade!"

"Maybe he was walking too close to the edge, slipped, and hit his head as he fell into the river?" Sadie, who obviously had a vested interest in this interrogation and was apparently fully engaged, speculated freely.

"That's one theory, but as you'll see, Mrs. Hawkins, we'll get to that."

My bottom ached possibly from my fall, but more than likely because the folding chair was as hard as ceramic flooring. As I switched from one butt cheek to the other, I noticed others doing the same. But they didn't fall. So maybe it was the chair's fault, or maybe it was the trepidation of what was to come. Personally, I blamed all three—the fall, the chair, and my fears.

Oscar shared that he initially thought solving what happened to Mrs. McGee would prove to be a simple case. One victim. One culprit. Case closed. But then unforeseen developments occurred, creating a puzzle that would take more than a list of suspects to solve.

Did he just insult me? I straightened in my chair, the pain in my backside be damned. I could feel everyone's eyes bearing down on me. Here I thought I was doing the good detective a favor—especially considering the additional insights I provided him first thing that morning.

"Don't get me wrong. This …" Oscar said, holding up our list for all to see, "is invaluable." I gave him a *thank you* thumbs up.

"But much more is required to solve complex cases such as we have here. A thorough investigation by the Chatham Crossing police includes photos of the crime scenes—plural; autopsy reports—plural; and lab reports—plural." Oscar stopped for what appeared to be a brief moment of self-congratulations. He was not accustomed to confronting an audience of suspects.

"Add to all of that, intense interrogations and background checks. Against all the evidence collected, I've concluded these three wicked incidents are connected. As are some of you sitting right here, right now, in the lovely Gardens of the Sofia Silva Whaling Museum."

At Oscar's accusation of a connection among us, there was an audible murmur.

Then, out of nowhere, Roger declared with more than a bit of a snark, "It's a whale of a mystery, wouldn't you say, hearties?"

CHAPTER FORTY-ONE

At first, no one responded to Roger, including me. I bet everyone, except me and my sister, was trying to figure out how they might be linked to each other, especially to Roger.

"He stole my line," Sherrie whispered to me. I tilted my head toward her and wrinkled my brow. Whatever was she talking about? "I already said it's a whale of a mystery," Sherrie explained. "A couple of days ago." Honestly, I didn't recall her saying that, but I took her word for it.

I cupped my left hand over my mouth and leaned toward her. "What do you expect?" I said as softly as possible. "He is a pirate, after all."

Sherrie folded her arms across her chest, scowling.

"You just might have something there, Mr. Drake," Oscar said, picking up on Roger's remark.

Before Oscar expounded on what he meant, Budd leaped off his chair, reached down and grabbed Roger by the neck of his black T-shirt, pulling him to an upright position; their noses almost touching. "Hearties, you say? I'm not your friend. Not now. Never was."

We all jumped from our seats in reaction. I was sure we were all expecting to separate these two grown men who were suddenly acting like teenagers. Well, at least one was acting that way. But Roger just stood there, not fighting back.

"Let him go, Mr. Nickerson," Oscar commanded, "before this all becomes even more complicated."

Budd shoved Roger slightly, then backed away. Roger pulled the white bandana from his pocket, wiped his forehead, and then tied it around his neck. Both men reclaimed their seats. Why Oscar didn't direct Budd to a chair away from Roger was beyond me. Despite how much I wished to be more involved, I accepted this was the detective's game to referee, not mine.

Oscar waved his hands at the rest of us, indicating we should assume our prior positions as well. Which we did.

"Well, that was interesting," Sherrie murmured as we nearly bumped into each other sitting down. I merely raised my eyebrows. My curiosity meter was rising faster than a high striker game at a carnival. When did Budd and Roger's paths cross? And why weren't they friends?

"Now, where was I? Oh, yes. Evidence. Facts." Oscar's pacing resumed as he mumbled *evidence, facts.* Hercule Poirot he was not. But I wouldn't be the one to tell him.

"Let's begin at the beginning. Last Saturday. With Mrs. McGee." Oscar stopped mid-stride and scanned his onlookers. "Whoever was the last one to see Mrs. McGee alive will help identify who may have harmed her, wouldn't you all agree?"

Most everyone nodded.

"So, let's construct a timeline of that morning."

Oscar tucked the Sisters' List of Suspects into his hip pocket. Luckily, I'd memorized its contents in case the good detective's power of retention faltered.

"Would a whiteboard help?" Jeremy asked, rising halfway out of his seat.

"Thanks, but no, Mr. Roserun. I'm all set," Oscar responded, fetching from his shirt what looked to be the same small notepad he carried with him wherever he went. He held it up for us all to see he was armed with the facts.

I watched as he licked the tip of his index finger and flipped from page to page. When was he going to get a move on?

"Ah, here we are." He rubbed his nose and then proceeded. "My investigation establishes Mrs. McGee's time of death sometime between 7:30 and 10:30 Saturday morning. And that each of you interacted with her during her last precious minutes on this good earth."

Sherrie raised her hand to capture Oscar's attention.

"I repeat what I said earlier, except our visitor from San Fran."

"With all due respect, sir, that's San Francisco," Sherrie corrected him.

Oscar nodded and continued. My eyes found my lap as I grinned ever so slightly.

"On Monday, *The Chatham Crossing Chronicle* reported that Ms. Venus Bixby was the last person to see Margaret McGee alive," Oscar said, looking directly at Carole. She opened her mouth to speak, but Oscar raised his palm to her, curtailing any opportunity for her to defend herself.

Further, he explained that since the closed circuit television cameras in the gardens were on the fritz that day, he couldn't prove beyond a doubt that I didn't meet Maggie face to face that morning. But, in his view, the multiple conversations he'd had with me over the last several days totally satisfied him that Mrs. Duffy's conjecture was inaccurate and her broadcasting it to the press was totally ill-served.

"A gentle word of warning," Oscar turned toward Carole once again. "In the future, Mrs. Duffy, as the mayor's wife, you might want to be more judicious before pointing a finger at someone without proof. Especially when talking with a reporter."

Oh, my. That's harsh. Relieved the attention was now off me, I empathized with how Carole must be feeling. The last thing I wanted to come out of this horrid week was for there to be a wedge between us. Sherrie rubbed my arm. She shifted her glance past Carole toward the cookie trays. "Want one?" she whispered. The rush of exasperation I felt for my sister at that moment escaped my nostrils so audibly, I lowered my face hoping no one would pin her comment on me.

When I looked up, everyone, even Roger, was staring at me, not Sherrie. "Sorry. Please continue, Detective."

"Thanks, Ms. Bixby, I will. Now, back to Saturday morning." Oscar exchanged his notebook for his phone, which was in his shirt pocket, and flipped through screen after screen. Not knowing where he was going with this, I drank some water to quench my inner hysteria, not my thirst.

"Ah, here they are. Photos from the crime scene." He held up the phone, facing it toward us, but of course, the screen was too small. For all I knew, he could be showing us a picture of his dog.

"Would a laptop and a screen help?" Jeremy asked, rising again from his seat.

Oscar tilted his head toward Jeremy and glared at him as if to say, "You've got to be kidding me." Jeremy got the message.

"This picture shows the crime scene. If we ignore the yellow tape, what's left?" Setting the stage, his eyes considered each of us. But no one answered his impossible question.

"I'll tell you what's left. Evidence. Tables. Chairs. One pedestal standing upright. One on the ground. Paper goods and utensils." He stopped and stared more closely at the screen, still not getting it that he was the only one who could see the photo. As I mentioned, he was no Agatha Christie detective. "I see salt and pepper shakers. And multiple trays of cookies," he said, with a side glance toward me.

I got the picture he was trying to convey. Oscar was about to tie the items in the picture to the scene currently in front of us.

"Now, just the facts," he proceeded. "Shortly after arriving at the museum that morning, probably around eight o'clock, Mr. Nickerson and Mr. Roserun retrieved the tables and chairs from the storage closet and brought them in through the side door."

Budd turned and looked at Jeremy, shaking his head affirmatively. With the mention of Budd, I sucked in some air and forgot to let it go. Instead, I concentrated on Oscar.

"It's safe to say, in the process of placing these items in their proper places, these two gentlemen had occasion to speak to Mrs. McGee. And, it's equally safe to say, that since three's generally considered a crowd, neither Mr. Nickerson nor Mr. Roserun would've caused Mrs. McGee any undue harm."

I exhaled. My shoulders collapsed ever so slightly.

"At least not at that time," Oscar said. I closed my eyes, desperately wanting this to be over. He certainly knew how to press my buttons.

"Now that the tables are in place, what happened next?" he asked, shifting his eyes onto Carole.

"I delivered the paper goods. Anything that was non-perishable," Carole said bluntly.

"And the time?"

She squinted her eyes, thinking.

"You opened the store at eight-thirty, right?" I said, trying to help a friend.

"I did. My van was already loaded, so I wasn't at the store long. Just double-checking that the bakers were already delivering their goods as planned and that Hannah had everything under control. Especially keeping Sonny and Cher away from the cookie trays."

"My cats," I said, for anyone who needed clarification or a reminder.

"Hannah's my daughter," Sadie piped in, stating the obvious with a wide, prideful smile. Most everyone knew Hannah had been dating Detective Donovan's son for about a year. They'd become quite the talk of the town. Nevertheless, Sadie added, "For the record, she had nothing to do with any of this."

"Duly noted, Mrs. Hawkins. Thank you." I hoped no one else noticed Oscar rolling his eyes. There was no reason he or anyone else would suspect Hannah was in any trouble.

"So, Mrs. Duffy, the time. What time?"

"Oh!" Carole lifted her chin toward the glass ceiling as if there were a timepiece floating around up there. "I'd guess around nine o'clock, maybe? And Maggie was very much alive then. In fact, she helped me unload the crates and arrange the tables. With my supervision, of course."

I accepted Carole's scenario as factual. Anything and everything related to her catering business required her seal of approval.

"Were you and Mrs. McGee alone during that time?"

"Yes. Even without bringing the food in then, setting up was still a two-person job."

"So, maybe *you* were the last one to see Mrs. McGee alive?" Oscar asked Carole.

She crossed her arms. "Couldn't have been. Poseidon wasn't there when Maggie and I arranged the tables. And why would I hurt her?"

"You had words with her on Friday," Sadie chimed in. "You told me so, remember?"

We all turned to look at Sadie, but only for a moment. Any attempt Carole wanted to make to explain her words with Maggie on Friday was quickly squashed.

"That's right, I'll second that," Roger said. With our heads bouncing from one of us to another, it was beginning to feel more like a tennis match than an inquisition. Roger still had the ball, and he delivered an ace in Carole's direction. "Maggie told me how jealous you are of Ms. Bixby. Kind of vying for who's top dog in this town."

I felt my sister's elbow in my ribs. I bit my lower lip and tried not to glare at Carole. It was not the time to challenge her feelings about me. After all these years. I wasn't the only one shocked by this revelation. You could hear a butterfly flutter.

Coming to our rescue—both Carole's and mine—Sadie jumped in. "But assuming Carole did not return after she dropped off her stuff Saturday morning, I can confirm, she was not the last one to see Maggie alive."

Despite filing away my need to confront Carole at some point, I was much relieved by Sadie's support of her. Carole was still my BFF.

"Carole is quite correct," Sadie continued. "After I watched her leave the museum through the lobby doors, I brought Poseidon into the garden. Maggie seemed to be quite content at that moment, strolling around. I imagine she was admiring Jeremy's handiwork." Sadie looked to her left, giving him an appreciative grin.

I noticed Jeremy touch his palm to his chest.

Oscar had been unusually quiet, observing and listening to our accusations and alibis. He was letting it all play out, but I still worried Budd was on shaky ground.

"Assuming you didn't come back to the museum, Carole—I mean Mrs. Duffy—it appears you're in the clear," Oscar said. "But what about you, Mrs. Hawkins? What happened when you brought Poseidon into the garden?"

"And why did you bring such a valuable possession into an unsecure location?" Sherrie asked Sadie innocently, though Roger prevented Sadie from responding.

"And you have some nerve singling out Mrs. Duffy alone," Roger said, preventing Sadie from answering

Sherrie's question. "What about you, Mrs. Hawkins? Maggie told me all about how poorly you treated her, excluding her—"

Sensing the lists of suspects (the Sisters' List and the detective's) were shrinking, the natives were getting restless; turning on each other. Somewhat like musical chairs, but would the person left sitting or standing be the guilty one?

Oh, God. Sadie was crying. I mean, she sobbed. "Why are you ganging up on me? I'm so ashamed."

Sherrie handed me a tissue, which I turned and handed to Sadie. She waved it at me in thanks.

"I made two mistakes," Sadie said. "First, I took too much time getting to know Maggie. I should've trusted Budd. He recommended her. Second, I had this whacky idea that by giving her responsibility for protecting Poseidon, we'd be able to mend our relationship. I even made sure we snapped pictures of each other with Poseidon. I hoped we could start anew."

"That will nev-never happen now," Jeremy said.

"True," Sadie said, wiping her nose. "But when I left the gardens and went back to my office, both Maggie and Poseidon were very much upright. She was standing next to the pedestal, guarding the statue. Now Maggie's gone and Poseidon is who knows where?"

"Okay, so the women appear to be innocent of any wrongdoing," Oscar reported, positioning himself at the side of the chairs where the three men resided.

Jeremy raised his hand. "Detective Donovan, you should count me with the women."

"Not so fast," Oscar said. "Didn't you have some issue with Mrs. McGee yourself?"

Knowing that accusation came from me, I pinched my lips and looked down, waiting to hear Jeremy's explanation. I could jar Jeremy's memory, but I refrained. He was a big boy and perfectly capable of standing up for himself.

"Ex-excuse me?"

"At the parade on Tuesday, did you tell Ms. Bixby that you and Mrs. McGee got along most of the time except …" Oscar stopped for a theatrical pause, then said, "Except for what, Mr. Roserun?"

Since the good detective had dragged me unwittingly into this line of questioning, I sat upright in my chair and looked directly at Jeremy. I had to take my medicine. Although he was never really high on the Sisters' List of Suspects, if there was an ounce of chance that he could absolve Budd, I wanted to hear it loud and clear.

"Except for my … stuttering," Jeremy whispered.

Oscar bent between Roger and Budd. "Come again?"

"Stuttering. She teased me about it. Not funny. But I did-didn't wish her any harm."

Heads shook, empathizing with Jeremy's plight. We all had our own little idiosyncrasies; things that drove others nuts. I joined Sadie with my own badge of shame. I should've known. Jeremy's a gardener. I looked around me. A masterful one at that. He put his love of plants and nature above himself. He wouldn't hurt a bee even if it landed on his nose.

"I think you can move on," I said, giving Oscar permission to finish what he'd started. Or, rather, what we'd started.

CHAPTER FORTY-TWO

As soon as I gave my blessing to Oscar to move on, I knew I was in big trouble. He didn't need my permission, but I needed closure. Would the *evidence and facts* I provided him stand up to scrutiny? If not, would Budd emerge as the more likely suspect?

This couldn't be happening.

Frankly, Oscar's process of eliminating us one by one was driving me out of my mind. He could've aimed right for the jugular, but he chose to put each of us through the wringer. For what purpose?

Were there three cases being investigated, or just one interrelated clustered mess?

Just thinking about it tired me to the point I almost wished we hadn't executed this little plan of ours. I could've left Oscar and the Chatham Crossing police to their own devices and minded my own business. Though, with Budd in the mix, I had a vested interest in seeing this to its conclusion. Wherever it led.

My weary eyes skirted over the backpack sitting to my left, drifted past Roger who was literally twiddling the thumbs of his still black-gloved hands, and landed squarely on Budd's eyes. He locked into mine as well.

It's okay, he mouthed, bobbed his head, and grinned slightly.

In response, I turned my palms up and shrugged, as if to ask *What do you mean by that?* Okay—he'd soon be acquitted? Okay—even if he was arrested, he was fine with it, and thus I should be too?

If Budd were arrested, I would not be fine with it. Not only would our mutually beneficial relationship end, but I'd need to be more vigilant in the future as to whom I rented the cottage or invited into my bed.

This is all Paul's fault. If he hadn't gone and died, we would've been off celebrating my fiftieth birthday somewhere charming and romantic. I gazed at my sister. *How selfish I'm being.* She left her family behind to be here sitting right next to me, supporting me through whatever happened in the next few minutes.

"Sorry, Detective," I said. "I don't know what got into me."

Just as it seemed Oscar was about to move along, a rush of cool air breezed through the gardens. Collectively and instinctively, we all turned toward the glass doors, the direction from which the sudden, though refreshing, disruption came.

"What now?" I mumbled.

Helen Davis took three steps into the gardens and halted. "What's going on here?"

"Who's that?" Sherrie asked me. I told her I'd tell her later. Not worth my energy at the moment to go into it.

"That's Helen Davis," Carole piped in, overhearing my sister. "Only one of the best of *Bixby's Dozen*, for your information." Was Carole copping an attitude toward my sister when it should be me who was calling her on the carpet for what she had to say about me to Maggie?

I let her slide. Not worth my time.

"What are you doing here, Ms. Davis," asked the detective. "This is a private—"

"Party?" Helen said. "If the party's started early, you'll need these." She raised a tray in front of her face, then brought it down to waist level. She rotated slightly, as Billy Bomba was close on her heels on the garden's path. "My apologies for being late this morning." She blushed from the neck up.

"No apology necessary, Ms. Davis," Roger said, coming to her rescue.

"There you are, Roger! I'm so glad you're here. Now, I can thank you in person." Helen shuffled toward our semi-circle, delivered the tray to Carole without so much as a *here take this*, and hightailed it toward Roger.

What the heck is happening? Helen and Billy showing up was not part of the master plan.

"Wait, Helen," Carole said, after sliding the tray onto the table. "How did you get in here? Wasn't the door locked? Didn't you see the sign the museum's closed this morning?"

Helen put her hands on her hips and pivoted toward Carole. "Show her, Billy." She jutted her chin in his direction.

He did as he was told. I gathered he always did what Helen told him to do. Reaching into his pocket, Billy fetched a carabiner and jiggled it in the air. "See, I still have a key," Helen responded to Carole with a how'd-you-forget kind of twinkle in her eye.

But, of course, she had a key. Her husband was the museum's caretaker before he died, many years before either Sadie or Budd arrived on the scene. What were the chances Helen had keys to other establishments in town where her husband had worked? Like my store or the dance studio? Her carabiner looked kind of crowded.

I didn't have time to explore this with Helen right then. But at some point, I would. Most definitely.

Helen pushed past Oscar so she was standing over Roger. She had the floor, or the pavement, as it were. At least for the moment. She reached into the ragged tote bag slung across her body and pulled out a piece of paper that looked like a letter from where I sat.

"Wherever did you find my binder, Roger?"

He opened his mouth to answer, but Helen was on a roll and didn't let him speak.

"Oh, never you mind. I'm flattered you trusted me enough to sign your note with your real name."

"His real name?" I blurted out. I started to lift myself out of my chair, but Sherrie pulled me back down.

"I'll be darned. Even you didn't know, Venus! His full name is Roger *'the Pirate'* Drake." Clearly, self-satisfied, Helen tipped her head up, lifting her nose in the air and grinning from ear to ear. Like the parrot who ate the canary.

I zipped my lips for a change. How was this such a big revelation? Roger wasn't shy about proclaiming himself a descendant of Sir Francis Drake, the infamous explorer and privateer of the sixteenth century. Look at the way he dressed. Always in black. How he talked, slipping in pirate slang whenever. Question was, how far had he taken this disguise beyond incorporating it into his name? And had he taken it too far?

Out of respect for Helen, I decided to let her have her fifteen minutes of fame, though it was short-lived as it turned out.

Without hesitation, Helen reached for Roger's backpack. "If you don't mind, I'll just sit …"

Roger grasped the straps of the pack before she got her hands on it, placed the pack on his lap, and wrapped his arms around it.

"I do mind," Roger and Oscar blurted out at exactly the same time.

Before Helen claimed the empty seat between me and Roger, the good detective patted her elbow. "Carole, do you mind showing Ms. Davis …" Carole was next to Helen in a flash and pointed toward the exit. "You, too, Mr. Bomba," Oscar said. "This isn't a party. And you're excused."

"Well, I've never …" Clinging to her tote bag, Helen rose and shuffled off behind Billy.

Under the circumstances, I expected Oscar would give us a few minutes to digest what had just happened and regain our composure. But such was not the case.

"Okay, Mr. Roger *P.* Drake," he said. "Let's see what you've got in there."

CHAPTER FORTY-THREE

"It's not what you think," Roger pleaded.

Detective Donovan stopped Roger from showing us what was in his pack. Instead, he removed the backpack from Roger's death grip and returned it to the chair between us. Was he suggesting I open it? I leaned left thinking so, but he called me up sharply.

"Not you, Ms. Bixby. Mrs. Hawkins."

Sadie got to her feet and wended her way left, behind Jeremy, around Budd, past Roger, until she was positioned in front of his backpack right next to me. Out of her hip pocket, Sadie whipped a pair of gloves I assumed all seasoned museum curators must be required to keep within their easy reach. She slipped them on with a snap. I jerked at the sound.

"Wait," Roger said. "I'm telling you, it's not what you think."

"We'll see," Sadie said as she unzipped the pack's main compartment. From where I sat, I could detect her lower lip quivering as she lifted Poseidon ever so gently up and out of its hiding place.

My mouth dropped, as did everyone else's. Who'd be the first to find the right words for the moment?

"Stand up," Detective Donovan commanded Roger. "You're under arrest, Roger Drake, for grand larceny and for the homicide of Margaret McGee."

"He forgot his middle initial," Sherrie hissed under her breath. I raised my index finger to my mouth, the universal sign for *shut up*.

As if they were off stage awaiting their cues, two armed police entered the scene through the side door. One handcuffed Roger. The other gave Oscar a friendly pat on the back.

No one had to tell us what to do next. With the sight of Chatham Crossing's finest in our midst, we got up and hustled to the far end of the tables where Carole had been sitting out of harm's way.

"You have the right …" said the cop with the handcuffs.

But Roger didn't remain silent. "I didn't steal that statue. Like Helen's precious binder, I found Poseidon. I came here this morning to return it and claim the reward money. Don't I get twenty-five thousand dollars?"

"You scoundrel!" Sadie broke away from us and charged toward him. "You plunderer! Pirate! Thief! You expect to be rewarded for stealing the museum's most prized possession?"

Ignoring my rising blood pressure as I processed the audacity of Roger's contention, I rushed to Sadie's defense. "You say you didn't steal Poseidon? Do tell us, then, what were you planning to do when you got a gander of Amphitrite this morning?"

Roger bowed his head.

"It looked to me like you were going to scoop her away just as you did the god of the sea. Add it to your black bag? Your booty bag?"

I felt the rest of the onlookers move in behind me; a hand gripped my arm.

"Stop. That's enough," Budd whispered in my ear.

But I didn't stop. I was only getting started. I shook off his hold.

"I suppose, Roger *P.* Drake, you would've clobbered me with Amphitrite, just the way you walloped Maggie with Poseidon?"

"That was an accident. She slipped and hit her head."

"Not according to the initial autopsy results," Oscar said, opening the door for me to demonstrate to everyone present my skill at connecting the findings of the autopsy report I'd read earlier that morning.

"An accident? I don't think so. How do you explain the remnants of your cookie in Maggie's mouth and stomach?" I added, as if saying *so-there, what do you think of them apples?*

"What do you think happened?" Sherrie asked me.

I stepped back from everyone. The circle forming around the prisoner widened.

"My theory? You want my theory?" I looked to Detective Donovan for permission. He nodded and gave me a go-ahead wave of his hand.

"It's really very simple. As Detective Donovan laid out, neither Budd, Jeremy, Carole, or Sadie could've killed Maggie. Oh, they each had the opportunity, but not everyone had a motive, from what I can tell." I shot Budd a glance and then swallowed hard. I believed in my heart of hearts he had nothing to do with what happened at the whaling museum last Saturday morning.

"And according to the sequence of how everything was set up here in the garden, they were not the last people to see Maggie alive. Whoever delivered the cookie trays was. That would be you, Mr. Drake."

"You're wrong," Roger said. "I was dating Maggie. We were having fun."

"Fun? Until she stood between you and a statue you could fence for a million dollars. I'd say that's a pretty clear motive."

I half expected some sort of recognition from everyone around me. An aye-aye, or at least a thumbs up. But everyone was silent, even Roger. So, I concluded.

"Your motive was greed. And the proof is in the cookie."

I lifted my left hand and gazed at my thumb. "If I hadn't stumbled over Maggie's shoes, who knows how long she would've been lying there. If only I'd come earlier …"

Suddenly, I was overwhelmed by the moment. I was standing where a young woman died only days earlier, confronting the man I believed responsible. And he wasn't even on the Sisters' List of Suspects. I turned toward Sherrie, who wrapped her arm around my shoulder.

"I'll take it from here, Venus," Oscar said.

The two police officers approached Roger, one on each side of him, and carted the suspect away through the side entrance.

"You can all go about your day," Oscar said, telling us the faux-party was over.

Sadie picked up Amphitrite and headed for the exit, carrying the treasured artifacts. I heard Carole ask Jeremy, "What should I do with all these cookies?" As if he had any clue. Budd folded and stacked chairs.

Leave it to my sister. She pulled me into a dancer's pose. Softly, she sang Peggy Lee's "Is That All There Is?" One of our mother's favorites. As Sherrie twirled me around, I pulled away from her embrace.

"Wait!" I shouted. "What about Brian McGee?" Everyone stopped in their respective tracks; Oscar made a U-turn so he faced me.

"Relax, Venus. That's a story for another time."

CHAPTER FORTY-FOUR

The Chatham Crossing Chronicle
Police Lower the Boom. Crime Spree Scuppered

By: Daniel DaRosa, Investigative Reporter

BREAKING NEWS! **Friday, July 9, 2010, 2:30 p.m.** Residents of Chatham Crossing can breathe a sigh of relief. The three successive crimes that rocked the town this past week have been solved.

Early this morning, in a clear stroke of genius and in relative secrecy, the Chatham Crossing police (led by Detective Oscar Donovan) and a cadre of concerned citizens (led by Venus Bixby, owner of Oldies & Goodies) reconstructed the incident that occurred last Saturday in the Gardens of the Sofia Silva Whaling Museum (SSWM).

At this early investigative stage, we can report that, at the conclusion of the reenactment, short-time Chatham Crossing resident, Roger Drake, was taken into custody in connection with the death of Margaret "Maggie" McGee and for stealing the Poseidon statue.

During the subsequent interrogation, Mr. Drake fessed up to being involved in the death of Brian McGee (Ms. McGee's husband): the body discovered in the Crescent River minutes before the parade horses crossed Morgan's Bridge on Tuesday.

While details are sketchy at this time, be sure to check our site daily as new information is sure to come to light. And starting a week from today, we will publish in serial format Ms. Bixby's theory on the motives for these crimes. All of us are indebted to her. Word has it, Ms. Bixby's sharp intuition and keen observations were crucial in aiding police in their arrest of Mr. Drake.

Needless to say, Sandra Hawkins, curator at SSWM, was thrilled by the recovery of Poseidon. When asked about the $25,000 reward the museum offered for the statue's safe return, Mrs. Hawkins said, "No one deserves it more than Venus Bixby."

Now, inquiring minds want to know ... what will Ms. Bixby do with all that cash?

According to Sherrie Moore, Ms. Bixby's twin sister: "Totally up to her. She worked hard for the money."

This reporter suspects there are more details to come. Keep following for the rest of this story.

Digital edition.

CHAPTER FORTY-FIVE

Following the arrest of Roger Drake on Friday morning, Sherrie and I could finally relax on my veranda that afternoon with a cold non-alcoholic drink. Sisters rehashing the day's and week's events.

Sherrie announced perhaps she'd head back home come Monday—to a life far less exciting than mine. I tried to convince her murder and mayhem were rare in Chatham Crossing and extended a sincere invitation for her to return soon. Perhaps during the holidays? The town knew how to do it up big. She should bring her daughter Lexi along. There were plenty of teenagers who'd show her a good time.

As Sherrie rolled her eyes and guffawed at that thought, a black car pulled in the driveway.

"Detective Donovan?" my sister asked and answered. "By now, I'd recognize his vehicle anywhere." She laughed as we linked arms to greet him. I'd laugh, too, except I was troubled as to why he was there. I rolled my hand across my waist, my stomach talking to me. When I asked earlier about solving Brian McGee's death, he'd said it was a story for a later time. Had that time come? Did he have news about Budd I didn't want to hear? News he'd decided was best delivered in person, somewhat privately? Was that why he flipped me off earlier?

"Hey there, ladies. Room for one more?"

I surrendered the Adirondack chair I'd been sitting on to him; Sherrie returned to her original place; and I, well, I leaned up against the railing, bracing for bad news.

Oscar looked at his watch. "Since you're out here enjoying the scenery, I gather you haven't caught the latest news *The Chronicle* just posted on their website?"

I looked at Sherrie. We both leaned forward, ready to move. "I'll get my phone," Sherrie said, bouncing up to head inside to get it.

"No need to. Take a seat," he said, meaning me, as well. I switched places with him. "I'll just read it to you. It's short enough."

He started. "Police Lower the Boom. Crime Spree Scuppered. Blah. Blah." He paused, then added, "That DaRosa chap sure knows how to be creative, doesn't he?" I nodded, knowing Daniel as I did. He continued. "*BREAKING NEWS!* Blah. Blah. Blah."

I scratched my head. How many blah, blah, blahs would I need to fill in when I read the story myself later?

When he was done in less than two minutes, I asked for his phone. I would not wait until he was gone to find out if anything was missing from his readout. I needed to see it myself.

"You were right, Venus. Totally right about Roger P. Drake. What a rascal."

"More than a rascal, wouldn't you say?" Sherrie piped in.

Scanning the article, I asked, "Why didn't you charge him with Brian McGee's murder this morning? I've been …"

"As it turns out, it's better that we got a confession out of him. Makes my job a whole lot easier. And like I told you earlier, Venus, you can relax."

"Easy for you to say," Sherrie countered. "With Budd and all."

"I get it. But think about it. If I really thought Budd Nickerson was involved in any of these crimes, would I have let him remain in such close proximity to you, living back there in your cottage? Give me some credit." Oscar paused, as if he needed time to think. "I must admit, Venus, you deserve much of the credit for solving this so quickly and helping return our little town here to some sense of normalcy."

"Thanks." I clutched his phone to my heart. Budd didn't do it. He didn't do any of it. Oh, happy days!

"Just don't try it again." With that, the good detective took his leave.

In Chatham Crossing, news traveled quickly. Sherrie and I still lingered on the porch, taking turns reading Daniel DaRosa's article from her phone. Within an hour and before I had time to do even one chorus of "Joy to the World" (either the Christmas hymn or Three Dog Night's version), a van pulled into the driveway. Two fellows I didn't recognize climbed out and began to unload their cargo. They looked to be around Hannah's age, late teens.

An energetic and somewhat materialistic generation always willing to work and make some quick dough to spend on video games.

"What's going on?" I rushed to head them off at the pass, thinking they must be at the wrong address.

"Oh, hi, Ms. Bixby," the fellow wearing a Patriots cap said. I'm embarrassed he knew my name, yet I couldn't put a name to his face. It occurred to me he may have been one of Paul's dance students. Was he there when Paul keeled over? Did I want to ask?

I was saved by the fellow in the Red Sox cap. "Mrs. Duffy's orders," he said. I got it. Nobody defied the mayor's wife. Nobody. So I moved aside to let them do whatever Carole had hired them to do.

In less than fifteen minutes, a large white tent, tables, and chairs were set up on the lawn area between the back of the main house and the cottage. They strategically placed four standalone portable lighting fixtures. It appeared Carole was expecting a late night. It'd been years since Paul and I did any entertaining out there.

While that was happening, Sherrie disappeared into the house. I really hadn't noticed until the screen door to the kitchen slammed, driving my shoulders up close to my ears. When she returned with a look like she thought I'd lost my manners, she handed me two twenties, jutting her chin toward the two guys.

"I would've taken care of it," I said with a glare. "You're slipping, though. You could've gotten my phone while you were at it. I need to call Carole."

Sherrie spun on her heels and went back into the house while I thanked the guys and tipped them accordingly.

A couple of hours later, as I stepped out of the shower and wrapped a towel around me and opened the door, I heard a husky "Ahem."

"You could've joined me," I said to Budd as he lifted himself off the rocking chair in the opposite corner of the bedroom, taking two steps toward me.

"I'm here now." He opened his arms wide. I didn't bite.

"That you are. But then I'd have to shower once more," I said cheekily, half hoping he'd ignore my brush off. I missed him. I checked the time on my phone. Just under an hour before folks would be arriving. Peeking through the curtain on the window overlooking the yard between my house and the cottage, I spotted Carole and her team busy doing whatever first-class caterers did. Owning an oldies music store just had to be easier than her line of work.

I sensed Budd approaching. "There's time," he advocated on his behalf, bolstering his case with a sweet kiss on my neck.

I swiveled around. The towel found its way to the floor. He was right.

CHAPTER FORTY-SIX

Carole's idea of an impromptu gathering was not quite an Open House, but without a doubt, the gang was all there. The entire cast of the Sisters' List of Suspects was accounted for. Besides Budd, who came early, Carole, of course, was already milling around when I made my entrance, damp hair and all. Luckily, the red and white floral V-neck half sleeve midi dress I'd slipped on needed no ironing, though my hair could've used more than a quick brushing.

The first to greet me was Simon Duffy, the mayor. Was he there for me? As his wife's date? Or to represent the town in thanking me for helping put Roger P. Drake behind bars?

Which made me wonder …

What were we celebrating? When I called Carole earlier, she only said there'd be a party going on this evening at the Hilltop. "Be there, or be square," she'd said. It was my house! Why wouldn't I be there?

I spotted Jeremy and his wife on the other side of the tent. Or perhaps it was the humongous bouquet he was holding that caught my eye as I scanned the crowd.

I made it easy for him and headed over to greet him. "Great job today," he said. "These are for you, Ms. Bixby."

I reminded him it's Venus. "Are these from your home garden?" Jeremy nodded; his wife grinned ear to ear. "Thank you. And welcome to my home. So nice of you to be here."

"I'll take those," Carole said, scurrying off inside the house. She'd visited enough times to know where I stored the vases. I trusted she'd find one big enough.

Minutes later, three bells chimed. "Dinner is served," the mayor declared. Ah, that was why he was there. He was Carole's wingman of sorts.

Carole gave Sherrie and me the high sign; we should start the buffet line. Carole outdid herself. There was something for everyone. Lobster sliders for seafood lovers. Prime rib, ready and carved to perfection for meat eaters. A huge green salad with every seasonal vegetable imaginable for just about everybody. As I was about to place a petite dinner roll on top of my overflowing plate, I turned and noticed a long line of hungry guests.

Besides the usual suspects (no pun intended), the entire gang of *Bixby's Dozen* (let's just say, the remaining twelve) and their significant others chatted amongst themselves, having a grand ol' time.

I felt my cheeks warm and flushed, and it wasn't just the result of the Sangria I'd been drinking. I was so thankful Paul brought me there to live so many years ago. Thankful for people like Helen Davis and Billy Bomba, who I recalled were extremely instrumental over the past week. First, with planning what ended up being my aborted birthday celebration, and then stepping in without a clue of what was happening during the reenactment that morning. Given all this hullabaloo, I wondered if the time had come for Helen to shut her precious binder once and for all?

Thankful, too, for the next generation. People like Cecilia Powers, who was also there. She was about the age I was when Paul and I married and settled down. With one foot in the museum as a docent, and the other in *Bixby's Dozen*, it seemed Cecilia decided to make Chatham Crossing her home for the foreseeable future. Lucky for us.

As Sherrie and I grabbed a table and were about to dig in, I caught sight of Sadie making nice with Detective Donovan and his wife at the end of the buffet line.

"Look who's here," I said to Sherrie between mouthfuls, waving my fork in the air. It was nice to see Oscar in street clothes for once, though he gave me a tip of his imaginary cap when he noticed me noticing him. I was also not at all surprised their respective offspring chose not to attend these festivities. After all, it was Friday. Date night.

I felt a hand on my shoulder. "You missed your appointment today," Gabby said. She touched my hair, dry and totally unruly. My natural waves had a life of their own. I apologized for forgetting. "None needed." She flashed the *call me* sign. "Whenever …"

As the sun set and the July temperature cooled ever so slightly, many of the guests guzzled their last drinks and bid goodnight to one another. Over and over again as they were leaving I said, "We should do this again sometime.

Soon." Except … I wasn't so sure I really meant *do this again*. Who in their right mind would want to get knee-deep into solving a murder, let alone two, ever again?

"They didn't stay for dessert!" Sherrie gasped as she tapped my arm.

I told her maybe there wasn't any dessert beyond the leftover cookies Carole had brought over from the museum. She frowned. We both inherited our mother's sweet tooth, among other things. Like our love of oldies music.

It'd been a long day. For everyone. Especially for those who decided to stick around. I was touched as I noticed Simon pitching in to help Carole package up the leftovers, gather up the trash. Not sure if she was in second, third, or fourth gear, but she showed no signs of slowing down. Bless her heart.

Sherrie appeared with a large pitcher of Sangria and announced coffee was brewing for those who'd prefer it. I saw her glance at Oscar. Knowing my sister as I did, if it were up to her, no one would receive a DUI driving home. Smartly, most hangers-on opted for either coffee or a bottle of water.

I hadn't seen Budd in a while. Not sure why, but he kept his distance during dinner, mingling with the guests instead of hanging with me. Or maybe it was just my imagination. The party foiled any prospect of our customary cuddling time earlier. Even so, I for one would've welcomed a gentle, familiar squeeze from him now and then. But never mind, I assured myself, there'd be plenty of time for that. His innocence meant I wouldn't have to find a new renter for the cottage any time soon.

While clean up continued and drinks refreshed, Jeremy and Budd folded up about half of the chairs, rearranging the tables while they were at it. On one of them, Budd set up a boom box, while Jeremy connected some speakers. It appeared the real party was about to begin.

CHAPTER FORTY-SEVEN

"Let's sit for a while," said Oscar, who apparently would rather chat than sing or dance. Once a copper, always a copper. No one countermanded him. The boom box remained silent as well.

Budd finally approached me and took the seat to my right. Sherrie, naturally, was still hovering nearby to my left.

Once everyone settled down, Budd said, "How about some closure? Shouldn't we tie up some loose ends?"

"You mean like how my sister was able to nab Roger?" Leave it to Sherrie to jump-start the conversation.

"Or, Mrs. Hawkins, here's a question," said Jeremy in a surprising show of confidence. "After Poseidon was stolen, weren't you afraid Amphi-Amphitrite would be too?"

"And how is it, Venus, that Budd was suspect number one?" Leave it to Carole to single out the elephant in the room, or maybe she was just relieved the elephant wasn't her.

"Easy," Budd said, not at all shy in his response to her. "I'm always first on her list, aren't I?" He reached over and put his arm around me. Finally, a public display of affection, even if it was just a shoulder hug.

"So many questions!" Oscar said. "We could be here all night!"

"Like that's gonna happen." Turning to Sadie, I said, "Let's start with Amphitrite. Wasn't having one treasured statue stolen enough? How could you risk losing another one?"

Sadie bent over her knees in a fit of laughter. "Gotcha! Amphitrite was a fake."

"You mean Amphitrite wasn't Poseidon's wife?" Sherrie asked.

"Of course, she was. The fake was that statue this morning! What do you all take me for? I'd never make the same mistake twice."

I could feel a collective sigh of relief.

"No one had laid eyes on the real Amphitrite, right?" Sadie reminded us.

We all nodded.

"She's hidden safely under lock and key. Once we set our plan in motion the other day, I simply drove over to the popular house wrecking place in Providence and found a statue that could pass as a beautiful goddess. Polished her up, and voila! No one would be the wiser. After all, no one can tell the difference—real or fake—between a Greek or Roman goddess."

"I can!" Budd lifted my hand in the air. My face contorted between a grin and a grimace. *Careful, my thumb,* I thought, but didn't say it.

"Since you've raised your hand, Budd," said Sherrie, "I think it's time for you to come clean about your involvement in this mess. You just about drove my sister to kick you to the curb."

He patted my lap. "Sorry about that."

"You've got a lot of *splainin'* to do. Get to it," I said.

Budd rose to his feet, as if he thought it was necessary to get our attention. He started by acknowledging how logical it was for me to consider him a suspect. After all, he'd known Ms. Margaret (as he referred to her) for a long time. They had a history together, but not the romantic kind. They'd worked together at the Chadborn estate in Maine. And, of course, he was the first one to see her at the museum Saturday morning when he unlocked the premises for her.

"But, as we know, I wasn't the last to see her alive."

"Nor was I," I said, shooting a glance at Carole, who simply shrugged and patted her chest. Must have been her way of admitting a mistake. Not quite a public apology, though.

"Why did Maggie follow you here from Maine?" Sherrie asked.

Budd explained that when he left Chadborn's, Maggie was the only person who knew his whereabouts—that he'd left the state. So, when she decided to leave Brian, she contacted him, hoping to get out of Maine too. He was sympathetic to her situation, having witnessed on occasion what a bastard Brian could be to her. He wanted to help her escape her life with him anyway he possibly could.

"I know how it goes. I, too, left some of my life behind when I arrived here in Chatham Crossing. A past I seldom talk about," Budd said, lowering his head.

What did he say? A past I didn't know about? I was all ears. But he didn't go down that path. Not yet, anyway.

Instead, he explained how Maggie had asked him if he knew where she could get a job and hide out for a while, especially until the divorce was final.

"That's when I recommended her to Sadie."

Sadie nodded.

"I could say the rest is history, but that would be a bit cruel under the circumstances."

"You could say that," Sherrie said.

Not knowing where he was headed with this, I shifted in my seat and reached for Sherrie's hand.

"So, Budd, how did you know Roger P. Drake?" I asked, sucking in as much air as possible.

Budd ran his fingers through his hair. "It's the part of my past I'm not proud of. And one of the reasons I left Maine. You know, the Pine Tree State can get pretty dull, especially during the winter. If you're not a skier, which I am not, there's not much to do besides drink and watch football. Pretty monotonous, if you ask me."

As an avid New England Patriots fan, I could not relate to his assessment of the season. But I wouldn't hold it against him.

"Ms. Margaret's husband introduced me to Roger Drake. He didn't include the *P* in his name at the time. Not sure when he started inserting it. In retrospect, not so important, eh?"

Unbeknownst to Budd, he just confirmed his connection to Brian and Roger. At least to me. I shot a glance in Oscar's direction. I bet he knew the rest of Budd's story.

Evidently, among his many talents, Roger was a bookmaker, and not the legitimate kind. He was a bookie who preyed on bored men who hung out in the dive bars in Maine on game days watching football on cable television.

"I'm embarrassed to say in front of all of you, especially you, Venus, that I got in over my head. So, when I got my chance, I hightailed it out of town and found a little piece of heaven right here in Chatham Crossing."

"More than a little piece it looks like," Sherrie said. I turned and looked daggers at her. Was she really making me the butt of her humor? I was not laughing. No one else was either. Thank goodness for the mayor.

"But Roger showed up here in town months ago. Back in September, right?" Simon said.

It was Budd's turn to sigh big time. "That he did. I never asked how he tracked me down. But once he did, we made a deal neither of us could refuse. I'd pay off my debt to him over time, which I did. In exchange, he'd stay out of my affairs and I'd stay out of his. Frankly, I was surprised he tried to settle down and become a good citizen of this community. He got an apartment, a job, was reading to elementary school kids. Even a gig with *Bixby's Dozen*!"

"Maybe he was trying to turn over a new leaf?" As soon as Sadie uttered those words, she looked at Jeremy, her master gardener, and then added, "Strike that. My bad."

"How did Roger hook up with Maggie … romantically? Did they know each other before? In Maine?" Jeremy's wife spoke up, asking questions I'm sure we were all thinking.

"The bars we hung out in up there were off limits to wives and girlfriends, as weird as that may sound. Roger pretty much operated under the radar." Budd said. "So, Ms. Margaret never laid eyes on Roger, or him on her. Until they met here in Chatham Crossing one night in February at Whaler's Watch Pub."

Budd admitted at first he didn't put two and two together when Maggie decided to move to Chatham Crossing. He didn't see any harm in it. Roger and she traveled in different circles. He figured the chances their lives would collide were slim. In his mind, anyway.

"This is a small town, Budd, if you haven't noticed," the mayor said.

"True. I found that out soon enough. And I tried to nip it in the bud before it went too far."

"What do you mean?" I asked.

"Like I said, I'd known Ms. Margaret for years, so she confided in me when she started seeing Roger. At that point, I had a choice to make. Do I tell her about the connection between Roger and Brian? Or do I warn Roger not to contact Brian and give him a heads up that his wife was here. If he did that, I'd reveal his past. He could lose a chance to start a new life." Budd looked at Sadie. "Because I believed both Ms. Margaret and Roger deserved a second chance, I chose the latter."

"Apparently, it didn't work," Sherrie said.

"Oh, but I think it did," Budd said. "For a while anyway. They seemed happy with whatever romantic relationship was brewing between them."

"So, why did he kill her?" Jeremy asked.

"It's my turn now," Oscar said. Both he and Budd were standing. "Those of you who were at the museum this morning heard Roger claim it was an accident, right?"

Everyone nodded, even folks like Simon and Jeremy's wife who didn't hear Roger say it firsthand, but most likely heard it indirectly from their spouses.

"Hardly matters what I think," Budd said, interrupting the detective. "But I believe Roger didn't intend to harm Ms. Margaret when he showed up Saturday morning. It was a cookie delivery gone bad. It's a shame the closed circuit cameras weren't working. If they had been, I bet we'd have seen Roger arrive just after nine-thirty. Soon thereafter, they argue about the statue. He probably saw an opportunity—steal it and then sell it to the highest bidder."

"But she fought for it, right?" Sadie said, her voice wobbling. "I knew I could count on her to protect Poseidon. I just couldn't have imagined doing so would cost Maggie her life." Sadie closed her eyes, placed her hands on her thighs, inhaled deeply, and bowed her head.

Best thing about meditation: *It's portable.*

"And in the struggle, she fell," Budd said, as he bowed his head.

Talk about putting a damper on a party. It must have been contagious because we all joined Budd and Sadie in a moment of silence without being encouraged to do so.

"If it was an accident, he could've run, or even called, to get some-some help. But he just left her there in the pachysandra?" Jeremy said.

"That's why we're considering charging him with involuntary manslaughter in the case of Margaret McGee. We'll see. Time and further forensic analysis will tell," Oscar said.

"So that explains two crimes. What about Brian McGee? Roger confessed, right?" Carole said.

"I should confess something, as well," Budd interjected. "I ran into Brian in the museum's lobby Monday afternoon. I guess he was there just to check out where Ms. Margaret had worked. So, I offered to buy him a drink at the Whaler's Watch later that evening. He was very much alive when I left him there."

"You're off the hook, Budd," Oscar said. "Others at the pub confirmed you left alone."

I let out a sigh. Budd smiled at me slightly.

"Because Drake came clean, that case is easier to solve," Oscar said. "You'll recall after Ms. McGee died, we searched for her next of kin. Someone on the force tracked down her husband, Brian, and gave him the news. After identifying her body, quite possibly he went to her apartment. That's when he probably spotted Roger's car in the parking lot. It's hard to miss. According to Roger's account, late Monday night they argued and had a fist fight on Morgan's Bridge. Brian lost. In the melee, Roger strangled him and tossed him over the side."

"Ouch," I said as I noticed everyone grimacing.

"Did they scuffle over Maggie?" Sherrie asked. "A crime of passion, perhaps?"

"Either that or greed, wouldn't you think?" Budd asked Oscar.

"Given Roger's past and what he was carrying around in his backpack, greed is a good guess. Or he panicked, fearing Brian would out him for who he really was. Not a pirate, after all."

"Once a scoundrel, always a scoundrel, if you ask me," Sherrie said.

"Strange, though, he stuck around," Jeremy said. "Did-didn't leave town Tuesday after Brian's b-body was found."

Oscar surmised Roger thought he was invincible. He could merely hide in plain sight. He'd left Maine without a trace. More than likely he would've beat it out of Chatham Crossing sooner rather than later. "We're checking on unsolved crimes, and aliases, too, throughout New England. Like Ms. Moore said, 'Once a scoundrel.'"

"Which brings us to Venus," Sherrie said. "Oh, sister extraordinaire, do tell us how you fingered Roger P. Drake?"

I could've stood like the two spokespeople before me, but I chose to stay anchored in my chair. I was going to make this short and sweet. No need for lengthy dramatics. Everyone knew the ending.

I simply said, "The autopsy." Why make things complicated when two words were more than enough? At first, I raised both palms in the air as if to say, "There you have it." Then I rested my case by interlacing my fingers, avoiding a collision with my thumb and placing my hands on my lap.

"Oh, poppycock, Venus. Go on. Out with it. No time to suddenly become shy." Sherrie bumped my elbow.

As if my sister had pushed *Play* on my voice box, I began to roll out the rest of the story. I was sure Paul was forgiving my verbosity from up above. He always did.

"Originally, when we put the plan together to stage the events of last Saturday morning, our intent was to pressure whoever was involved in the mess to confess under the stress of the reenactment. And yes, I had a list. Or rather, Sherrie and I had a list of people we identified as having the opportunity ... since they'd seen Maggie that day. Figuring out their motives, though, stumped us royally." I glanced at Sherrie who flipped two thumbs up.

"They shared their list with me," Oscar confirmed as he looked around the group. "And, let's see, we know Budd was on it. Sadie, and Jeremy. Oh, and you, too, Carole."

"Carole?" Simon roared, "that's absurd!"

"Chill, Simon," I said. "We quickly ruled out Sadie, Jeremy, and yes, Carole." Then, I turned to Budd. "Unfortunately, you were a conundrum. You don't know what I've been going through all week." I sucked in some air and then let out a hefty sigh. "All's well that ends well ..."

"Little did we expect Roger P. Drake would climb aboard the list, so to speak. But leave it to my sister," Sherrie boasted.

"She's right," I said. "Roger wasn't on our list until breakfast this morning. The autopsy changed all that."

"Suddenly, Budd had some competition for *Villain of Chatham Crossing*," Sherrie said.

"Not funny." I gave her a slight, but emphatic, punch in the arm.

"Not funny," Budd said, leaning past me and glaring at her. If looks could speak, I was confident he'd be suggesting she hop the next flight to San Francisco.

Anyway, I continued with the tale of how I parsed together somewhat unrelated details for the investigators. I purposely refrained from calling out Detective Donovan, in particular, for not solving these crimes himself. Instead, I stuck with the facts and my observations.

While I acknowledged I couldn't tie Roger to Poseidon, I stated unequivocally that I believed the autopsy proved Roger was the last one to see Maggie alive.

"Besides that, Venus's eagle-eye account of Roger interacting with a stranger in front of his apartment set off even more bells and whistles," Oscar said.

"Thanks," I said. On a roll, I took back an imaginary microphone. "As it happened, I shared with the good detective a very pleasant, though impromptu, lunch and repartee I had on Monday with Roger at Captain's Catch—their lobster roll is to die for …" Oops, I stopped, caught my blunder momentarily, then continued.

"I can report, he was quite the gentleman—the vintage Roger we all thought we were beginning to know and accept into our fold. Attired in full pirate mode, of course. All in black, except for his white bandana. When I asked for a dab of his hand sanitizer, I even noticed a ring he was wearing. Kind of dull, unlike the diamond pierced earring he always wore. The ring had some letters on it I didn't recognize then.

"Anyway, I digress. After he disposed of our lunch litter, he walked me back to my car that just happened to be parked in the lot next to the apartment complex that he … and Maggie, by the way … lived. 'Neighbors with benefits,' he said."

I couldn't help but notice more than one set of eyebrows raised, coupled with multiple side glances. Not sure if the reaction was to Roger and Maggie's living and relationship arrangements or present company's. Neither Budd nor I offered any explanation or apologies. If the shoe fits.

"In any event, we chatted briefly among the cars. Then, Roger seemed distracted by a man standing in front of what I assumed was his apartment door. He waved to the fellow, shouted 'What a surprise,' and politely excused himself."

"Did you recognize him, Venus? The other man?" Sadie asked, as if I didn't know which fellow she meant.

"Goodness, no! He had to have been new in town. He was wearing a New York Yankees jersey."

"Heaven forbid," Sherrie said, somewhat under her breath.

"Don't be so fast to criticize your sister, Ms. Moore," Oscar said. "That detail, along with the white bandana, was critical in our connecting Roger to Brian."

"White bandana?" I heard at least three among us say at the same time.

"When we found him floating in the Crescent River, Brian McGee was wearing a New York Yankees shirt and he was clutching a white bandana. As Venus noted, a signature trademark of one Roger P. Drake."

Everyone but Sherrie and I gasped. She was with me when I met with Oscar earlier in the day when I handed him everything I knew on a silver platter, including what leaped out at me on the autopsy report.

"Not his only trademark," I said. "It seems he took this whole pirating thing way too seriously, even down to the ring I mentioned … and his license plate."

"How's that?" Sadie asked.

"Apparently, the ring he wore is associated with the explorer Francis Drake. In his day, some considered him a privateer, a pirate. Sherrie and I spotted similar rings yesterday in Nantucket."

Sherrie nodded.

"But it was his license plate that completed the triangle: cookies, ring, and car."

Mostly everyone looked at me like I was from outer space. I glanced at Sherrie assuming she'd appreciate the triangle reference. "Go on," she said with a wink.

"Jolly! His license plate is Jolly. Jolly Roger! Get it? The Jolly Roger is the pirate flag! And the decoration on the cookies he made for last weekend's event, as well as for today's. He passed them around the store on Monday and even gave a couple to me. They're probably still in my purse. Shall I get them?"

"No need to," Carole said, reassuringly. "Go on with your story."

Since I'd read the words in the autopsy report often enough since early that morning, I was confident I had them right. In an instant, they flowed off my tongue as if I was singing "Sweet Caroline" during a Red Sox game.

"The autopsy said, '*The stomach contains undigested sugar cookies and white and black gel food coloring.*'"

"There you have it," Sherrie said, "his Jolly Roger cookie nailed him."

"If only he'd stuck to making chocolate chips. But no, his obsession with being a pirate busted him," Carole said.

"I guess that's the way the cookie crumbles." Budd added. I rubbed the back of my neck, pleasantly humored at his attempt at a joke. So uncharacteristic of him. I guess it was another side of him I didn't know before.

Of course, the first being his history of being a gamblin'
man.

"And that's all I have to say about Roger P. Drake.
This case is closed as far as I'm concerned." I raised my
left thumb up as best as I could, knowing a replacement
splint was in my future.

"This calls for dessert." Carole rushed into the house
with Sadie close behind.

Minutes later, Sadie emerged from the kitchen with
Carole in tow, carrying a cake with way too many candles blazing. Couldn't she have lit just two candles: a 5
and a 0? On Sadie's signal, the gathering sang "Happy
Birthday"—with the refrain, *happy birthday dear Venus
and Sherrie, happy birthday to … you both!*

Cheers and applause abounded.

As each of my friends wished my sister and me health
and happiness, I felt rewarded and blessed. For the first
time in a week, I was optimistic happy days were certainly
ahead in Chatham Crossing.

I was content knowing that Sadie could showcase
Poseidon and his goddess side by side at the Sofia Silva
Whaling Museum, never again removing them from behind the locked glass display. That Jeremy would never
permit another party to be scheduled in the gardens as
long as he was in charge. That Carole would delight in the
fact that she needed to make a critical decision. Should
Bixby's Dozen add one more cookie baker, or should she
leave it at twelve, since Roger was in the clink?

I was confident Detective Donovan would ultimately
determine whether Margaret McGee's death was an accident or not. When I imagined offering to read the final

forensic results, I also imagined he'd date himself and hum a few bars of Hank Williams's 1986 song "Mind Your Own Business." If and when that happened, rather than respond with a witty rejoinder, I would keep my options open and merely mumble, "We'll see about that."

I was relieved Budd wouldn't be going anywhere soon, especially not to jail. He'd probably be called as a witness if Roger ever came to trial. For that matter, that probably made the two of us. I'd cross that bridge whenever. Until then, I intended to spend quality time getting to know the fellow who resided in my cottage better than I obviously already did. Who knew what the future would bring?

Speaking of the future. In just a couple of days Sherrie would be heading back to San Francisco, where she had left her heart and her family. My invitation stood for her to celebrate the holidays with me. She'd yet to make a commitment. "I'll surprise you," she said.

I soaked in the moment. The smiles on the faces of everyone around me brought me joy—like New England clam chowder for my soul. Time had come to give back the best way I knew how.

Over their clamoring and laughter, I shouted, "Hey, what's your favorite song?" That got their attention.

Never one to be first on the dance floor, Budd volunteered to be our disc jockey. Safely sequestered behind the table with the boom box, he was obviously having a whale of a time taking our requests.

It was getting close to midnight when we sang and rocked out to "Birthday" by the Beatles. After Budd whispered something to Jeremy, the stand-alone lights went dark, leaving just the spotlights on my house and the cottage illuminating the yard. Then Budd announced, "Final dance," and offered me his hand. "Shall we?"

I could name the song he chose for us in one note. "At Last" gave new meaning to oldies and goodies.

CHAPTER FORTY-EIGHT

The Chatham Crossing Chronicle
Cat-astrophe Averted to Purr-fection

By: Daniel DaRosa, Investigative Reporter

BREAKING NEWS! **Saturday, July 17, 2010, 1:30 p.m.** Good times, or at least better times, were celebrated at the Sofia Silva Whaling Museum (SSWM) this morning. If you don't believe the ancient Greek poet Menander who said time heals all wounds, just ask Sandra Hawkins, the museum's curator.

Two weeks ago, SSWM was rocked by the its first ever double scandal—a murder and a robbery. But thanks to the combined investigative prowess of Chatham Crossing's police department and one of our own long-time residents, the crimes were solved quicker than a rainbow evaporates after a thunderstorm. According to Mayor Simon Duffy, a lengthy investigation could have been detrimental to the town's tourist industry.

In a ceremony at the museum earlier today, Mrs. Hawkins made good on her offer of a $25,000 reward to whoever provided information leading to the safe return of the nearly priceless Poseidon statue.

Mrs. Hawkins expressed her gratitude when she presented a certified check to Venus Bixby, owner of Oldies & Goodies. "Ms. Bixby's dogged determination was instrumental in returning Poseidon to his rightful home."

When asked what she planned to do with this windfall, Ms. Bixby announced she'll be expanding her business portfolio right here in Chatham Crossing. Rumor had it she was interested in owning the museum's gift shop. Apparently, that was just a rumor. Instead, she told the story of having to travel upstate to Newburyport to adopt her two kitties, Sonny and Cher, and of the challenge of finding day care for them in her absence.

"The days of our town not offering premium and dependable resources for cat lovers are coming to an end," Ms. Bixby said. "I intend to open Cats & Their Cradle—the first cat adoption and pet sitting service in Chatham

Crossing. If all goes according to plan, our cats will no longer need to be caged when their owners take a vacation, and kiddies will have new kitties to play with by the time the upcoming holiday season is upon us."

As a cat lover, this reporter applauds Ms. Bixby for her generosity. But is there anyone in town truly qualified to manage this new venture? And where in town will it be located?

To find out if the Town Committee approves Ms. Bixby's proposal, follow this story.

Print and digital editions.

Thank you for reading A WHALE OF A MURDER, the first book in the Venus Bixby Mystery series.

A story about oldies music and a cookie bakery would not be complete without a playlist and recipes. I do hope you enjoy what follows!

A WHALE OF A MURDER PLAYLIST
On Spotify.com

https://spoti.fi/3SuJGcE

Access songs depicting the story on the *A Whale of a Murder Playlist* on Spotify.com, which is free*!

Tall Paul, *Annette Funicello*
Venus, *Frankie Avalon*
Oh! Carol, *Neil Sedaka*
We're Off To See The Wizard, *Judy Garland, Ray Bolger*
Garden Party, *Ricky Nelson, The Stone Canyon Band*
Don't Worry Be Happy, *Bobby McFerrin*
Memory, *Andrew Lloyd Webber, "Cats"*
Ticket to Ride, *The Beatles*
The Lusty Month of May, *Vanessa Redgrave, Lee Herschberg*
Bridge Over Troubled Water, *Simon & Garfunkel*
A Pirate's Life for Me, *Scarecrow Jack*
Only In America, *Brooks & Dunn*
I Heard It Through The Grapevine, *Marvin Gaye*
Love and Marriage, *Frank Sinatra*
Light My Fire, *The Doors*
Sherry, *Frankie Valli & The Four Seasons*
You're So Vain, *Carly Simon*
Kumbaya, *Peter, Paul and Mary*
Oh, What A Beautiful Morning, *Gordon Macrae, Darcy M. Proper*

Pirates Of The Caribbean, *The Intermezzo Orchestra*
It's Five O'Clock Somewhere, *Alan Jackson, Jimmy Buffett*
Magical Mystery Tour, *The Beatles*
I Got You Babe, *Sonny & Cher*
I Feel the Earth Move, *Carole King*
Is That All There Is?, *Peggy Lee*
She Works Hard For The Money, *Donna Summer*
Joy To The World, *Three Dog Night*
Sweet Caroline, *Neil Diamond*
Splish Splash, *Bobby Darin*
Mind Your Own Business, *Hank Williams, Reba McEntire*
Birthday, *The Beatles*
At Last, *Etta James*

*Best browsers for Spotify's Web Player are Google Chrome, Firefox, Edge, and Opera.

RECIPES

Many thanks to my friends who graciously responded to my request for their favorite recipe.

While not directly attributable to *Bixby's Dozen*, we can imagine the residents of Chatham Crossing and the tourists who make their annual pilgrimages there savoring each and every one of these goodies. I hope you will too!

RAINBOW COOKIES
From the kitchen of Kathleen Craig

INGREDIENTS & INSTRUCTIONS
In a large bowl, cream:
- 1 cup butter/shortening
- ¾ cup white sugar
- ¾ cup packed brown sugar
- 2 eggs
- 1 teaspoon vanilla extract

Blend in:
- 3 ¾ cups sifted all-purpose flour
- ½ teaspoon salt
- 1 teaspoon baking soda

Divide the dough into 4 sections:
- Add a few drops of different colors of food coloring to each (1 color per section).
- On wax paper pat each color into strips 8 inches long and 4 inches wide and ¼ inch thick.
- Stack 4 sections on top of each other.
- Refrigerate a few hours.
- Cut into ¼ inch slices and curve into arches.

Bake at 375°F on ungreased cookie sheet about 7 minutes or until done.

TOFFEEDODDLES

From the kitchen of Kathy Danheim

INGREDIENTS

- 1 cup unsalted butter, room temperature
- 1 ½ cups plus 2 tablespoons Imperial Sugar Extra Fine Granulated Sugar
- 1 teaspoon vanilla extract
- 2 eggs
- 2 ¾ cups all-purpose flour*
- 1 teaspoon cream of tartar
- ½ teaspoon baking soda
- ¼ teaspoon salt
- 1 cup toffee bits
- 2 teaspoons cinnamon

INSTRUCTIONS

- Preheat oven to 350°F.
- Line two baking sheets with parchment paper. Set aside.
- Cream butter and 1 ½ cups sugar in bowl of an electric mixer until light and fluffy (about 5 minutes).
- Add vanilla and eggs.
- Slowly add flour, cream of tartar, baking soda, and salt. Mix until combined.
- Reduce speed to low and add toffee bits.
- In a small bowl, combine remaining sugar and cinnamon.
- Use a tablespoon scoop to portion cookies and roll into a ball.

- Coat dough in cinnamon sugar.
- Place on prepared sheets, 2 inches apart.
- Bake 10 to 12 minutes.
- Let cool on pans for 2 minutes, then transfer to a wire rack to cool completely.

*SPECIAL NOTE: Spoon & Sweep method. Use a spoon to fill measuring cup with flour until required amount is obtained. Scooping measuring cup directly into flour bag will firmly pack flour resulting in too much flour required for recipe!

SPICY CHOCOLATE CHIP COOKIES
(a.k.a. Mexican Chocolate Icebox Cookies)
From the kitchen of Renee Mirsky

INGREDIENTS

- 2 cups all-purpose flour
- 2 teaspoons baking powder
- ½ teaspoon cayenne pepper
- 1 teaspoon ground cinnamon
- ¼ teaspoon salt
- 8 tablespoons unsalted butter (1 stick), room temperature
- ½ cup granulated sugar
- ½ cup lightly packed light brown sugar
- ¼ cup milk
- ½ teaspoon vanilla extract
- 1 large egg, room temperature
- 2 cups semisweet chocolate chips or finely chopped dark chocolate

INSTRUCTIONS

- Preheat oven to 350°F and arrange rack in the middle.
- In a medium bowl, whisk together the flour, baking powder, cayenne, cinnamon and salt. Set aside.
- Mix the butter and sugar in a large mixing bowl on medium speed until light and fluffy, about 3 to 5 minutes.
- Add milk and vanilla, blend well.
- Add egg and mix well.

- On low speed, add flour mixture and mix until just incorporated.
- Fold in chocolate chips or chopped chocolate.
- Turn dough onto a piece of plastic wrap, shape it into a log about 12 inches long and 1 ½ inches in diameter. Wrap tight. *(You can totally skip forming it into a log. Just place covered cookie dough in the fridge and form into balls later.)* Place in the refrigerator until firm, at least 1 hour but preferably 8 hours.
- Remove cookie dough from the refrigerator and form into 1/5 inch sized balls.
- Place on an ungreased baking sheet and bake until golden brown on the bottom, about 12 to 14 minutes.

SOFT AND CHEWY CHOCOLATE CHIP COOKIES
Recommended by Karen Plaster
Recipe from the *Martha Stewart Test Kitchen*

INGREDIENTS

- 2 ¼ cups all-purpose flour
- ½ teaspoon baking soda
- 2 sticks (1 cup) unsalted butter, room temperature
- ½ cup granulated sugar
- 1 cup packed light brown sugar
- 1 teaspoon kosher salt
- 2 teaspoons pure vanilla extract
- 2 large eggs
- 12 ounces semisweet chocolate chips (2 cups)

INSTRUCTIONS

- Preheat oven to 350°F with racks in the upper and lower third positions. Line baking sheets with parchment paper.
- In a small bowl, whisk together flour and baking soda; set aside.
- In the bowl of a stand mixer fitted with the paddle attachment, beat butter and both sugars.
- Add salt, vanilla, and eggs; mix to combine. Reduce speed to low.
- Gradually add flour mixture, mixing until just combined.
- Mix in chocolate chips.
- Using a tablespoon measure or a small ice-cream scoop (for uniform cookies), drop heaping

portions of dough about 2 inches apart onto prepared baking sheets.

- Bake until cookies are golden around the edges, but still soft in the center, 8 to 10 minutes.
- Remove from oven, and let cool on baking sheet 1 to 2 minutes.
- Transfer cookies to a wire rack and let cool completely.
- Store cookies in an airtight container at room temperature up to 1 week.

VANISHING RAISIN OATMEAL COOKIES
From the kitchen of Tambi Smith

INGREDIENTS

- 1 cup softened butter
- 1 cup brown sugar -- packed
- ½ cup granulated sugar
- 2 large eggs
- 1 teaspoon vanilla
- 1 ½ cup all-purpose flour
- 1 teaspoon cinnamon
- ½ teaspoon salt (optional)
- 3 cups uncooked quick oats
- 1 cup raisins (or craisins, nuts, chocolate chips, or a combination)

INSTRUCTIONS

- Preheat oven to 350°F.
- In bowl, beat together the brown sugar, sugar, and butter.
- Add eggs. Mix well.
- Add vanilla. Mix well.
- Add flour, cinnamon, and salt. Mix well.
- Stir in oats and raisins.
- Drop by tablespoon on ungreased cookie sheet.
- Bake 10 to 12 minutes until golden brown.
- Cool for 1 minute on cookie sheet before moving to cooling rack.
- Store airtight.
- Makes 4 dozen 2 ½ inch cookies.

CHOCOLATE CHIP COOKIES

From the kitchen of Tammy Pasterick, author of
Beneath the Veil of Smoke and Ash

INGREDIENTS

- 2 ¼ cups all-purpose flour
- 1 teaspoon baking soda
- 1 cup butter (softened)
- ¼ cup sugar
- ¾ cup light brown sugar
- 1 teaspoon vanilla
- 1 4-serving package vanilla instant pudding
- 2 eggs
- 1 12-ounce package chocolate chips

INSTRUCTIONS

- Preheat oven to 375°F.
- Mix flour with baking soda.
- Combine butter, sugar, pudding mix, and vanilla in a bowl. Beat until smooth and creamy. Then, beat in eggs.
- Gradually add flour mixture.
- Stir in chocolate chips.
- Place drops of batter (rounded teaspoons) two inches apart on ungreased cookie sheets.
- Bake for 8 to 10 minutes.

AUNT HONEY'S BUTTER COOKIES

From the kitchen of Deborah K. Shepherd, author of
So Happy Together

INGREDIENTS

- 2 sticks butter
- 2 egg yolks
- 2/3 cup sugar
- Salt
- 1 teaspoon vanilla
- 2 ¼ cups all-purpose flour
- 1 teaspoon baking powder

INSTRUCTIONS

- Preheat oven to 350°F.
- Cream butter and sugar.
- Add egg yolks and vanilla and a little salt.
- Add rest of ingredients.
- Mix and roll into ball.
- Refrigerate overnight (or at least a few hours).
- Roll by teaspoonful and press each ball with a fork.
- Bake for 11-13 minutes.
- Do not brown.

GINGERBREAD MEN

From Kim Gravell, author of *The Dark Places* trilogy, from her kitchen in Wales, U.K.

INGREDIENTS

- 1 ¾ cups (13 ounces) all-purpose flour
- 1 teaspoon baking soda (a.k.a. bicarbonate of soda)
- 3 teaspoons ground ginger
- 4 ounces unsalted butter (cold & cubed)
- 6 ounces light brown sugar, softened
- 5 tablespoons golden syrup (or maple syrup or honey)
- 1 large egg

INSTRUCTIONS

- Preheat oven to 375°F (190°C/180°C fan) and line 3 baking trays with parchment paper.
- Add the flour, baking soda, and ground ginger to a large bowl and add the cold, cubed unsalted butter to the bowl.
- Rub the mixture together with your fingertips until it resembles breadcrumbs! (Or mix the four ingredients in a food processor till it's breadcrumbs!)
- Mix the sugar into the mix and combine, and then add the golden syrup and egg— beat with a spatula (or your hands) until it is a smooth dough.
- Knead the biscuit dough in the bowl slightly to bring it together and then roll the dough out onto a lightly floured work surface.

- Roll it out to a ¼ inch (or ½ centimeter) thickness and cut out your desired shapes (approximately 16 gingerbread men).
- Place them on the lined baking trays and bake in the oven for 10-11 minutes, cool on a wire rack fully.

PUMPKIN BREAD

From the kitchen of Jan Hill, author of the
Rock, Paper, Scissors Series

INGREDIENTS
(Yields three breads)
- 3 ½ cups all-purpose flour
- 3 cups sugar
- 2 teaspoon baking soda
- 1 ½ teaspoon salt
- 1 teaspoon cinnamon
- 15 ounce can of pumpkin or 15 ounce cooked, ground pumpkin
- 1 cup oil or applesauce
- 2/3 cup water
- 4 eggs
- 1 12 oz package of peanut butter, chocolate, or butterscotch chips
- 1 cup chopped nuts (optional)
- 1 cup raisins (optional)

INSTRUCTIONS
- Preheat oven to 350°F.
- Grease and flour three loaf pans (8 ½ x 4 ½ x 2 ½ inches).
- In medium mixing bowl, combine: flour, sugar, baking soda, salt, cinnamon.
- Blend in: pumpkin, oil (applesauce), water, eggs.
- Stir in: chips, nuts, raisins.
- Split mixture between the prepared pans.
- Bake 50-60 minutes or until toothpick comes out clean.

CREAM CHEESE BARS
Recommended by Leslie Rasmussen,
author of *After Happily Ever After* and
The Stories We Cannot Tell;
From the kitchen of Julia Kahan

INGREDIENTS for Crust
- · 1 cup melted butter
- · 1 cup brown sugar (packed)
- · 3 cups flour
- · ½ cup chopped nuts

INSTRUCTIONS for Crust
- · Preheat oven at 350° F.
- · Mix above ingredients into crumbs. Remove 1 ½ cups and set aside.
- · Pack the remaining crumbs into a 9 in. x 13 in. baking pan; pat hard.
- · Bake crust 12 to 15 minutes.

INGREDIENTS for Filling
- · 1 pound cream cheese
- · ½ cup sugar
- · 2 eggs
- · 4 tablespoons milk
- · 2 tablespoons lemon juice
- · 1 teaspoon vanilla

INSTRUCNS for Filling
- · Blend above filling ingredients until smooth.
- · Pour into crust.

- Sprinkle crumbs that were set aside on top of filling.

TO COMPLETE:
- Bake at 350° F for 25 minutes.
- Cool and cut into bars.
- Keep cold.

HOLLY WREATH COOKIES
From the kitchen of Monica Calzolari

INGREDIENTS
- 1 package Philadelphia Cream Cheese (1 ½ oz.)
- 1 cup sifted all-purpose flour
- ½ cup butter
- ¼ cup sugar
- ½ teaspoon vanilla extract
- Green food coloring
- Sugar sprinkles

INSTRUCTIONS
- Preheat oven to 400°F.
- This recipe, though called Holly Wreaths, requires a cookie press (consider a Christmas tree shape).
- Let butter and cream cheese sit for an hour so ingredients are room temp or soft.
- Combine butter and cream cheese; add the sugar and blend well.
- Then, add the vanilla extract and food coloring. (Green for trees; red for stars)
- Slowly add the sifted flour. Mix well.
- Put through cookie press on ungreased aluminum cookie sheets; using the star or Christmas tree plate.
- Add sprinkles or sugar and bake.
- Bake 8 to 10 minutes. Watch these cookies carefully so they don't burn.
- Yields approx. 2 dozen cookies.

JOLLY ROGER COOKIES
From Suwannee Rose at https://suwanneerose.com

A Whale of a Murder must include a Jolly Roger cookie recipe! If you are an adventurous pirate (or baker), give this recipe a try! I discovered it online. Access it at the Suwannee Rose website above.

For The Meyer Lemon Cookies
INGREDIENTS
- 2 cups unsalted butter (room temperature)
- 2 cups sugar
- 2 large eggs (room temperature)
- 1 teaspoon vanilla extract
- 1 teaspoon lemon extract
- 2 tablespoons Meyer lemon zest
- 6 cups all-purpose flour
- ½ teaspoon salt

INSTRUCTIONS
- Preheat the oven to 350°F.
- Add the butter and sugar to the bowl of a stand mixer fitted with a flat beater. Beat on medium speed until light and fluffy. Add the eggs, vanilla extract, lemon extract, and Meyer lemon zest, and beat until combined.
- In a large bowl, whisk together the flour and salt.
- If you have a bowl guard, use it. Otherwise wrap a towel around the mixer while you slowly add the flour to the mixture, half a cup at a time, while the machine is running (starting on low speed

and increasing after you've added all of it). Keep beating until a stiff dough forms in the center.

- Divide the dough into quarters and pat into discs. Wrap in plastic wrap and refrigerate until you're ready to roll.
- Roll out the dough between two sheets of wax paper (so you don't dry out your cookies with more flour) until it's ¼ inch thick. Cut cookies with a rectangular cutter, transfer to a parchment-lined baking sheet, then re-roll and cut more.
- Bake for 12-15 minutes, or until the edges are lightly golden. Repeat with the remaining dough.
- Allow the cookies to cool completely before decorating.

For the Coconut Rum Royal Icing

INGREDIENTS

- ½ cup warm water
- 6 tablespoons meringue powder
- ¾ teaspoon cream of tartar
- 1 teaspoon coconut extract
- 1 teaspoon rum extract
- 2 tablespoons Meyer lemon juice
- 2 pounds confectioner's sugar
- 1 tablespoon light corn syrup
- .5 to .75 ounce black gel food coloring
- .25 ounce white gel food coloring*

INSTRUCTIONS

- Combine the water, meringue powder, and cream of tartar in the bowl of a stand mixer fitted with

a whisk attachment. Mix on high for about 2
minutes.

- Add the coconut and rum extracts and Meyer
  lemon juice and blend again until incorporated.
- Slowly add the confectioner's sugar, about a cup at
  a time. Once you've added about half, drizzle in the
  corn syrup, then finish with the rest of the sugar.
- Divide the icing into thirds. Place one third in
  one bowl or measuring cup, and the other two
  thirds in a separate bowl or measuring cup.
- For the cup with one third, add drops of food
  coloring until it's bright white*. Once there, add
  teaspoons of water until it's the consistency of
  toothpaste. Cover and refrigerate until ready to use.
- *At this point, you might want to wear gloves
  to prevent looking as if you were juggling open
  Sharpies (as Suwannee Rose did).*
- Blend the reserved two-thirds icing with a
  tablespoon of water and 20 drops of black food
  coloring. Keep adding more food coloring while
  mixing well and it's truly, evenly black. Slowly
  add more water until it's the consistency of
  honey. Add the final icing to a squeeze bottle or a
  pastry bag fitted with a round tip.
- Once the cookies are cool, use the black icing to
  trace the outline of your flag, then squeeze on a
  dollop in the center and spread it with an offset
  spatula, butter knife, etc.
- Allow the cookies to dry for at least 5 hours.
- *Now it's time to stencil on the skull and crossbones.*
  Suwannee Rose uses a Stencil Genie to hold the

stencil in place. Dollop the white icing over the stencil, then use a plastic scraper to drag off the excess. It's best if you can do it in one motion. Gently lift up on the stencil. Repeat with the remaining cookies. *Every few cookies, you'll need to wash and dry your scraper and stencil.*

- Allow that layer to dry for another few hours and they're ready to be looted by pirates of all sizes.

NOTES

*If you want bright white, you've got to actually dye it that way, otherwise the skull and crossbones will be off-white or even yellow, depending on your extracts.

ACKNOWLEDGMENTS

How do you write an Acknowledgments page when the power goes out? When the day is dark, wet, and dreary, and there's no Internet?

As it happened, overnight a storm was so ferocious that its driving downpour and wild wind not only knocked down powerlines, but also toppled three reindeer decorations on my neighbor's lawn across the street. Yet, because I obsess over my daily checklist and crafting this page was first on today's, I'm sitting in my kitchen writing by candlelight on a purple lined pad with a felt tip pen (that I first thought was black but later discovered when power returned, that it's purple).

Nevertheless, perched here as I am, gazing at the gray fog through windows covered with pearls of raindrops, I'm motivated just thinking about writers who would never have let this incident impede their routines. Authors like Charlotte Bronte, Ernest Hemingway, Stephen King, and Joyce Carol Oates and many others who were (or are) known to write longhand rain or shine.

For all of them, I am grateful for their inspiration and am determined to not let little things like the lack of daylight or technology get in the way of jump-starting my day. As Stephen King said, "Amateurs sit and wait for inspiration; the rest of us get up and go to work."

So to work, I go … on this mission to express gratitude to the many people who encouraged me to launch the Venus Bixby Mystery series.

Starting with my *dear readers*. Thank you for taking a chance on the *What's Not* trilogy and then urging me to tackle a different genre. Along this new journey, I discovered mystery writing is extraordinarily challenging. I've a renewed admiration for mystery writers everywhere.

Further, I'm grateful to my partners in crime, as it were, that were instrumental in producing *A Whale of a Murder*. For her editing and proofreading prowess, no one is better than Melissa Norton Carro. And for her cover and interior design talent, no one can compare to Danna Mathias Steele of *Dearly Creative*. Collaborating with you both reminds me: there's no *I* in team.

Nearly seven years ago when I decided to write my first novel, I envisioned it a solo adventure. Boy, was I wrong. I quickly learned it takes a community: a group of likeminded people who unselfishly give their time and expertise to help initiate and deliver a project as intimate as a book idea.

I am blessed to have an enormous community of writing, publishing, and marketing professionals, any of whom I can reach out to even if my Internet is down. (There are far too many to name here, but you know who you are!) However, to KISS (a.k.a. to keep it simple sweety), I wouldn't have been able to write this particular book without Leslie Rasmussen, Suzanne Simonetti, and Meg Nocero (authors who "get me"); and Jan Hill and Kim Gravell (authors who share their tricks of the trade on a regular basis); or Meryl Ain and Eileen Sanchez (my Facebook buddies who are always a text away to save me when social media drives me insane).

Since the pandemic forced all of us who published in 2020 and 2021 to discover how to market our books online, the world has now opened up to book clubs, sign-ings, festivals, and fairs. I'm indebted to all the organizers and influencers that support me in my journey wherever and whenever. Special thanks to Michelle Smith of The BookSmiths Shoppe in Danbury, CT, and Amy Sheehan of The Coffee Spot of Simsbury, CT, for opening up your establishments and spotlighting my books.

You may have noticed I dedicated this book to Jimmy Buffett and wondered why. If you've finished reading *A Whale of a Murder*, you'll understand the connection. The manuscript was well underway when he died in September. Jimmy Buffett's music inspired me before and during my writing this story. He'll inspire me forever. He was, after all, the most talented of all pirates. Without specifically citing the titles of his songs in the chapters, I embedded infer-ences to two of his greatest hits. Did you happen to notice?

Last, but certainly not least, I bestow hugs and kisses onto my granddaughter, Cecilia. At eleven-years-old, my "Little Miss Idea Generator" enthusiastically engages with me in what-if banter that ultimately steers me through twists and turns that even surprise me. She empowers me to do better even when storm clouds try to get in the way.

Obviously, the electricity eventually came back on, al-lowing me to continue with my latest obsession: to write the next Venus Bixby Mystery.

So, with love, laughter, and light …

Valerie Taylor
December 18, 2023

ABOUT THE AUTHOR

Valerie Taylor is the author of the award-winning romantic comedy trilogy: *What's Not Said*, *What's Not True*, and *What's Not Lost*. She lives in Shelton, Connecticut, where she's an active member in several book clubs, an expert sports spectator, and a proud grandmother. *A Whale of a Murder* is the first in the Venus Bixby Mystery series.

CONNECT ONLINE
WWW.VALERIETAYLORAUTHOR.COM

valerietaylorauthor

@valerieemtaylor

ValerieETaylor

www.ingramcontent.com/pod-product-compliance
Lightning Source LLC
Chambersburg PA
CBHW061415160726
47995CB00003B/615